Renewed Redemption

ANDREW ROTH

COPYRIGHT NOTICE

Renewed Redemption

First edition. Copyright © 2020 by Andrew Roth. The information contained in this book is the intellectual property of Andrew Roth and is governed by United States and International copyright laws. All rights reserved. No part of this publication, either text or image, may be used for any purpose other than personal use. Therefore, reproduction, modification, storage in a retrieval system, or retransmission, in any form or by any means, electronic, mechanical, or otherwise, for reasons other than personal use, except for brief quotations for reviews or articles and promotions, is strictly prohibited without prior written permission by the publisher.

This is a work of fiction. Names, characters, businesses, places, events, locales, and incidents are either the products of the author's imagination or used in a fictitious manner. Any resemblance to actual persons, living or dead, or actual events is purely coincidental.

Scriptures taken from the King James Bible, public domain

Cover and Interior Design: Derinda Babcock

Editor(s): Cristel Phelps, Deb Haggerty

Author Represented By: Hartline Literary Agency

PUBLISHED BY: Elk Lake Publishing, Inc., 35 Dogwood Drive, Plymouth, MA 02360, 2020

Library Cataloging Data

Names: Roth, Andrew (Andrew Roth)

Renewed Redemption / Andrew Roth

262 p. 23cm × 15cm (9in × 6 in.)

Description: Mandy, a single mom, has been doing all she could to keep her family fed and clothed. When her house and livelihood is taken away, she must depend on others and on God.

Identifiers: ISBN-13: 978-1-951970-17-8 (paperback) | 978-1-951970-18-5 (trade paperback) | 978-1-951970-19-2 (e-book)

Key Words: Old West, California Gold Rush, Pioneers, Single Mom, redemption, family, faith

LCCN: 2020934069 Fiction

To my children; David and Kate, Cameron and Sara—
You have no idea how much your kindness and support encouraged me through the tough times.

"… and I will build you up again and you will be rebuilt."—Jeremiah 31:4

CHAPTER 1

Mandy Barrett arched her aching back as her gaze traveled up the bleak slopes of the valley to the pine-covered ridges above. Patches of snow gleamed in the shadows of granite outcroppings and under the protective branches of the dark conifers.

A chilled breeze from the heights fanned her heated cheeks. She shivered and wiped her clammy brow with the back of her hand.

She glanced at the lowering sun, gauging how much work she could accomplish in the fading light.

Waves splashed over the bucket's rim as she plunged her reddened hands into the steaming water once more. She bent to her work, her shoulders rocking as she scrubbed.

Long strings of hair lay matted to her sweaty forehead, draping her eyes, but she didn't bother to brush them aside. Instead, she sighed, eager to complete this final task before preparing supper.

A wave of exhaustion and nausea swept over her, and she wondered if she had the influenza. She clenched her teeth. She had no time to be sick.

Certainly, she had no time to rest now. These shirts needed to be washed and hung up, but food was her primary concern. They were almost out and had maybe enough for today, but no more. Other necessities haunted her as well.

Mandy pressed her lips tightly together as she worked. She hadn't slept well last night. Sounds of revelry—pistol shots and even some fireworks marking the beginning of yet another New Year—had erupted until early this morning.

Renewed Redemption

She hadn't felt any need to participate in the festivities. Life wasn't what she'd hoped it would be. Would 1861 be any better than 1860? Regardless of a different year, her future looked just as dreary. Granted, the country had elected a new president, but Mandy held small hope a change in leadership would affect her in any way.

She drew a ragged breath and tried to ignore the stabbing pain in her chest. Her lungs felt on fire, and she doubled over, grasping the bucket with both hands as cough after cough racked her. Paroxysms shuddered through her chest until finally the fit passed, and she could breathe and drink in the cold air.

She wiped her mouth across the wet sleeve of her faded dress, scuffing her chapped lips.

Returning to the task at hand, she lifted a dripping shirt from the bucket, scowling at it, willing the garment to be clean. The sodden shirt slipped from her numb fingers and tumbled again into the bucket, splashing soapy water onto Mandy's already wet dress.

She stared down at herself, too weary to care.

A hasty glance to the west alerted her to the diminishing light, and she reluctantly plunged her hands back into the water. She worked the last article of clothing, shoving it across the washboard, her knuckles reddening from the hot water and effort, pushing herself to finish.

Steam rose from the bucket, darting in ghost-like wisps that melted into the brisk chill of the mountain air around her. Her calloused hands halted once again in the soapy water, and Mandy looked up at the ridges towering above her lonely shanty.

A knot formed in her gut as she thought of Richard. He'd been ten years her senior and had captured her heart with promises of wealth and travel.

She curled her mouth into a bitter smile. Wealth had eluded them, but they had traveled to California. Or was it *fled* to California?

Andrew Roth

This normally hot, dry state differed from her native Virginia in so many ways. Richard had assured her settlers in California were raking up gold by the tons. A man could make his fortune in the gold fields here.

After the Gold Rush began, the population had ballooned out west, and California gained its statehood. She and Richard married that very year.

Mandy tilted her head and surveyed her drab surroundings again. Well, it wasn't warm now, that was plain. Today had been gray and cold with a hint of moisture in the frigid air. This had been the coldest winter they had spent so far in California. It might even snow.

She lowered her gaze to the bucket of dirty water and made herself refocus.

Quit daydreaming. There is plenty to get done before sundown. It only makes you angry, anyway. You know Richard hoodwinked you, and you let him.

She lifted the final checkered flannel shirt from the bucket and wrung the sodden garment out before tossing it over the clothesline tied to the corner of her shanty. She eyed the dingy shack. It wasn't really her shanty, she remembered with a tinge of guilt. Last summer, she'd found the dreary hovel abandoned and moved in. Finders keepers, she figured, lifting her chin.

The thud of an axe startled Mandy from her muddled thoughts. Her brow furrowed. She swiped her wet hands on her dress and hurried around the corner.

Tiny wood chips lay scattered across the uneven ground, and she watched in horror as a young boy lifted the heavy axe for another whack.

"Jack," Mandy scolded her youngest son, her voice raspy. "Put that down. You'll cut off your foot. Where's Sam?"

Jack dropped the rusty tool in the dust. He looked up at his mother, his face smudged with dirt, his eyes glowering.

Renewed Redemption

"Mother, I am old enough to use the axe now. Really, I am. Besides, Sam doesn't like to cut wood."

"I don't care what Sam *likes* to do," Mandy snapped, brushing a length of lank hair from her face with the back of her wrist. "It's his chore to cut wood. Go fetch him."

Jack hesitated, and Mandy clapped her hands, her eyes narrowing.

"Go on, now. Fetch Sam," Mandy repeated, her voice taking on a more severe tone.

Jack lowered his head but not before Mandy saw the frown on his face as he turned and started down the trail toward the river.

Mandy watched him go, sad she'd spoken so sternly to him. She knew he only wanted to help, but it had to be done. If Jack injured himself with their dull axe, a boy with one foot was no help at all.

And Mandy desperately needed all the help she could muster.

She turned from watching Jack's departure, and her gaze strayed to the trail beyond where something caught her eye. She lifted a hand, shielding her eyes for a better view.

A stranger walked along the trail that followed the river, leading a lame horse.

His presence did not alarm her. Men constantly moved up and down that trail. Yet this man seemed to intrigue her. But why?

Her eyes lingered on the traveler a moment more, and a strange, unfamiliar emotion welled within her. Confused by the unexpected sensation, she squinted and shook her head before turning once more to the little shack.

"I must be truly ill," she muttered. She glanced back over her shoulder, annoyed that she did so, and considered the horse instead of the man. The geography of the Feather River made lameness for horses fairly common. Though the rich soil would grow anything planted, nothing grew here except oak trees, scrub oak, Manzanita, and cactus. Rocks and boulders covered most of the ground along both banks of the river's rapid waters. Pine trees flanked the higher slopes, but none grew at this lower elevation, although the boys had discovered wild berries and grapes along the river.

Only a few hundred yards farther along lay Yuba City, where the Yuba River emptied into the Feather River. Mandy hoped to deliver the clean laundry there tomorrow.

Before entering, she peered at the stranger and his horse a third time, studying the pair a moment longer. Finally, Mandy walked into her shanty. It was time to start dinner.

A final glance at the dull sun revealed a lowering sunset, disappearing over the ridges that bordered the other side of the long valley. She had to hurry to get something on the table if she wished to take advantage of the declining light. Soon it would be too dark to do much in the shanty, and she would not light the lone stub of a candle she possessed, wanting to hoard it for special occasions.

A wave of nausea swept over Mandy as she rushed about her work, but she ignored it and set to preparing the meal.

She had added their last two small potatoes to the simmering stew when she heard a horse whinny. Taking a step to the door, she looked out into the gathering gloom of the hard-packed dirt yard. Her eyes widened.

There stood the stranger she'd seen on the trail. Even at this distance, he was a striking figure. He stood tall with a gray shirt stretched over his broad shoulders and tucked into black trousers. Heavy leather work boots completed his outfit.

She lifted her gaze to his clean-shaven face, uncommon for a miner. Her breath caught in her throat as she peered into his clear eyes. They seemed so peaceful, content. Like he had all that he wanted.

His peacefulness contrasted sharply with the greedy, hawk-eyed men on the trail who were never satisfied, always searching for the precious yellow metal.

Renewed Redemption

His peace also contrasted with her own countenance.

"Howdy, stranger." Her words came slowly, hesitantly, and she eyed him with caution, for she was a woman alone.

Mandy's gaze strayed over his shoulder toward the river. Where were those boys? Was she safe?

"Good evening, ma'am," the visitor replied. "I smelled your cooking from the trail yonder and was hopeful for a bite to eat. I can cut wood or anything that needs doing."

He held his hat in hand and spoke with a sort of gentility she was unused to. Sure, she'd heard the tone often along the Atlantic Seaboard, but that sort of behavior was rare out here in the camps.

"Sorry, miner. I … we just don't have any to spare. Go on to Yuba City. It isn't far." She glanced again toward the river. Irritation rose within her. Where were they? Oh, she'd tan Sam's backside if he was gambling again.

"Ma'am, I'm no miner." He grinned, softening his tanned face. "My horse went lame, and I don't want to push him into Yuba City tonight. I won't eat much. Let me cut some firewood for you and maybe fix this sagging door." The man motioned toward the stretched leather hinges of the shanty's plank door.

The old, dried hinges had cracked long before Mandy's arrival. Before this shanty, she'd lived in Sacramento, slinging hash in a café right after she lost Richard for good. Sometimes, the café owner allowed her to bring leftover food home to the boys. It had been a big help.

Since bringing her to California, Richard had disappeared often, traveling through the gold country, gambling, hunting work that a lazy man would do. He occasionally returned after long absences, rarely bringing money to her. Once, he even showed up wounded, shot in the shoulder.

Before Mandy could argue further, a fresh coughing fit shook her. She wished to chase the hungry stranger off, not wanting to share her last remnants of food with him.

But the stranger waved and bent to pick up the axe. Without waiting for a reply, he tethered his horse and began cutting wood. Mandy scowled as she regained her breath. She did need the firewood, and soon it would be too dark to cut logs. The boys still hadn't returned, and they'd need the wood to keep warm for the night.

A shiver ran down her back as she felt the cold air that drafted through the wide cracks in the shanty's thin walls.

Too tired to debate further, she reentered the shanty. Another cup of water should stretch the soup. Mandy leaned on the table and closed her eyes as she pushed another rebellious strand of hair from her face. She considered again how ill she might be.

Whack!

She looked out the open door into the gloomy yard. The stranger raised the axe for another swing and brought it down. Huge chips flew from each strike. He would make short work of the pile of driftwood Sam had retrieved from the river.

Mandy marveled at how easily the tall man wielded the heavy axe. The muscles in his big shoulders rolled with each swing, his movements graceful and fluid.

Something stirred in her chest as she watched the stranger work. Mandy felt her eyes widen in recognition of the unwelcome feeling, and she turned away quickly, annoyed at herself.

She stirred the stew on the small, pot-bellied stove. Mandy never thought of herself as a girl anymore. Her wonderful youth had passed far too quickly. Too many years behind her now, she reckoned, although she was not yet thirty. Eleven years ago, she and Richard had married. She'd been seventeen then.

Despite her slight frame, Mandy had carried this very stove with the aid of Sam, her ten-year-old son. They'd found it in an abandoned miner's cabin farther up the river.

When the stew bubbled in the pot and she heard the boys running up the trail, Mandy dished up four chipped bowls and set them on the unsteady table. Only two of the dishes matched.

She kicked a box from a corner of the small room to serve as another seat. They only had two chairs anyway.

Through the walls, she clearly heard the conversation between the stranger and the boys outside. "You've cut more wood than Sam does in a whole day," Jack announced as the trio marched into the tiny shanty and crowded around the table.

Sam and Jack scampered to their usual seats, but the tall stranger waited patiently. A sharp look from Mandy told the boys to share the other chair as she sat upon the box. Sam averted his eyes from Mandy's searching scrutiny. His obvious guilt conveyed he'd been gambling again. She would deal with him later.

"Stranger, we don't stand on ceremony out here. Take your seat," Mandy said, a bit gruffer than intended. She remembered a time when men stood by their chairs and waited for ladies to be seated. That was a long time ago.

The stranger glanced at the boys, then took his seat. The chair creaked as he shifted, placing his hands on the edge of the table before dropping them to his lap.

Mandy decided this would be a candle night. She wasn't sure what inspired her decision, but she retrieved the stub from next to the stove, nonetheless. She lit it with one of her few remaining matches and placed it in the center of the table, its feeble glow providing a dim light.

The boys watched, wide-eyed. Candle nights were rare.

Mandy sat and looked at the stranger. Sam and Jack had started eating, but the man waited.

"Eat up, stranger. It's not bad for stew without meat." She dipped her spoon into her dish and lifted the utensil to her mouth.

Mandy had been hungry all afternoon, waiting for suppertime to finally eat something. Now that the moment was at hand, she wondered at her lack of appetite. Her head swam as her stomach gave a lurch at the smell of the thin stew.

Despite her vanishing hunger, she choked a spoonful down her throat. She would need her strength.

Obtaining food had proven difficult these past couple of years. Often, she went without so the boys would have enough. She worked hard all day, eager to reach the time when she could sit and enjoy something to eat with her tiny family. Now was that time.

She dipped her spoon for another scoop and peered through the veil of her loose hair. A muscle tightened in her jaw when she realized the stranger still hadn't lifted his spoon. He sat with his hands in his lap as if waiting for something. Mandy bristled, offended by his inaction. Did he not like her cooking? Was it not good enough for the likes of him?

She cast a sidelong glance at the boys. Sam, too, had noticed. He'd stopped eating and now watched the stranger with suspicious eyes.

"What's wrong, mister? Aren't you going to eat?"

"I was waiting for someone to say grace." The tall man smiled a lopsided smile.

Mandy blinked. Grace? It'd been years since she'd said grace at the table. Not since Richard had entered her life.

"What's he mean, Mother?" Jack held his spoon in midair, his eyes on Mandy.

"He means *prayer*," Sam whispered.

Mandy glanced at the boys again as a flush of heat came to her cheeks. "Well, of course, prayer. That's a nice idea. Mister, being as you're a guest, will you say grace this evening?"

The boys gawked at her unaccustomed formality.

The tall stranger pressed his hands together and bowed his head. The boys watched Mandy. She gave them a nod, and they all mimicked the stranger.

"Dear Lord, thank you for your many blessings, and thank you for this very kind woman who took pity on a stranger and allowed him to join her family for dinner. You are gracious, Lord, and you richly provide for our needs. Amen."

Jack chuckled. "Mister, I don't know who you're talking about, but he surely doesn't provide for our needs."

Mandy stared at her youngest son, dismayed. If her father back in Virginia had heard her son speak so, he would die of shame. In her father's day, small children were raised not to speak in such a manner at mealtimes. Children were to be seen and not heard, unless properly addressed.

The stranger glanced at Mandy and then turned back to the boy. "I'm speaking of the Creator, the Lord of Lords, God. He made us, he loves us, and he wants good things for us."

Jack laughed out loud.

Wide eyed, Sam peered through hooded eyelids at his mother and then kicked Jack under the table. Jack howled.

"You'll have to excuse Jack. He's young and doesn't understand such things." Sam gestured with his spoon toward a now-whimpering Jack. "Jack, this man is talking about God. God is kind of like Santa Claus. If you're good, good things come to you."

Mandy choked.

"Well, then, we haven't been good 'cause nothing good happens to us," Jack persisted.

The man in the gray shirt held up a hand. "Wait. I am talking about God, but you have him figured wrong. He is not like Santa Claus. He doesn't keep a list of those who are naughty or nice. In God's eyes, we've all been naughty.

"But by the blood of his son, Jesus Christ, God cleanses us of our naughtiness. We don't deserve this gift because we do bad things and are selfish. God is merciful and kind. Jesus paid the price for our wrongdoing by his sacrifice on the cross and his coming alive again. Now, we can stand sinless before a holy God."

Mandy and her sons gaped at the stranger.

Andrew Roth

The box creaked beneath her as she shifted. She'd been raised in a Christian home and knew what the man was saying, but the boys simply stared at him. This was all new to them.

Finally, Mandy broke the uncomfortable silence. "Eat up before your stew gets cold," she barked, glaring openly at them all.

Everyone bent to their bowls. Mandy ground her teeth. As if she needed more proof she'd failed as a mother.

She cast furtive glances around the bare room, remembering each foray into empty buildings to acquire the battered and discarded belongings she now called her own. They had so little, and all of it came from their own efforts.

Mandy only earned a small income from taking in laundry. To supply their home, she'd foraged through the gold camps, retrieving abandoned furniture, clothing, and utensils. Mended miner's cast-offs were worn by Sam, and Jack wore his older brother's hand-me-downs.

Now, as her eyes swept the shadowed items around the dingy shanty, Mandy felt her heart sink in her chest. Not only had she neglected a proper Christian upbringing for her boys, but she'd stolen all their belongings as well. Nothing remained of the good things she'd grown up with in Virginia.

Mandy's gaze came to rest upon the tall stranger. He watched her too, and for a brief moment, their gazes locked. She could read the look of pity in his gentle, brown eyes.

Anger surged within her, and the heated wave of shame crept up her neck as she hastily turned away. She would have no man pity her.

"If you're finished eating, stranger, you're free to be on your way." Mandy rose, almost upsetting the wooden box as she snatched the stranger's bowl. "Thank you kindly for the firewood."

The man rose slowly. "My name is Brian Dawson, ma'am. Thank you for the stew. I'll spread my bedroll outside and get to work in the morning. Goodnight, ma'am."

Renewed Redemption

Mandy tilted her head, not sure she heard right. "Morning?"

"Why, sure." The stranger nodded toward the shanty door. "I told you I'd fix those old hinges. Won't take me but a few minutes. Goodnight."

Brian moved around the table toward the door and was outside before Mandy could respond. The door closed quietly behind him.

She stared at the door, her eyes narrowing, as a wave of livid anger rose from her belly. Who did this stranger think he was? First, he'd made her acutely aware of her inadequacies and shortcomings, now he presumed on her hospitality to stay the night. She didn't like this man, this Brian Dawson.

Mandy blew out the candle, casting the little room into darkness except for the ruddy glow from the tiny stove. Their special night was over.

She could hear Brian settling down outside as she got the boys ready for bed. By the dim light of the pot-bellied stove, the boys rolled into their blanket.

Jack protested, arguing it was too early for bed.

Mandy leaned close to the boys so the stranger outside couldn't hear through the thin walls.

"Go to sleep now or get a switching," she hissed.

Sam lay quietly in the bed he shared with Jack, and Mandy fixed her attention on him next. "Sam, don't think I've forgotten how you shirked your chores today. Jack almost killed himself attempting to cut the firewood with that dull axe. What do you have to say for yourself?"

Sam reached into his pants, which he still wore, and retrieved a handful of coins. "Mother, I was gambling with the town boys. I'm sorry. But I won a dollar and six bits."

He handed the coins to Mandy, then turned his back to the pot-bellied stove. Jack curled close to his older brother, his small head nestled near to Sam's larger one. She noticed they both needed haircuts.

Mandy deposited the coins in her dress pocket without looking at them, then stared down at these two little boys. She bent and kissed each of their heads and pulled the single blanket up a little higher. She hadn't done right by them.

That night, she sat for a long time beside the small stove, feeding it tidbits of firewood. Mandy knew she should conserve the wood the stranger had cut. Sam's even breathing told her he'd fallen asleep. She couldn't hear Jack, but she knew he'd be sleeping too.

She stared into the flames leaping through the slits in the stove's grate. Brian Dawson's visit to their shanty rekindled memories she had long tried to forget. Although he'd attempted to respect her by standing behind his chair, waiting for her to sit first, the action hearkened back to a time she wished to remove from her memory.

After midnight, Mandy finally crawled into her own bed. Despite extreme fatigue and a clammy brow, she didn't want to sleep. The day had exhausted her but paled in comparison to the ordeal of remembering her past, which opened wounds she'd tried hard to seal.

Why did the stranger's arrival have such an effect on her? He was nobody, and yet, she felt she hated him. After tomorrow, she would never see him again. Why did thoughts of him and memories of home in Virginia now consume her mind?

She lay in the darkness with her thoughts. The glow of the dying fire cast shadows upon the rough-cut plank wall, and pine pitch snapped inside the little stove. She'd have to fetch more driftwood from the river tomorrow. She sighed. Always more work to be done than hours in the day.

Abruptly, the sharp image of her father filled her mind, disappointment flooding his eyes as Richard lifted her hand, revealing the small ring on Mandy's finger. She'd broken her father's heart, but she'd been in love. Hadn't she?

She tugged the worn, woolen blanket tight up to her shoulders, her body shivering as sweat streamed down her face.

Renewed Redemption

Regret and sorrow swirled in her feverish mind as she slept fitfully, dreaming of standing on the brink of a precipice, too frightened to peer over the edge but powerless not to.

CHAPTER 2

Mandy awoke in the morning and, for an instant, felt uncertain of her location. She looked wildly around the dingy clapboard shanty until her present condition came flooding over her like a brick wall crashing upon her.

She sighed and swiped her hands through the tangled mess of her hair.

She rolled from the hard bed in the predawn gloom and poked a few sticks into the grate of the old, pot-bellied stove. She placed a pan of water on top to boil for tea.

Out of habit, Mandy began the day by mentally listing the tasks that lay before her, according to priority. First, go to Yuba City to deliver and fetch customers' laundry, hopefully collecting pay. If paid, she would stop by the store for some food—food they desperately needed. Then, she would return to their shanty and help the boys gather more driftwood. They needed her to lift the big pieces.

She thought suddenly of the coins Sam had given her the previous night. Those funds would help. Perhaps she wouldn't be so hard on her eldest boy for gambling again. After all, the money was appreciated.

Richard had taught the boy some gambling tricks, and Sam had used them on more than one occasion to furnish money for the family. Mandy hated this, but she also realized how helpful it had proven but not helpful when he lost.

She coughed as she continued to poke the fire, her thin shoulders shook from the force. She held one hand over her mouth, trying not to wake the sleeping boys.

Renewed Redemption

Mandy didn't feel well, and she was both concerned and bothered. She didn't have time for this. She shook her head. No matter. She needed to keep moving—things to be done if they wanted to survive.

The water began to boil on the stove, and she added the tea. The shriveled leaves had been boiled more than once, but it was all they had for their morning meal today. They'd gone without before, though, and today probably wouldn't be the last time.

With a glance at the sleeping boys, Mandy pushed the door open. The shack had no windows, and opening the door was necessary to determine both the day's weather and to obtain some fresh air for the inside of the stuffy hut. If it were raining, she couldn't hang laundry outside.

The door dragged on its stretched leather hinges as she looked out to a gray, ominous sky. She searched the sky for a hint of blue—a bit of hope—but there was none. The storm would come soon.

Sighing heavily, she was pulling the door closed when a hand shot in, gripping the edge of the door. Startled, she jerked back and saw the man from last evening standing before her. She'd forgotten him.

"Good morning, ma'am." He beamed a smile at her, and his bright, happy greeting annoyed her.

"What do you want?" Mandy demanded, trying to pull the door in after her, ignoring his firm grip on the plank door.

"Ma'am, I promised to help around the place to pay for the soup you gave me last night," he explained, his eyes on the rotting hinges. "I was thinking about starting on these loose hinges, but how about I fetch wood for you as well?"

She looked hard at him, seeing him in the dull light of the early morning. He seemed lively and energetic, freshly washed, hair brushed. She had to admit he was handsome, though irritating.

His words from the night before reminding her about her mothering skill came back to her. She'd not raised the boys well and knew so, but she hated to be reminded of this harsh fact. This stranger also made her think of her past. She frowned now as she recalled his perfect manners and courtesy.

"Mister," she began with an agitated ring to her voice.

"Brian," he corrected her, still smiling.

Mandy bristled. "*Brian*, I'm grateful you chopped that wood last evening. Your debt is paid. I don't want you to fix these hinges, and I don't need your help fetching wood. You are released from further obligations. Please go," she finished and tried to pull the door shut once more.

The taunting memories he'd conjured up last night still rankled in her mind. She wanted this bothersome man to disappear.

He looked down at her, his smile faltering as his brown eyes clouded with confusion. "Ma'am, if you don't mind me saying, it doesn't look like you're doing all that well. Now," he stood tall in the doorway, arms crossed, "I have a proposition for you and your boys."

Mandy stopped trying to close the door and stood opposite him, mirroring his stance. She was always on the lookout for more opportunities to make money.

Let's hear what he has to say.

She pushed a strand of hair from her eyes and nodded for him to continue.

"You see," Brian went on, now more animated, "I made the trip to Sacramento to buy alfalfa seed. I figured it'd be cheaper if I went for it myself rather than paying a higher price locally. Well, it was cheaper, but then my horse came up lame on the way home. Now, being a Christian man, I always study each event, each situation, to see if the Lord is trying to tell me something. To ask if there's something I'm supposed to do."

He paused and leaned a shoulder against the shack. Mandy peered up at him with impatience broiling in her chest.

Renewed Redemption

She glowered at the gathering dark clouds amassing above the ridge. She needed to get to town with that clean laundry before the storm.

"So?" she prodded, turning back to him with raised eyebrows.

Brian nodded and rubbed the back of his neck with one hand. "Yes. Like I said, I wondered what God wanted me to do. I mean, look, he even allowed my horse to go lame right here by your shack." He gestured to his horse. The animal stared back at them with baleful eyes.

Mandy nodded, wishing he'd speak faster. Was he going to give her a job or not?

"Anyway, I trust the Lord. I know he brought me here. And then the answer came to me." He snapped his fingers. "He's telling me to help you." He smiled again and she blinked. This could take a while. She motioned for him inside the shack. He followed her, and she poured two cups of tea. As they seated themselves at the table, he glanced at the sleeping boys before continuing.

"I have a farm about three or four miles up the Yuba River trail from town. Cross the bridge and take the Middle Fork trail when you come to it, but it leads from the main trail to a nice valley. Quail Valley, it's called."

He sipped his tea, wrinkling his nose at the taste, which annoyed her further. "Anyway, I purchased Quail Valley from a homesteader a couple of years ago and been making improvements right along. I have a garden and fruit trees on all the higher ground. But I've decided to dam the creek and irrigate alfalfa. I need the rocks removed from the fields for this, though. It's more than I can do in a season, and I want to start planting this spring."

Mandy held up a hand. Obviously this man liked to hear himself speak, but she was in no mood to hear him talk all day.

"Mister, get to the point. What do you want me to do?" Brian lifted his cup for another drink, hesitated, thought better of it, and returned the cup to the table. "I need your boys to clear the rocks from the land. While we work the land, I'd want you to run the house, do the laundry, the cooking, and run errands to town."

She stared at him, her mental wheels turning swiftly. He was asking her to move. To his house. His land. Mandy already knew her answer. It was out of the question. If he didn't like her work or if the boys caused trouble, she'd be fired, and this place would be occupied by someone else by then. There was no way she'd move to be this man's housekeeper.

She shook her head. Then a thought occurred to her. "How do you know I'm not married? My husband could be home any minute."

Brian smiled before he answered. He smiled too much, Mandy thought. "Jack told me his father was dead. I asked him yesterday where his daddy was when I first came here from the river." He tilted his head. "Why not accept the job? I can tell you need the work."

Mandy sipped her tea, watching Brian over the rim of the dented tin cup. She did need the work but wouldn't risk vacating this shack for a temporary proposition. She couldn't work for this annoying man anyway. He was too happy and sure of himself.

"No," she said.

She read the curiosity in his eyes, but something else too. Pity. She didn't want anyone's pity. Her hand tightened on her cup.

"No, Brian Dawson," Mandy repeated more forcefully, not wishing to explain herself to this man. "Thank you for your offer, but I am not interested."

Mandy rose quickly from her seat. Too quickly, and her head began to spin. She gripped the edge of the rickety table and ignored the temporary dizziness and nausea churning in her belly.

Renewed Redemption

Brian stood too, his chair scraping on the hard-packed dirt. "Are you all right?"

Spots floated before her eyes, but she nodded. "I'm fine," she lied. The spots cleared, and she saw the look of confusion cross his face. "Is something bothering you?" she asked flippantly, feigning a confidence she didn't feel.

He scowled and pursed his lips. "It's just that usually I can tell when the Lord is guiding me. I thought he wanted me to help you."

Mandy narrowed her eyes. "Well, I guess you're mistaken. Maybe the Lord got this one wrong." She gestured toward the door. "Thank you and good day. If you don't mind, I have a lot to do."

He stepped backward, his hand groping for the latch. "Yes, ma'am. Well, if you change your mind, you know where to find me," he sputtered as he found his way out of the shack. She pulled the door closed behind him, the latch falling into place, and resumed her seat at the table.

Leaning her aching head against her palms, Mandy rested a moment and allowed the nausea to pass. Soon, the dizziness left her. Her long, dirty hair fell in her eyes and she angrily brushed it aside. This was terrible timing for her to be sick. Then again, she thought grimly, when *would* be a good time?

Picking up her cold cup of tea, she thought a moment longer about the stranger. A busy-body, do-gooder trying to give her a handout, Mandy figured. Well, she would have none of that nonsense.

Mandy heard Brian's horse snort as he loaded the heavy sack of seed. Drawn to the door, Mandy peered through a wide crack and watched the retreating man. Hooves thudded as the pair went down the path to the larger trail along the river. She noticed with a curious twinge the horse seemed to no longer be lame.

She sighed, glad to be rid of him.

"I liked him. Why don't we go to live with him?"

Mandy whirled. Jack was sitting up in bed, studying her. He'd heard everything.

She leaned wearily against the door. "I have other things to do." She closed her eyes for a moment, then opened them. "Which reminds me. You get your brother out of bed and start fetching wood. It looks like a storm is brewing, and we'll need the wood to be dry. I'm going to town with the clean laundry. I hope to stop by the market and buy some food as well."

Making sure the money Sam had given her was safe in her pocket, Mandy picked up the folded laundry and started for the door.

She glanced back once more at the two boys and gave Jack the briefest of smiles. "I'll be back soon," she promised as she stepped outside and pushed the door closed behind her.

CHAPTER 3

Mandy walked down to the river trail, the same trail Brian Dawson had just traveled, and cast a nervous glance at the lowering, dark clouds overhead. She gritted her teeth, hurrying her pace. It would just be her luck if a huge storm hit today. She turned into the wide trail that followed the river.

The hour was early, and few businesses would be open at this time of day, yet Mandy hoped her customers were at work. She crossed the bridge spanning the Feather River and entered town.

Yuba City was only a few hundred yards from the bridge. She wondered why the stranger hadn't pushed on, despite the lame horse, to find lodging in town. Why stop at her shack?

She passed a number of businesses before she came to the blacksmith shop. A few early risers peered at her with curiosity, but no one called to her.

The ringing of the hammer on the anvil told her the smithy was already at work. Mandy walked in the open door, the powerful bang of the hammer growing louder as she entered.

She allowed a minute for her eyes to grow accustomed to the dim light of the blacksmith shop. Only the bright glow of the fire was clear until her eyes adjusted.

After a moment, the smithy noticed her presence. When he did, Mr. Bricker put his hammer down and wiped his large hands on his leather apron, sweat pouring from his red face.

"Aw ... Mrs. Barrett, it is you."

Mandy wondered at the hesitation in his greeting.

"Mr. Bricker, here's your mending and the three shirts I cleaned for you." She handed the stack of clothes to the blacksmith, but he shook his head and pointed to a nearby work bench. Mandy searched for a place on the crowded table, then deposited them. "Mr. Bricker," Mandy continued, trying hard not to wring her hands. "I was hoping you'd pay me today what you owe me."

He moved to the light near the open door, reaching for his pocket. The burly blacksmith hurriedly counted out some coins. Mr. Bricker handed them to Mandy and cleared his throat. "Mrs. Barrett, I will not be needing your services further. Thank you for doing my mending and all, but I won't be needing further help."

He nodded, pleased at the rehearsed speech. Mandy glared at him, and he lowered his eyes.

Mr. Bricker nudged the dirt on the floor with the toe of his boot as Mandy considered, not surprised at this news. She recognized the familiar feeling of another horrible day. She sighed.

"Mr. Bricker, why will you no longer need me? Is something wrong with my work?" Mandy hated to argue, and she already knew the business arrangement she had with the blacksmith was finished. Her luck had run out.

"No, no, ma'am," the big man hastened, looking at her once more. He wiped his forehead with the back of his huge hand. "It's just that I'm getting married, and my wife will be doing my laundry."

Even in the dim light, Mandy could see he blushed a rosy pink as he spoke. Mandy wanted to warn him. *Don't do it, Bricker. You'll regret it.*

Instead, she pursed her lips and nodded, slipping the few coins in her pocket before leaving the shop.

Another glance at the sky increased her worry. The clouds appeared darker than before.

She wended her way to the livery barn next, sidestepping moving wagons and men. Mr. Bricker was getting married.

Well, he would soon realize how simple life was with just a wash woman to consider. Now, the poor man would be burdened with a wife who would need to be fed and might even want children one day. He would surely come to regret his intention of finding a mate, Mandy mused.

Mr. Stine stood in front of his business, holding a lead rope on a horse at the water trough. He saw Mandy coming and hastily moved to the other side of the drinking horse.

Was he hiding from her, Mandy wondered as she approached?

"Good morning, Mr. Stine," Mandy called to the concealed man. Sheepishly, he peered at her over the back of the red mare.

"Here is your mending." She handed the hostler his clothes over the drinking animal. Mr. Stine took them, then shuffled his feet. Mandy watched this little dance, fearing what was to come.

"Uh, Mrs. Barrett," the balding man started, "I'm afraid I'll have to let you go. My business is not doing as well as I'd like, and I'm going to do my own laundry. I figure I can handle the additional work if I don't change my shirt regularly." Mr. Stine smiled weakly. "Thank you for helping me out for these past months, but now I'll be doing my own clothes."

Mandy received the few coins he paid her, and then spun on her heel and marched away. She didn't even attempt to question the livery man.

She scowled as a distant rumble of thunder rolled. What was going on? She was used to bad luck, but this was getting out of control.

Mandy glanced again at the darkening sky and decided she would not go to any of her other customers but would hurry to the general store and buy some food. She was suddenly eager to return to the shanty across the river and her boys. She felt weak and her back ached.

Renewed Redemption

Stepping into the busy store, Mandy drew the money from her pocket and then waited her turn. When a clerk was free, he turned toward Mandy.

He froze when he recognized her. The young clerk turned quickly and motioned to an older man some yards distant. Catching the clerk's gesture, the older man noticed Mandy as well. A scowl crossed the man's face, and he nodded to the young clerk, hurrying through stacks of store goods and supplies toward her.

A chill ran down her back. Whether from fear or the bothersome sickness that surged within her, she was unsure.

"Mrs. Barrett," the shopkeeper began, looking disdainfully at Mandy. "I hoped you'd come in soon."

She drew a deep breath and painted her best smile on her face, preparing for battle. She'd fought in these wars before and was not daunted.

"Good morning, Mr. Ambrose," she purred sweetly. "You look almighty wonderful this day. I was just going to buy some food. Look, I have money." She jingled the coins in her outstretched palm.

Mr. Ambrose did not return her smile. "Mrs. Barrett, you already owe a considerable amount to this business, and the new policy is no tab for customers who do not pay monthly."

"But, sir, I have cash to pay for my purchases today," Mandy countered, attempting to keep her inflated, false cheer. Inside, she wanted to punch him.

"I will get to my tab as soon as I can," Mandy promised, her heart beating rapidly. Her cheeks felt flushed and she could feel the clamminess across her brow. Mandy wondered if her knees would give way. She leaned against the counter to steady herself.

She'd battled this old storekeeper before and always won. Why did she feel so ill-equipped today for this fight?

Mr. Ambrose scooped up the money in Mandy's hand. Before she could realize what he was doing, Mr. Ambrose handed the coins to the young clerk behind the counter.

"Hey!" Mandy protested, her fake smile replaced by genuine concern. She noticed her cry had brought the attention of other patrons and felt the flush on her cheeks deepen.

Mr. Ambrose spoke over his shoulder to the other clerk, never taking his eyes from Mandy. "Apply this amount to what Mrs. Barrett owes the store, Herbert. Let me know the balance still due."

"I was going to use that to buy some food today," Mandy pleaded. She felt as if she might cry. *Don't cry*, she told herself sternly. *Don't do it.*

"This money will be applied to your credit owed. You still owe us more money, Mrs. Barrett." The old shopkeeper spoke loudly for all to hear. A number of other people crowded closer, watching the show.

"You can't do this." Mandy squeezed her eyes closed. Why was this happening today?

She opened her eyes to glare at Mr. Ambrose. "My boys have nothing to eat. I need to buy some food."

Mandy could feel the hot tears rolling down her cheeks. This day was rapidly going from bad to worse. Now, she couldn't stop crying.

"I am sorry, Mrs. Barrett," the storekeeper replied in a softer tone. "But this is a business, not a charity. No more credit. You still owe additional funds."

Mr. Ambrose stood tall, his legs wide, hands on hips, as he lectured her. He reminded Mandy of a sea captain, waging war with another vessel. He'd won this battle, she admitted as her shoulders slumped, and she rushed through the crowd for the door.

The door slammed loudly behind her as Mandy halted on the stoop outside to gather her wits. She fought the sobs back and wiped an angry hand across her wet eyes. She would not cry anymore, she told herself. Experience had taught her of its uselessness. She was determined to be strong and not cry further.

As she stepped off the stoop, Mandy heard the distant peal of another thunderclap, and a spattering of rain struck her face. She looked up as the heavens opened. She couldn't hold the tears back now as she trudged back down main street to the bridge. She crossed and joined the river trail to her shack, her dress soaked from the downpour. She started to shiver even though her head burned.

The cold rainwater ran with the hot tears down her cheeks as she allowed herself to cry freely now, her hated tears concealed by the rain. She would allow this one indulgence, rarely permitted, but the rain made it permissible. No one could see.

Her shoulders heaved as the sobs wracked her thin body. She was defeated. In fact, things hadn't gone well for the past ten years, she reminded herself bitterly. Richard Barrett had been the beginning of the end of Mandy Mulligan. Her father had told her not to marry him, but she'd ignored his wisdom. She'd been in love or at least thought she was. Richard convinced her she was special, and he truly loved her. He said Mandy's father was old-fashioned and didn't understand true love anymore. He'd made eloping sound so romantic.

Mandy had disappointed her father, but he'd paid a dowry, nonetheless, much to Richard's expectation and delight. Not until later did Mandy realize the depth of Richard's scheme to secure finances for gambling. He had cared nothing for her.

Ashamed and desperate to believe that Richard might still pull things together and redeem himself in the eyes of her father, Mandy had consented to give the last of the dowry for tickets on the windjammer to California.

She had been such a fool. Her pride had not allowed Mandy to seek forgiveness from her family. Indeed, that would mean she admitted she'd been wrong about Richard, and her father had been correct all along. Mandy couldn't do it.

And now she was stuck here in Yuba City. No hope, no options, no food.

As she neared the shanty on the outskirts of town, she saw a commotion ahead. Men shouted, and despite the rain, several gathered in the trail.

Mandy looked ahead, her eyes widening when she saw they were at her shack.

Her tears forgotten, she broke into a stumbling run.

CHAPTER 4

Shoving and shouldering her way through the noisy crowd, Mandy gained the door of the shanty. Jack sat crying in the mud, rain soaking his clothes, his unkempt hair plastered to his head. Beside him, Sam stood, hitting a man busily throwing their personal things into the yard.

"What's this all about? Who are you?" Mandy demanded of the big miner who had just deposited her cooking pots at his feet.

"This is my shack, and I've come home to find it occupied by squatters," he bellowed to all within listening range.

"We moved here last summer, and this place was abandoned," Mandy wailed, kneeling to hold Jack. His sobbing subsided at sight of his mother.

"I went to Angel's Camp to work at a mine for the summer and fall. Jim here will vouch for me. I never abandoned my shack. Hey, I even had a lock on the door. Where's that, now?" The big miner shouted this last, turning to the crowd for support.

Mandy pursed her lips and hugged Jack closer. Well, indeed, Mandy remembered the lock on the door. She'd used a large stone to break it loose from its clasp. Crestfallen, she peered at the pitifully small pile of goods she could call her own. Jack sat among them, rain mingling with his tears as Sam backed up beside her, his eyes full of anger and embarrassment. He knew they'd moved into this shanty without permission.

The big miner dragged the door closed and the crowd slowly drifted away, leaving Mandy and the boys with their meager belongings in the steel gray rain. There was nothing she could do. The owner's unexpected return was a surprise, and she had no legal claim to this little shack on the outskirts of Yuba City.

Gesturing to Sam to help gather their things, she lifted Jack by his arm and turned to walk up the trail toward town.

Mandy stared wild-eyed around her. She had nowhere to go. The rain was steadily falling now, the heavy downpour lessening somewhat.

She shivered and looked at her boys. Only Jack had a coat, one she'd made with her own hands from old clothes. Sam wore a thick flannel shirt, too big for him. She wore a miner's shirt, a torn and bedraggled thing she found in a cabin and had mended and cleaned. She knew they must look a sight as they walked along the muddy trail, their arms full of blankets and cooking pots.

Mandy used to feel shame. Not now. Long ago, when Richard left them with nothing, she learned to fend for her small family. She understood shame was a luxury for people with options. Mandy had none.

Mandy had given up caring what others thought. Only food and shelter mattered to her now. Protection from the cold for her boys. Pride was an extravagance she could not afford.

They crossed the bridge and trooped up the empty street. An awning attached to Mr. Bricker's blacksmith shop offered some relief from the pouring rain. Jack stumbled ahead of Mandy as she pointed the way to the smithy's. The small boy dropped to the ground, his face reflecting shock and grief.

Mandy dropped her armload of things and leaned heavily against the awning post, staring out dismally into the leaden sky. Sam followed close on her heels and found a seat next to Jack.

This is what she deserved, Mandy thought glumly, watching the rain with unseeing eyes. She should never have come to California—a mistake from the beginning. All of it. Richard, the elopement, the escape from Richmond.

The warmth of her parent's house haunted her now. The delicious smells of her mother's cooking, the coats and shoes and clothes that filled her closet. Why had she not been satisfied?

She watched a miner trudge through the rain, his boots splashing through the deep puddles.

Mandy could feel a shiver coming up her back. *Go ahead*, she thought, urging the unwanted sensation to fruition. *I deserve this.*

"I'm hungry."

Jack's whimper broke through Mandy's self-pity and reminded her of their plight.

"We're all hungry," Mandy snapped, angry she couldn't do anything about it.

"Mother, what are we going to do? Where are we going to go?" Sam asked quietly, hesitant to voice his question lest he, too, receive his mother's bark.

Mandy gritted her teeth. She had no answer. Perhaps she deserved this, but the boys did not. They were innocent of the crime of selfishness. They were mere pawns in this ugly game she'd been forced to play out.

She looked up at the heavy, dark clouds and began to cry again. *Only a little, just a tear or two*, Mandy promised herself. She didn't want the boys to see the tears, so she leaned forward, just enough for the rain to strike her face.

She choked back a sob, realizing she'd cried more today than she had in the past few years.

With a shudder, Mandy knew she'd lost. She had no idea what they would do now. No possibilities came to her. Her plans had all failed, and she was out of fresh ideas. She stared into the rain, panic filling her.

"We could go to that nice stranger's house." Jack shifted behind her, sniffling.

Mandy glanced over her shoulder as Sam sat up. "What nice stranger?" She detected the smallest note of hope in his voice.

Renewed Redemption

Jack dragged a wet sleeve across his face. "Brian. Brian Dawson. He offered Mother and us a job and a house." Jack straightened as he spoke.

Mandy squinted, studying the two soaking wet boys. Sam held his arms crossed tight over his chest, shivering. Despite the cold, Jack was smiling a little now.

"What are you talking about, Jack?" Sam turned to Mandy. "Mother, is it true?"

"He offered Mother a job," the small boy continued. "You were still asleep, but I heard it." Jack looked up at Mandy. "Mother, do you think we could go there? I'm awfully hungry and cold."

Sam looked up at her, and Mandy read the gleam of hope in his hollow eyes.

She looked away, staring into the steel gray rain. Could she crush them so easily? She had no intention of going to that stranger and taking the job he'd offered. Brian Dawson made her feel inadequate. He was too sure of himself, too confident. She didn't trust him. There was something about him she didn't understand.

"Boys, I don't think he was serious. He seemed kind of odd to me. Too cocky. He probably doesn't even have a farm." Mandy shrugged casually, dismissing Brian Dawson. There was no sense in lifting their hopes only to have them dashed again.

"He does so," Jack protested loudly. "He even gave us directions to his place. I remember them, Mother. I could take us there."

Sam looked again at Mandy, seeking leadership. There didn't seem to be an alternative plan.

"Boys," Mandy began quietly, knowing this was probably not a good idea. "Boys, I don't know …"

"I know, Mother. I'm sure he's going to help us. He said he would. He even prayed at dinner. He will help us, Mother," Jack went on, slowly rising to his feet.

Andrew Roth

Sam looked from his younger brother back again to his mother, his big eyes looking for direction, a way to go.

Mandy sighed. She'd tried her best to provide for this little family when Richard left them. She'd truly done her best. It was all over now, though. There was nothing else to do.

With another glance at the falling rain, she turned to the boys and put on a fake smile. "Okay, then, we try to find this stranger's farm. What was his name, Jack?"

"Brian, Mother. His name is Brian Dawson."

CHAPTER 5

Her fever had started earlier, but Mandy ignored the symptoms. A deep throbbing in her temples, almost imperceptible at first, now beat like drums in her head and persisted. She could ignore the pain no longer—but she must.

Mandy helped Sam and Jack pick up their meager belongings, each taking a small load. Then they started walking through Yuba City. They'd crossed the bridge over the Feather River to come to town and now followed the smaller river as Jack led them up the Yuba River trail.

The rain continued. At first, Mandy felt greatly bothered by the rain's chill and irritated by the wet clothes against her skin. But as they trudged up the incline of the trail along the Yuba, she realized the walking helped warm them all. They plodded on.

The weather seemed to have convinced many travelers to stay indoors, so the trail was not busy. Nonetheless, Mandy and the boys did pass prospectors undaunted by the wet weather who gave the trio curious glances.

Her vision blurred, making her headache worse. Mandy stumbled but tried to carefully navigate the path Jack led them on, wondering if they were going the right way. He was, after all, only eight years old. However, the pain and fever dulled her senses. The boys could have led her off a cliff and she would have blindly followed.

Mandy found herself staring at the heels of Sam's shoes in the trail. She could not lift her head and gave up trying. Her teeth chattered as sweat covered her brow. Even the cold rain couldn't quench the fire in her head.

Renewed Redemption

Suddenly, the heels before her stopped moving. With great effort, Mandy looked about her. The bleak and wet landscape was unfamiliar, new to her.

"Brian said to turn off this trail at the junction and take the Middle Fork trail." Jack pointed to a small bridge and another, smaller trail.

Sam scowled and glanced at Mandy. "Are you sure this is the way, Jack? It doesn't look as well-traveled as this trail we're on."

Jack nodded rapidly. "Mother heard him too. Brian said to go this way. Isn't that right, Mother?" Jack turned to Mandy for corroboration.

Sam followed his younger brother's gaze. They stared at her, demanding direction.

Mandy staggered and would've fallen if not for Sam's steadying hand on her elbow.

"Mother, are you all right?" Sam's brow furrowed. "You're so pale, and your eyes look funny."

"Fine," Mandy mumbled. With great effort, she raised a hand and indicated the side trail they were to take. "Lead on."

Jack again took point. He crossed the little bridge and led up the trail.

Mandy followed, her hand gripping the rough wooden railing of the small bridge with one hand. Again, she attempted to focus on Sam's heels as she tramped behind her oldest son.

The stupor had overcome her now, and she simply put one foot in front of another, having no idea where they were or how long they'd been walking. The trail they followed suddenly turned away from the small river and began to perceptibly climb.

After a great while, Jack stopped. With difficulty, Mandy lifted her head and peered around once more. Her back ached, making it difficult to stand erect. Her vision foggy, Mandy blinked several times, trying to clear her blurred sight.

Sam and Mandy crowded near Jack, peering down into the fertile valley below. They stood on the high rim of a basin, snowcapped mountains towering around them.

They seemed to be poised on the lip of a bowl. Mandy squinted at the verdant valley that spread out a hundred feet below them.

"Quail Valley," breathed Jack.

Brown fields and green foliage dotted the rough terrain, creating a colorful patchwork of various pieces. A winding thread of a small river passed through the center of this valley. Tucked inside a fold of the land, she made out a house and a barn. Brian's farm?

Sam laid a hand on her arm. "Almost there, Mother. Come on." Taking her by the elbow, he gently steered her forward.

"It's stopped raining, Sam," said Jack. Then, he pointed across the valley. "Look, Sam, a rainbow."

Turning her head stiffly, Mandy's distorted gaze followed his small hand. It was indeed there, leaning from a dark cloud, colorful shafts of sunlight illuminated against the gray sky behind. Multi-colored, bright rays of sunlight streaked through the leaden sky above. The rainbow stretched over the valley, covering it like a shield.

With incredible effort, Mandy followed the boys the remaining half mile to the house, glad the way was downhill now.

Each step seemed like torture. Chills racked her thin frame, and occasional coughing spells left her exhausted. Mandy desperately wanted to stop and lie down under one of the leafless trees that lined the trail. She repeatedly told herself she could go no further, she had to rest. Then she would push herself on. The boys needed to get somewhere. They could not be left alongside the trail.

She wondered if she were dying. It didn't bother her terribly much to be dying, she only feared for the boys. She wasn't overly attached to this life, she decided grimly. She hoped the boys would be okay without her.

After an endless span of time, a house loomed only yards away. She had succeeded. The boys would be safe.

Then there was no rain, no light, no mud. She was in a dark cave and nothing mattered anymore. Had she died?

At first, Mandy felt she liked the cave. There were no responsibilities for her, and she didn't have to take care of anyone, even herself. She enjoyed this feeling of freedom. It was quiet here in the dark.

But then she started remembering. She did not like this at all.

She remembered her home in Virginia. Comfortable, loving, encouraging, warm. She didn't like to remember what she'd turned her back on. Father had been so angry when Richard and she returned from eloping and announced they were married. Father predicted awful things, and Mother had cried.

Mandy remembered the various taverns they'd lived in for the next two years in Richmond. At first, they'd been grand and clean when the dowry money was still available. Later, they'd stayed in some disreputable places with bugs and dirty linens.

Mandy remembered the sea voyage to California. She'd been pregnant with Jack then and spent most of the trip with her head hanging over the railing. Not behavior befitting a lady.

Richard had not cared and only laughed at her discomfort. He'd spent his days gambling with the men and sailors aboard the windjammer. Sam was but a toddler then and didn't like the confining ship any more than she did.

Despite Richard's promises this move to California would greatly improve their situation, the opposite had proven true from the first. In San Francisco, her luggage had been stolen. When it finally occurred to her later that only *her* luggage had disappeared, Mandy wondered if Richard had sold her dresses for money.

It hadn't taken long for Richard to begin his ventures into the gold fields. He would be gone for months and rarely returned to see his young family. One time, Mandy had taken a job in a café in Sacramento and had run into Richard. He came into the diner with some friends to have dinner. He was shocked at first to see her, then feigned happiness. Whatever his true feelings for her, he returned to the gambling dens of the gold towns within the week.

Mandy floated through her memories, unaware of hunger or feelings, thinking over events she'd been too frightened to allow herself to consider these past several years. As if released from a locked box, they played across her mind, terrifying her once again.

She was only twenty-five when she found Richard that night in Sacramento, dead in a gutter, robbed and knifed. She hadn't even felt sad when she'd found him dead. Their love had died long ago, if he ever had any for her to begin with. She hadn't seen him in two years at that point and had almost given up ever seeing him again.

She stayed working in the Sacramento café until the proprietor had gotten the gold fever and closed the doors of his business, heading for the hills of Hangtown. She'd heard there were many jobs to be had in Yuba City and moved there, hopeful of employment. The reports had been false, however, and she ended up washing laundry for whoever would pay.

The cave was safe now, though, above the horrible existence Mandy had lived these past years. She floated above the events that unfolded below her, not really a part and yet not unattached, either. She watched as if from a safe distance.

She heard voices before she came to consciousness. She was shocked to hear laughter. When was the last time she had heard laughter?

Renewed Redemption

Slowly, the haze cleared. Desperately, Mandy tried to cling to the dark cave. She liked not having to work so hard and to watch the boys continue to struggle. The bizarre respite was coming to an end, and she knew she was not ready to return to reality.

The fog parted, the sun burning away the haze.

Someone sat on her bed. Bed? Why was she in bed?

Mandy opened her eyes hesitantly, the light from the window momentarily blinding her. She blinked, trying to focus.

With a gasp, Mandy recognized the man beside her. It was the stranger from her shack, the farmer. Brian Dawson.

CHAPTER 6

He sat on the edge of her bed, spooning broth into her mouth. Mandy stared.

Brian smiled at her. This time, she liked his smile, she thought. He looked happy.

"Hello, Mrs. Barrett," he said softly, lifting a spoon towards her. "I'm glad you've awakened. Try to take some more soup. It'll help you regain your strength."

Obediently, Mandy opened her mouth, not thinking she had a choice.

She did not remember granting this man permission to feed her, but she secretly enjoyed it. The soup was warm and tasty.

Mandy took a few more spoonsful of the soup before she held up a hand.

"Where am I?" she whispered. Her voice seemed hoarse and sounded odd in her ears.

"You're in my farmhouse in Quail Valley." Brian fed her another spoonful.

She swallowed. "How long have I been here?" Her voice sounded stronger, yet still tentative.

He pursed his lips and arched an eyebrow. "You came to my door five days ago. You've been sleeping."

"Where are Sam and Jack?" She didn't know why she hadn't asked about them first thing.

"They are removing rocks from a field. They're safe." He pushed the final spoon of soup into her, then dabbed her lips with a linen napkin.

Renewed Redemption

Brian placed the empty bowl on a stand beside the bed and lifted a glass of water. A real glass, Mandy noticed. Not a tin cup.

He held the water to her lips, and she drank sparingly. A tiny dribble escaped and rolled over her lips. He dabbed the napkin again.

Without moving her head, Mandy looked slowly around the room. The yellow walls made her think of sunshine, and light streamed brightly through the glass window. She was reminded vaguely of home.

Mandy studied the comforter more closely, noting its intricate stitching. Then, her eyes bulged at sight of her bare arms, exposed for all to see, laying on the comforter, pale and thin. Her dress had been removed and she wore only her undergarments.

Shamefully, she closed her eyes. She could feel her cheeks burn in disgrace.

Ashamed, she looked swiftly at Brian.

"How come I'm not in my dress?" she demanded, her eyes narrowing with accusation. Was this man to be trusted? Suspicion and doubt flooded over her, and Mandy wondered bitterly what new mishap she would now add to her list of regrets.

A crimson wave crept up his neck, and he glanced away, pretending to retrieve the water glass once more. "Sam and Jack took the dress off you. It was dirty. You collapsed outside in a mud puddle," he explained.

Mandy relaxed. She remembered the muddy trail to Quail Valley.

He helped her drink, the glass pressed to her lips, while Mandy stared at him.

"Rest now. I'll see you later." He rose. Brian collected the empty dishes and left the room, lightly closing the door behind him.

Mandy smoothed the comforter, feeling the cleanliness and softness of the bedding. She hadn't been in a bed in a house for over ten years. She'd missed it without realizing the difference. Mandy had gotten used to strange beds in taverns, on the ship, and the many places she'd lived in since coming to California. But she hadn't slept in a house in years.

Her hand swept the soft bed cover, marveling how clean the sheets and blankets were. The whole room spoke of someone who cared for cleanliness.

The warm meal was having its effect. Unable to keep her eyes open, Mandy dozed the rest of the afternoon.

∞∞∞∞∞

That evening, a pair of excited, shining-faced boys came bounding into the room. Mandy brightened at the sight of them. She also noticed their hair was washed and their ears spotless. The clothes they wore were not the ones they'd arrived in. Not quite fitting correctly, they were nonetheless of a better quality than what they'd worn.

Mandy stared at Sam and Jack, studying their scrubbed, shining faces as they shared their news. She noticed the hollow look in their cheeks had faded. The boys were eating well.

"Oh, Mother, it's so good to be here. Brian works hard every day, but he lets us take breaks, and we eat breakfast and lunch and dinner each day. I am so glad God has brought us here," Jack reported upon first seeing his recovering mother.

She looked at him closely, wide-eyed at his comment. "God? Did God bring us here?" she questioned, her curious glance taking in her eldest son too.

Sam nodded. "Mother, I've learned more about God in the last four days than I ever knew in my whole life," Sam reported happily, a peculiar smile on his lips that Mandy did not remember seeing there before.

Renewed Redemption

"God is good. Brian says you can see his goodness all around us. He does beautiful things. Just look at nature. It worships God always," Sam explained, still smiling.

"Well, you two sound like regular preachers." Mandy eyed them disapprovingly. "Did Brian teach you all these things about God?"

She shifted uneasily. Mandy was suddenly not sure they should stay. Maybe this was not a good idea after all.

She tried to sit up, struggled and then fell back with a grunt, realizing she was not ready for travel. The sickness had taken its toll, and she lacked strength and stamina. They might have to stay a while longer. Just until she regained her strength, she told herself.

"Brian has taught us a lot of new things, Mother. Like praying before meals and even when we wake up in the morning. To give God the day, to allow him to guide our steps," Sam spoke up, almost mimicking Brian's pleasant voice. Mandy could imagine the tall farmer saying these very words. The thought made her shiver

"He has, has he?" she mused, her eyes narrowing as anger and distrust burned within her. Was this stranger trying to influence her children behind her back? She told herself she'd have to get better fast before Brian had the boys in a monastery.

"Mother," Jack added, "I haven't eaten so well in all my life. I'm learning lots, and Brian lets us read any book we want from his library. We have reading time every day."

Mandy tilted her head, and her anger waned. She'd always sought books from the various cabins and shacks they searched for anything of value. She enjoyed reading and placed a high worth on books. Reading was one of the things she and the boys liked to do together. They would take turns reading aloud and then discuss the book. It had proved to be an escape from their daily tasks.

And eating well, huh? That was big. Maybe she'd been hasty in thinking they might have to leave this place soon. Food everyday was hard to beat.

She relaxed then, her shoulders releasing the tension that formed there. Her boys seemed happy and well cared for—more than she'd been able to do for them, she thought bitterly.

Mandy didn't like the boys being taught so much about God, but having a lot of food might make this bitter pill more palatable.

Before she could question them further, Brian stuck his head in the door. "Hey, boys, it's time to help prepare dinner. I'll need wood in the wood box and someone to help peel potatoes."

Jack kissed Mandy lightly on the cheek and jumped off the bed to run from the room. Sam followed with a smile and a wave to Mandy.

She frowned. Their eager response to Brian's instructions shocked her. No fight, no arguing, no defiance. The boys had immediately obeyed. They even seemed happy to do so. Why?

She could hear light conversation coming from down the hall and guessed that was the direction of the kitchen. Nestling deeper into her blankets, Mandy savored the warmth and comfort of the little room. She knew this couldn't last and was intent on enjoying it while she could.

Brian later appeared with another bowl of soup and a plate of mashed potatoes. Her mouth fairly watered at the sight of the potatoes. When was the last time she'd eaten mashed potatoes?

Mandy felt she could manage feeding herself this time, her arms worked fine, but something held her back from speaking up. She thrilled at the idea of being fed one more time.

Again, Brian sat on the edge of the bed and fed her dinner. His familiarity somehow didn't bother her now. She felt silly having this man feed her, but she had to admit that she enjoyed it too. She felt as if she were being given the royal treatment.

"I want to ask you some questions," Mandy began between swallows of soup.

The tall man held the spoon again to her mouth. "Sure, anything."

Mandy watched him closely as she swallowed. "Why all this talk about God? Is it really good for small children to hear so much about God?"

Brian almost dropped his spoon. He stared at Mandy, his eyes widening.

"Well, yes. It is good for Jack and Sam to get some Bible teaching," he said slowly, his eyes wary. "It is truth. They seem eager to hear about Jesus."

He paused a moment between another spoonful of soup.

"Don't you believe in God, Mandy?" It was the first time he'd used her given name.

Mandy nodded. "Oh, I believe in God, all right." The bitterness in her tone was obvious. "I think of him every day. He's the one who's done this to me."

Brian fed her another spoonful of potatoes, a curious look in his eye. "Did what to you?"

Mandy swallowed. "Punished me for my selfishness," she replied quickly. "I knew it then, and I know it now. God has been with me this whole time, frowning on me every day."

Mandy gestured to the water glass, and Brian hastened to retrieve it. He held it to her lips.

"What do you believe God is punishing you for?" he asked as he returned the glass to the bedside table.

Mandy glanced worriedly at the door and lowered her voice. "God did not want me to marry Richard. My father didn't, either. I wouldn't heed his warning, and I married Richard anyway. I was wrong, and I know it. God has punished me ever since."

A long silence followed while Mandy finished her dinner.

"Why do you think he is punishing you?" Brian wiped her mouth with the napkin.

"It says in the Bible to not be unequally yoked," Mandy whispered, glancing furtively at the door again. "I knew Richard wasn't a believer, and I married him anyway."

Brian tilted his head. "I believe God disciplines those he loves. Like it says in the Book of Hebrews, but God isn't mean. He loves us. His intent is always to build our character, to draw us to him."

Mandy shook her head, defiant. "You're wrong, mister. God is mean, and he doesn't love me. He watches me like a bug under a magnifying glass, waiting for a chance to knock me down."

Mandy scowled, suddenly annoyed at herself for opening to this complete stranger. He wasn't part of her family and yet she'd let down her guard, confided in him. He'd gotten her to talk about things she didn't want others to know. She'd kept these feelings locked within, deep inside the small box in the shadows of her mind.

Now, exposed and vulnerable, Mandy turned on him.

"What do you know of hard times?" She almost yelled now, her voice rising. She could tell she was on the verge of tears, which made her angrier. She would not cry in front of this man.

Mandy saw the sudden pain that came to his soft, brown eyes, but she had gone too far and couldn't stop herself now.

"You live in this perfect house with plenty of food. What do you know of real hardship and struggle?" she demanded, glaring at Brian with narrowed eyes.

Mandy stared as the man seemed frozen in place. He held her glass of water in one hand, the napkin in the other, but didn't move a muscle for a full minute. He simply stared at her, his look seeming far away, seeing something in the distance.

Renewed Redemption

Brian slowly placed the half-full glass on the bed stand, rising to his feet as if he carried a heavy weight on his back, turned and walked from the room.

CHAPTER 7

For the next three days, Mandy saw nothing of Brian. Sam and Jack alternated bringing her meals, and each time, they acquainted her with the goings-on of the farm.

"It's bigger than you think, Mother," Jack reported one day at breakfast. "Brian even has bees. I haven't seen them, though. Brian says it's too cold right now, and there are no flowers for the bees to get honey from. That will happen later, when it warms up. They fly around the boxes by the hundreds, and Brian told me they'll be busy bringing honey to the hive. I told him I was afraid of bees because they sting, and he said that all things have stingers if you are not careful."

Mandy jerked. Had that comment been meant for her?

"He said rattlesnakes have poison, some fish have barbs that poke, and even roses have thorns. Brian says the secret is to be patient with them, not pushy, and treat them with gentleness," Jack went on, his young eyes glowing with excitement.

The small boy kissed his mother and carried the empty dishes from the room.

Thoughts of Brian's remarks to Jack occupied Mandy's hour after breakfast. The farmer sure had a lot of things to say to her sons. She felt concerned but knew she needed her strength before she could completely reenter their daily activities. Sleep seemed to claim her often. The fever had taken a lot out of Mandy, and she knew she needed to recover fully before attempting to get out of bed. She was beginning to feed herself again, at least.

Mandy tried to take her mind from her worries by reading the outdated newspaper Brian had left beside her bed.

Renewed Redemption

The political events of the nation were highlighted, including articles of electing an anti-slavery president and southerners' distrust of one. She gathered they would not support the new man in the White House.

Later, Mandy dozed, happy to rest in her quiet room.

She had to admit she was not eager to get back on her feet. Not just yet. She hadn't enjoyed any kind of a break in over ten years, and now, suddenly, she was in bed being fed with lots of food and rest in very clean and charming surroundings. It was more than Mandy could've hoped for.

Each mealtime was a treat with her boys. They were so full of joy, and, she noticed with delight, starting to fill out from the regular meals. She hadn't ever seen them so happy. They worked hard all day out in the fields, and yet, they loved it. Their faces shone with a sense of intense contentment like she had never known in her own life, at least not in the past decade.

Mandy wondered about these things as she read and napped the days away. By her calculations, she'd been at Brian's farm for eight full days. She felt as if she were on an exclusive holiday. The past day or so, she'd begun to feel guilty. The boys worked hard, if she was to believe their accounts of the labor in the fields, while she did nothing.

During this time, most mornings she'd simply rolled over and gone back to sleep—a luxury she hadn't enjoyed since her youth. On this particular morning, Mandy stirred before the sun began to make an appearance. She slipped from the covers and stood next to the bed.

A wave of dizziness swept over her, and she held to the headboard to steady herself. After a few moments, the sensation passed. Mandy struck a match and lit the candle on her nightstand.

A closet on one wall of the little room drew her attention. For the duration of her confinement, Mandy had wondered what the small closet might contain. Now, she turned the door handle. Unused hinges creaked, and she held the candle higher, exploring the closet's interior. Inside hung five dresses and a house robe. Three colorful every day dresses were flanked by a plain gray travel dress and a fancy burgundy dress for special occasions.

A warm looking black fleece coat hung at one end.

Donning the floral-patterned house robe, she picked up the candle again and walked to her door on the tips of her toes, careful to not make a sound. Easing the door open, she peered down the dark hallway to the left. Dimly, she could make out a pair of closed doors. Glancing to the right, she discerned a subtle glow.

Moving on cat's feet, she crept down the hallway toward the glow, which grew as she approached. Her feet made no sound on the hard, stone floor. When was the last time she'd been in a house with real floors? She brushed the thought from her mind as she continued forward. Finally, she paused and stared at the entrance to a cozy sitting room.

A fire crackled merrily in a large, open, stone fireplace at one end of a spacious room. Mandy let her gaze travel. Rugs lay in a plentiful array on the flagstone floor. There was even a mountain lion pelt on the hearth. An unlit kerosene lamp sat on the dining room table behind the semicircle of furniture facing the fireplace. A kitchen filled the far corner, copper pots gleaming dully. The fire cast a ruddy glow into the darkness, and by this light, Brian held a thick book on his lap, studying it intently.

An elegant couch faced the fireplace, and a pair of wing-backed chairs flanked each end. The room was not lavish but felt extremely comfortable and warm.

As her gaze came back to Brian, she started. He stared at her now as intently as he had the book but with a gentle smile on his face.

Embarrassed, she smoothed a hand over her robe. "Oh. I didn't know anyone was awake." Mandy moved her feet forward to stand at the edge of the room.

"I get up early every day for my morning devotions. Habit, I guess." He paused, his gaze traveling over her. "You're looking better."

Mandy smiled. She hoped he'd forgotten the argument of the other day. "Yes, I feel much better, thank you. A little unsteady on my feet, but much better." She came farther into the room and slipped into the big chair at the end of the couch. Facing him, she continued. "I haven't had a chance to thank you properly for your kindness and hospitality to me and my boys. They seem very happy, and that means a lot to me. I don't know how I will ever repay you for the food and rest you've allowed me."

Brian leaned back, closing the book on his lap. "I was hoping you were coming here to take me up on my offer of employment. You can repay me by accepting the job and running the house when you feel up to the task. I confess, I've been hard pressed to come up with meal options that anyone but me would eat."

He smiled again. He had a nice smile that looked comfortable on his face, like it was often there. It made her feel at ease, peaceful even.

"Well, it seems you've already enlisted the boys into your rock clearing army, and they appear content with the position, so I guess I must accept on their behalf. I will begin duties as soon as I receive a list of responsibilities from my employer."

Brian rose suddenly and walked into the dark kitchen behind the sitting room. He returned in a minute with two cups of tea. Handing one to Mandy, he resumed his seat on the couch.

"Well, let's see," he began and then blew gently on his tea. "I've never had employees before, so this is all very new to me. I'd have the boys work outside with me, working the farm and doing any chores I assign them. Currently, we are clearing fields of stones in preparation for planting alfalfa. They are a tremendous help. As for household duties, I guess they would include cleaning, laundry, cooking, and occasionally running to town to buy supplies or fetch something required on the farm."

Pausing, he lifted his mug and sipped his tea. Then he draped a casual arm on the back of the couch, facing her as he spoke once more. "Last week, I had to make a special trip to retrieve a tool I dropped off at the blacksmith shop for repair. It would be nice to send you on such errands so I can continue working here."

Mandy sipped her tea, listening. This job sounded too good to be true. She couldn't believe this was all she was to do. No babies to tend, no rough, hungry miners to serve, no dirty shanty to live in. She shifted, dreading this next part. What aspect of the new job would she have to refuse? It couldn't all be this simple.

She drew a deep breath. "Now that I'm feeling better, where would you like me to move to? The boys and I can bunk in one room. We're used to that." Mandy would miss the small room with the yellow walls, but this was Brian's house, and surely he'd have her move to less desirable accommodations.

Brian waved a dismissive hand. "Oh, no, there's no need for that. I have plenty of room, so you might as well stay in the room you're in."

Mandy nodded slowly, surprised by his response. Her own room? She couldn't believe it.

Then she frowned. Perhaps he meant to cheat her on pay because she had her own room. She narrowed her eyes.

"What about wages? Room and board are very generous, but I will need some wages," Mandy said, feeling like she was pushing her luck. No matter, she thought. He could only say no if he wouldn't pay wages. She'd be content for now with just room and board anyway.

"Of course." Brian nodded in agreement. "What's fair in your estimation?"

Mandy blinked. She didn't know what was fair. She'd earned wages for cleaning laundry or working in the Sacramento café, but she'd never been a housekeeper. She thought quickly and then decided to ask for high wages. She'd prefer to dicker with him for some lesser amount rather than miss out on what could be possible.

"I will require two dollars a week for wages. I can promise you I am worth it," Mandy answered, waiting for his rebuttal. But it was not forthcoming. Brian nodded agreeably and, putting down his cup, clapped his hands together.

"There, I have hired a housekeeper and cook. I'm pleased. You can start when you feel up to it. I'll want to give you household expenses to make purchases at town when need be."

He rose to his feet and crossed the room to a large maple desk that stood in one corner. As he pulled a drawer open and extracted a small box, Mandy glanced quickly at the book he'd laid on the couch beside him. She scowled when she realized it was a Bible.

Brian strode back to her and, opening the box, removed several dollar bills and started to hand them to her when he suddenly hesitated.

Mandy could guess his reasons for not handing her the money. He didn't trust her, she thought grimly. And why should he? They'd only just met.

Brian put the money back into the small box. "Mrs. Barrett, this is the money for the running of the house. I'll leave it in this box in the desk and you take whatever you need when you go to town, all right?"

She sat stunned, unable to speak. He was trusting her with the whole box of money. It probably contained more than she'd seen in years. She nodded mutely, her mind awhirl.

As Brian returned the box to the desk, she pursed her lips. What was he thinking? Was he playing with her, testing her? Why was he being so kind and generous to her and the boys? What did he hope to gain from this extreme kindness?

Her suspicious mind struck on a possibility and she froze, anxiety filling her as she explored the idea.

Of course, that must be it. Mandy could feel the anger surge within her, and her stomach heated with fire. Oh, no, a man would never take advantage of her again. What other motive could there be for such kindness?

Mandy's back stiffened and she glared at Brian.

"Mr. Dawson," she began, shifting in her seat. "I am not the kind of woman that maybe you are assuming I am. I will not be presumed upon in any capacity or indecent manner, and my room will always be for me alone. Do I make myself perfectly clear?"

He cocked his head to one side as if confused. Then, his face reddened with comprehension, and he laughed nervously. "Mrs. Barrett, let me assure you of my true intentions. You are merely the housekeeper, and I am your employer—nothing more. We will maintain the utmost respectable relationship. Strictly business."

Mandy nodded and held out her hand. "Good. Then it's a deal. I'll begin today." Even if he had other intentions in the future, she thought, she would set him to rights.

Brian shook her hand but eyed her skeptically. "I think you should take another day or two to fully recover."

"Nonsense. I'm on the mend," Mandy asserted with a laugh. However, as she stood, dizziness overtook her, and she sank to the chair once more.

Renewed Redemption

Brian moved swiftly to her side. "Can you walk?" He peered down at her, genuine concern in his eyes.

Mandy shook her head weakly. "No, but I'll be okay. Give me a minute."

Brian shook his head. "No. You're being stubborn." He swept her into his arms and pressed her to his chest. It happened so fast, Mandy didn't have time to protest. Within moments, he was placing her gently on her bed.

He pulled the blankets over her and stepped back. "You need more time. Don't worry about work, it'll be there tomorrow."

He strode to the door, and with his hand on the knob, grinned at her before retreating from the room.

Mandy stared at the closed door, her heart pounding. Brian had lifted her with such ease, and the feel of his muscular chest and arms thrilled her in a way she didn't fully comprehend. It had been years since she'd been held by a man.

Within the hour, Sam brought her breakfast, but she couldn't concentrate on his prattling about his workday. Her mind whirled with memories of Brian and his kindness and strength.

Mandy found herself thinking about little else the remainder of the day until that evening when Jack brought her dinner. She listened patiently at his tale of a raccoon that had eaten part of their lunch they'd taken with them to the fields.

"Brian says we have lots of land to clear but that we're doing a terrific job. He says soon he'll bring out the harrow and try to pull more rocks from the ground. We need to get the land ready for planting." The small boy gave his report with some importance, his chest puffing out. "I'm working my best. We're doing all things to the glory of God."

She narrowed her eyes. *There they go again, talking about God.* She chewed her lip thoughtfully and decided she'd have to put a stop to this constant talking about the Lord. It would have a negative effect the first time the boys encountered a struggle that God refused to help them with. In truth, her own difficulty with the Lord prompted her to protect the boys from his intervention. She would need to have a discussion with Brian.

The next morning, Mandy repeated her actions of the previous day and crawled out of bed before sunrise. She guessed Brian would be in the sitting room reading. Noticing with some satisfaction that she was not as dizzy this morning when she stood, Mandy moved stealthily down the hallway, this time with no candle.

The glow of the fire drew her along the dark corridor. As she reached the sitting room, she saw Brian in the precise position as before.

Her pulse quickened at the sight of him, and she frowned, nettled at the unwanted sensation. Steeling herself, she squared her shoulders and strode into the room. She hoped her face revealed nothing of the tumult she felt.

Brian lifted his eyes from the book at her approach. A smile came easily once again to his clean-shaven face. "Good morning, Mrs. Barrett. How do you feel today? Better, I hope."

"Better," she agreed, and sat down in her chair. "Mr. Dawson—"

Brian quickly held up a hand, interrupting her. "Brian. I insist."

Mandy huffed. "All right, Brian." She pursed her lips and scanned the room, noticing the ruddy shadows on the wall as she gathered her wits. She drew a deep breath and turned back to him, lifting her chin. "I am greatly concerned by the constant references to God the boys are making," she began, sounding more confident than she felt. "I think they are too young to hear so much about religious things. After all, what will they do when they discover he does not answer every prayer, or when God chooses not to fix a broken situation? I think it best if you lay off the Bible teaching for a while."

Renewed Redemption

Brian stared at her a moment, letting her words sink in, then shook his head slowly. "No, I don't agree."

She tilted her head, her eyebrows arching at his response. "Well, I appreciate that you don't agree, but I don't really see what difference that makes. I mean, I am their mother, and you are only their employer. I think you should respect my request and leave it at that." Mandy noticed the harsh tone of her voice, impatient with his argument.

Brian closed the thick book and looked at her, one hand stroking his chin.

"When the Jews told Peter and John in the Book of Acts to stop telling the people about Jesus, they replied with this question; 'Who should we obey? You or God?' It is my job to tell people about Jesus. It is what God would have me do. Should I obey you or God?"

His calm voice irritated her, but she sat straighter and nodded. "That's easy. Me. I'm the mother."

Mandy paused, then went on swiftly. "If they were your children, I would respect what you had to say about their upbringing. In this case, I am the parent and you should respect my decision." She felt herself start to get angry.

Brian smiled, and the action no longer soothed her. Mandy wanted to strike him. "With all due respect to you and your position as a parent, I believe I'm a better judge of what God would have me do than you are. God is good, loving, forgiving, and desires good things for his people. Sam and Jack deserve to know that."

Knots twisted in her belly, and her face flushed with heat. Mandy thought fire would leap from her eyes. Suddenly, she was on her feet. "Forgiving? Desires good things? Who are you talking about?"

She was shouting now but didn't care. "That is not the God I know. I know God, and he is vindictive, not letting me forget what I've done. I know I've made mistakes, but he will not forgive me."

Mandy could feel her chest tighten, and she struggled to draw breath. God had been cruel to her, never letting her forget how her mistakes haunted her every step. Now they had affected her sons as well.

She pointed a trembling finger at Brian. "You're wrong, Mr. Dawson, when you speak about God. I have lived under his wrath."

She turned to flee, but Brian stood and grasped her arm.

"Wait, Mandy. Let me show you the true God of Holy Scripture. Let me show you the Bible and what it says about God. I know he is good and forgiving. I, too, have lived with him, and he's shown me his grace and love."

She wrenched free from Brian's grip and ran down the hallway, her vision blurred in the dark passageway. She slammed the door behind her and threw herself across the unmade bed, sobbing as she clutched the blankets.

CHAPTER 8

Mandy lay in the total darkness, the emotion spilling from her as she let herself cry. God had been so mean to her, never giving her a break. She knew she didn't deserve one, either. Her own selfishness had ignored her father's wisdom and urged her to marry Richard. Oh, what a mess she'd made of her life.

Mandy cried until the disturbing passion drained her. With a sniffle, she dried her puffy eyes on her robe sleeve. Her hands trembled as she fumbled to strike a match and light her candle.

She lay back for a moment, thinking before she would rise and begin to pack. She stared at the ceiling, putting her whirling thoughts in order.

A sigh escaped her. She'd have to leave. It was all too good to be true, anyway. Good things never happened to her, not really. Even if they appeared good, they were taken from her soon enough, taunting her with things hoped for. Things that were not for her. Not anymore.

Things like love, home, peace, security. Mandy had these things back in Virginia, but she'd given them up to pursue her own path, forsaking God's way.

Now he hounded her, never allowing her to forget her mistakes.

She sighed again, the sigh of resignation and acceptance. She'd made her bed, her mother would say. Now she had to lie in it. Sin had consequences.

Mandy turned her head and peered at the closet. What would she take with her? With a heave, she rolled over and sat on the edge of the bed.

Renewed Redemption

Dim light stretched to the corners of the room and Mandy picked up the candle, taking it with her to the closet. She studied the dresses, her fingers caressing the soft material. She considered taking one of them with her. Brian could spare a dress. He would probably never even miss one of these fine garments.

Then she found her own dress hanging on a hook. She pulled it from the closet and examined it by the dull candlelight.

It'd been cleaned, that was obvious. But there was a rent in one sleeve and the garment was faded and badly worn. With longing, Mandy looked again at the other dresses hanging in the closet, then turned back to her own.

Placing the candle on the bed stand, she almost tore the house robe off herself. Quickly, she pulled her dingy dress over her head and looked at herself in the tiny square of a mirror mounted on the wall.

Rough, she admitted, but it would have to do. It had served her now for a couple of years, and she could squeeze a bit more time from the threadbare dress, she decided, gritting her teeth. She would have to.

She couldn't stay here another minute. This man was intolerable. He had no intention of listening to her or respecting her opinion. He as much as told her that his judgment was better because he knew the Bible. She bristled at the memory.

Brian was so sure of himself, Mandy fumed, her hands clenching and unclenching. He knew the Bible, and she did not. He was too self-righteous. It made her furious. He wasn't even a father, she reminded herself smugly, he had no children. She was the boys' mother and she knew best.

Mandy quickly pulled her blonde hair into a ponytail, tying it with a ribbon as she ignored the stringy, greasy feel of the long locks. She dearly would've enjoyed a bath, but there wasn't time for that now. She was leaving this place. She would gather the boys and be gone within the next few minutes. She didn't have to take any guff from this mister-know-it-all.

Abruptly, she stopped, the color fading from her cheeks as she considered a disturbing thought. What if the boys wouldn't go with her? They seemed so happy here. As for that, where would they go? They had no place to move to, no job awaited them. They had no money.

Mandy sat on the edge of the bed, her hand sliding lovingly over the soft sheets. She would miss this bed.

She arched an eyebrow and scanned the little yellow room. She would miss more than just the bed. The food. Three meals a day was hard to ignore. The comfort of the snug little house, the warmth and the protection it provided. She would miss all these things.

A scowl crossed her face and she shifted uneasily. What was she thinking? Would she move her children from such a wonderful place as this because of her pride? Would she never learn from her past? Hadn't pride been the cause of many of her current problems? Could she give all this up because she disliked Brian Dawson?

Sure, he was annoying, but he'd given shelter and food to her hurting family. Mandy had recovered her health here, taking time to rest while others worked. She did owe Brian for all of that, she grudgingly admitted. It was more rest than she'd known in years.

Letting her eyes roam her little yellow room again, her resolve softened.

Perhaps she could shield the boys from Brian's constant preaching while she worked here and saved her money before searching out another job. She'd be a fool to walk away from this situation because of her personal feelings. Pride does not feed people, she reminded herself grimly. Pride was a luxury for people who had food and shelter, not for homeless widows with two small boys.

Mandy would swallow her pride temporarily and work hard, grateful for what this house provided to her family. In the meantime, she'd keep an eye out for other employment opportunities that might come her way.

She sat there for a minute longer, gathering her ideas around her, and then she rose, standing tall, ready for battle again. Life had always been a battle, a war she was caught up in where she fought alone. She had learned quickly in her marriage that not even her husband would help her fight this war. Richard had not been concerned if his family won or not, if they were fed or went without. She'd always hoped one day she would marry a man who could help her, a fellow warrior in the struggle of life. But, sadly, Richard had proven to not be that kind of soldier. No, he'd been a deserter in the struggle to provide for his family, a quitter. He'd been a terrible soldier.

Her knees felt suddenly weak, and she lowered to the bed again. Mandy was a good soldier and was concerned about success in this battle. Success meant her boys were fed and safe, taken care of, warm. This war had many casualties. She had seen those who'd lost. People who'd starved or lived on the streets, begging for handouts and scraps. Mandy was determined not to be one of those casualties. She was in this battle to win. She stroked the bed again and set her jaw, resolution filling her as she determined to do what best served her family.

My sons deserve better, even if I don't.

Mandy sighed heavily and stroked the fine bed linen once more. She would swallow her anger and submit to this man, for a while anyway—but only to a point. She would work for him but would badger him to leave her boys alone. She would protect her children from this Bible-thumping farmer.

Mandy got slowly to her feet and walked back down the hallway to the living room. Brian hadn't moved. He still sat reading his Bible. He looked up at the sound of her approach.

"All right, listen, mister," she began, scowling solemnly at him. "I'll stay and work for you. I will clean and sew and cook. But you are to stay away from my boys with your religious teaching. They're off limits. Let me be the spiritual guide for them, not you."

Brian smiled, his even, white teeth gleaming in the dim light. Mandy grudgingly admitted he had a perfect smile.

He nodded. "I'm glad you've agreed to stay. I believe there's a real purpose in this arrangement. But you will not work today. You will wash yourself and find some other clothes to wear. I've already put pots of water on to boil."

He laid aside the thick book and rose to his feet, walking toward her. "Mrs. Rogers left a number of dresses in the closet of that room, I believe. They were here when I purchased the house. You may wear them. Meanwhile, I'll prepare breakfast for you."

He walked past Mandy and showed her where the bathtub was located, then returned to the kitchen.

Biting her tongue in order to hold back stinging retorts, Mandy carried the hot water to her room and bathed while Brian cooked.

The complete luxury of the event made Mandy take her time. The steaming water and the clean dress felt so amazing to her. She was reminded briefly of her youth, when she'd bathed often and only wore clean clothes, but she hastily brushed the memory away. It was painful to remember those wonderful days before she'd left home.

She didn't want to hurry, but upon hearing the boys scampering down the hall, she hastened to complete her preparations.

Mandy entered the kitchen and all eyes turned. She'd washed in clean, warm water for the first time in months and donned the blue gingham dress from the closet. Her long, blonde hair hung loosely over her shoulders and draped down her back. She had brushed the locks of hair until they shone gold in the morning sunlight streaming through the window.

Sam and Jack gasped at the sight of her and Brian dropped his stirring spoon.

Renewed Redemption

"Mother, you are beautiful," Jack breathed in a whisper.

"Wow, Mother. I've never seen you like this." Sam gestured at her costume. "That dress makes your eyes look so blue."

Mandy smiled weakly, self-conscious of the attention and praise. She'd been a local beauty back home, but years had passed without any encouraging compliments about her looks. She was unused to the positive observations now directed at her.

Suddenly uncomfortable and shy, Mandy simply stared back at the boys, unsure how to respond to their kind comments. She smoothed the pretty blue dress with her hands, liking how the material felt beneath her touch.

Brian turned back toward the stove and dished a plate of eggs and potatoes. He placed it on the table before an empty chair.

"Sit, Mrs. Barrett, and have some breakfast. The boys and I were just commenting on how nice it is you've joined us at the table."

Brian averted his eyes and helped serve more food to the hungry boys. Mandy could not help but notice how he avoided looking at her.

He's so disgusted with me he can't even look at me.

Well, so be it. She would do her work so well he couldn't deny she was a fit mother, and there'd be no more doubts from Brian Dawson.

Over breakfast, which Brian opened with a prayer, he outlined the day's tasks. He wanted to clear and level a section of land above the small waterfall of the river. He planned to dam this water course to flood the alfalfa field they would plant.

"I can plant at least a hundred acres if the land is cleared of stone and will allow flooding. That means I must level that ground for when I dam the river. We have a lot of work ahead of us, boys, if we're to be ready by spring planting." He shoveled another forkful of potatoes into his mouth.

Sam looked at Mandy. "What will you do, Mother, while we work outside?"

Mandy glanced at Brian. "I am to clean and run the house. I will be busy in here. Cooking and washing for three men will keep me very busy, I daresay."

"Well, it's good to have someone else to clean the kitchen this morning." Brian rose to leave. Again, he averted his eyes from Mandy, but she didn't care. She pursed her lips tightly as she rolled up her sleeves.

Chairs scraped as the boys quickly stood. She was surprised at the lack of arguments as they hastened to follow Brian out the door, no prompting necessary.

"Goodbye, Mother," Jack quipped as he tagged after Brian and Sam. "We'll see you later. We men must go to work now."

They trooped out the front door with a sack lunch, and in an instant, Mandy stood alone. She surveyed her surroundings, liking the way the sun shone through the glass windows.

A shiver ran down her back as she remembered the squalid, windowless shanty by the river. She wished to never see the little shack again.

Mandy pushed the memory of the disgusting shack aside and reached for the dirty breakfast dishes, eager to get to work. Mandy had immediately noticed the convenience of an indoor water pump mounted to the counter above the porcelain sink. It was a luxury she was unused to, but quickly learned to appreciate. Indoor pumps were for rich people, far above Mandy's expectations.

She worked diligently, one task leading to another, until she'd cleaned the whole kitchen.

Shiny copper kettles and steel pots hung on hooks from the walls and the dishes were stacked neatly on the sideboard. She boiled water and mopped the flagstone floor until it fairly shone.

Renewed Redemption

A man could eat off this floor, Mandy thought to herself with satisfaction, wiping a loose strand of hair from her face with the back of her wrist. Perhaps a particular farmer she was now acquainted with, she mused slyly.

Brian Dawson would be impressed indeed when he returned that evening.

She noted with worry that her fatigue still plagued her, but she kept moving. Mandy would not let Brian think she couldn't keep up her end of the deal. She'd have to push herself to complete all the tasks she wished to accomplish this day, but it'd be done. There was no way Mandy would shirk her responsibilities, she would finish them all.

Late afternoon found her preparing a dinner with the food from the pantry and whatever the root cellar offered. The smell of frying bacon filled the kitchen along with the aroma of boiled potatoes. Dinner was on the table when Brian and the boys returned from the fields. The mouthwatering scent of fresh baked bread greeted the men as they opened the door of the small cottage.

"It's been a long time since I've enjoyed bacon potato soup," Brian commented as he washed his hands at the sink. "The last time I had potato soup," Brian continued as he moved to his chair, "I think I was still back in Maryland."

"Where is Maryland, Mother?" Sam asked as he, too, washed his hands and then sat down.

Mandy helped Jack dry his hands. "It is near Virginia." She hefted the heavy soup pot and carried it to the table. Grabbing the cutting board with the fresh bread, Mandy moved it as well.

"Virginia is where Mother and Sam are from," Jack informed Brian. "I was born here in California."

"You were born here, Jack?" Brian questioned, glancing at Mandy. His curiosity was obvious, but she tried to ignore it. However, the staring faces around the table said this was not possible.

Mandy felt reluctant to explain but saw no way out of it. She sighed, giving in. "Yes. I had Sam while I lived in Virginia, near Richmond. Jack was born in San Francisco, right after we landed."

"We?" Brian pressed, his eyes on Mandy.

"Father was a no-account. He died," Jack cut in, reaching for the soup ladle.

Mandy gaped at the things Jack said. Sure, they'd been the exact words from her own lips but were not to be shared with strangers.

She glanced uneasily at Brian and interjected before either boy could say more. "Mr. Dawson, I am sure you will want to pray before dinner?"

He hesitated, irritation showing on his face. Mandy congratulated herself at diverting the conversation.

Brian bowed his head.

"Dear heavenly Father, you are always good and kind. You make our lives work together in such a way as to bring glory to your holy name. Thank you for bringing these two wonderful boys to help me develop this land. They are a blessing to me, and I thank you. Thank you also for this food. Amen."

As Brian finished, Mandy opened her eyes and studied Sam and Jack, now sitting very tall in their chairs. They liked what Brian had said in his prayer. Mandy also noticed Brian had not mentioned her.

Mandy stood to serve soup, and soon the table was full of lively conversation of the day's events and accomplishments. While the boys told her about their work, Mandy observed Brian covertly surveying the room. She felt a grim satisfaction he could not find fault with the kitchen, nothing out of place, everything clean. She smiled to herself with pride that she'd done a good job. He would soon compliment her, she was sure. He was always complimenting the boys.

"Mandy," Brian spoke casually, turning his gaze upon her. Mandy thrilled, trying hard to look at ease while her heart fluttered with anticipation. *Here it comes.* She was surprised how eagerly she looked forward to a kind word from this man. Richard had never been one to compliment her on anything.

"I see you've worked hard in the kitchen. I'm sure I left it in a frightful mess after my attempts to navigate it properly for my new crew." He gestured to the two beaming boys. "Thank you for this delicious meal and a day's work."

He turned back to Jack and asked him some pleasantry, but Mandy was deaf to further table talk. Although she'd awaited the praise, deep down, perhaps, she felt it would not come. But Brian had noticed her effort. More than that, he had noted her singularly, and it deeply touched her. She basked in his approval.

Suddenly, she felt ill at ease. It rankled her stomach she had so eagerly awaited a kind word from this obstinate, opinionated man. She was no silly schoolgirl looking for verbal praise from the school headmaster for correct mathematics. She was a woman who had single-handedly raised two good boys and kept them fed. No one had helped her. She sat straighter in her chair as she scooped a spoonful of soup to her lips.

A quick realization followed on the footsteps of her initial idea. Had she truly done that well by her boys? They were not in school, they often wore discarded rags, and there were more times than she cared to remember when she could not provide a hot meal for them.

As conversation went on around her, Mandy's shoulders fell, and she seethed inwardly. God was doing it again, she thought. He was reminding her of her failings, her many shortcomings. He always did this when she thought too highly of herself. He would never let her forget how she had disappointed her family and then barely survived, not letting her boys know the normal things in life like going to school or fishing with their father. All the things she remembered fondly about her youth were things not to be experienced by her boys.

Because of her. Because of the selfish decision she had made to disobey her father and do what she'd wanted to do. She had wanted so badly to marry Richard.

Mandy had realized too late that her father's wisdom and experience about men was something she should have heeded. Too late, she discovered how much her father had tried to protect her from marrying the wrong man—Richard. Her father wanted better for her, but she had been too stubborn.

Even after she and Richard had eloped and then told of their secret wedding, Jack Mulligan had reluctantly given opportunities for his new son-in-law to prove himself worthy. She knew her father's opportunities had only been to help her—not for the benefit of her husband. Richard failed on every score. Richard had even stolen from her father. That had been the straw that broke the camel's back. Jack Mulligan had ordered his daughter's husband from his property. His parting words still played in Mandy's ears.

"Richard, the love of God is not in you. You will destroy yourself with your thieving and gambling. My worry is you will take my daughter down with you in the process." He had turned then to face Mandy, his eyes softening. "Mandy girl, if ever you need to come home, know you will always be welcome. I love you, daughter."

Mandy had squared her shoulders, her chin rising, and glared defiantly at her father. The same Irish pride and strength that was in Jack Mulligan flowed in his daughter's veins. The bitter words she spoke then still rang in her mind.

"Father, you cannot speak so harshly to my husband and then try and sweet talk me. I will never leave my husband to come home, and you shall not see me again."

Mandy and Richard had left the farm then. Soon after, they departed for California. Neither had returned to Richmond since.

"Mandy," Brian spoke loudly, and she came back to herself, aware everyone at the table was now staring at her. Why did these haunting memories seem to be coming to her more frequently? It was as if the box lid was coming loose and she could not keep it closed any longer.

Wide-eyed, she stared in return. "What? Is something wrong?"

"Mother, we asked you about the bread." Sam looked at her sharply, his eyes full of concern. "We were discussing honey, and you seemed far away."

"Honey? What are you talking about?" Mandy felt confused and not sure what was going on around her. She had been very far away, she knew. All the way home.

"Brian was telling us about the honeybees," said Jack. "They give him honey every year. Sam and I want some for our bread, but Brian says not yet." Mandy could tell her youngest had not caught on she'd been deep in thought.

"Well, Jack, Brian must give you some honey, then," Mandy managed with a weak smile, trying to recover her wits.

"Mother." Jack laughed and rolled his eyes. "Have you not heard anything we've said? The bees eat the honey for their winter food. Brian says we cannot take their honey now, or they'll die. We must be patient for spring, then we will gather honey to sell."

Mandy felt like her head was made of wood. She slowly turned her gaze from the small boy to Brian. He was staring at her, a quizzical look on his face.

Brian nodded slowly. "Yes. We take the honey from the hive in spring and sell it at the market in Yuba City. I've even taken some to Sacramento. It brings a good price," he explained, his words pronounced clearly. He spoke as if Mandy was too simple to grasp complex concepts.

Once again, her anger boiled. She'd allowed herself to remember the old days when she had promised herself not to think on them anymore. Like a ghost, these memories haunted her waking and sleeping hours—she couldn't escape them. And now she'd been caught unawares while sulking in one of her memory moods. She didn't like how Brian and the boys acted overly polite and patronizing towards her. She felt heat rise in her cheeks.

"I heard you the first time," she snapped, lying to them. "You don't have to speak to me like I'm stupid."

Ignoring the startled hurt in Brian's eyes, she rose quickly and started clearing the table.

"Mother, I'm not finished with my bread," Sam protested as she took his plate. With an impatient flick of her wrist, she made the bread bounce from his plate. Sam awkwardly caught the slice, and Mandy turned to carry the dishes to the sink, ignoring the sudden silence that fell like a shroud over the room.

The dishes clattered noisily in the sink, and Mandy returned to the table for another load, the uncomfortable quiet weighing on her heavily. Mandy could feel the heat steal up her neck and splash across her cheeks, but she couldn't bring herself to say anything more.

Mandy knew she'd done wrong, and it bothered her anew she was constantly making mistakes. She couldn't seem to stop.

Convicted of her poor behavior, Mandy felt unable to do anything about it. Trying to ignore the wretched feeling in the pit of her stomach, she hurried to clear the table, attempting to keep her hands busy.

Brian rose suddenly and began to help her. The boys quietly slunk from the room, retreating to the sitting room.

For the next half hour, she and Brian worked to wash the dishes and put them away. She furiously scrubbed each plate in the hot soapy water and then handed it to Brian to rinse and dry. The silence between them was deafening.

Mandy cleaned the hard plank table next and stowed all the pots and plates away in their proper place. Finally, she turned to Brian and broke the awkward quiet.

Renewed Redemption

"Well, what now?" she demanded, her hands on her hips, glowering at him. She defied him, challenged him, wanted him to say something about her poor behavior.

Brian looked at her, his eyes piercing into her. She wondered if he could see into her soul, and it scared her what he might see there.

"I'm going to warm some apple cider. It's a cool night outside and a good evening for reading and hot apple cider." He reached for a copper kettle, his arm brushing her shoulder. She jumped involuntarily.

Taking the kettle from its hook, he walked to the root cellar.

Mandy chewed her lip. Would he never take her challenge? She was used to arguing and fighting for what she wanted or to defend herself. Fights with Richard had been common. But Brian played with different rules. When she prepared for battle, he wanted to talk. Why? Why was it so important they work things out, to compromise or communicate, rather than fight? She was confused and shook her head, trying to clear her conflicting thoughts. Hot tears brimmed in her eyes, and she knew she was acting foolish.

Quickly brushing the tears from her eyes before the boys could see them, she marched into the sitting room. Jack and Sam were quietly sitting on the couch. They studied her face when she approached, searching for the anger they'd seen before.

Sensing their fear, she stopped. Mandy didn't like the alarm she saw in their eyes. Taking a deep breath, Mandy gripped the dish towel in her hand. "Sam? Jack? Mother was wrong to act as I did at dinner. You're good boys, and I love you. Please forgive me."

Mandy felt even worse as she watched their eyes widen at her surprising words. The two boys nodded appropriately but said nothing, their hands crossed in their laps.

CHAPTER 9

Nothing was said the next morning about the happenings of the previous evening. The boys had never experienced their mother asking for forgiveness, and Mandy herself was somewhat confused as to why she'd done so.

An unspoken understanding seemed to have been reached, and no one said anything further about the peculiar event.

Mandy made sure breakfast was prompt and hearty. She took her job seriously to keep the men well fed for their day's work. Also, she wanted to impress Brian with her abilities and efficiency. She hadn't slept well, checking repeatedly throughout the night to make sure she rose on time. In addition, she'd racked her brain to remember favorite meals from the farm in Virginia.

Meals and details she had not thought of for ten years slowly started to come back to her. This morning, she made apple turnovers with cinnamon sugar sprinkled on top of the doughy concoctions.

Sam and Jack gobbled them with loud acclaim. She smiled as they eagerly chewed, but she watched Brian from the corner of her eye as he reached for a turnover. She tensed, anticipation filling her as she studied his reaction. A warmth radiated through her as Brian agreed with her boys that the apple turnovers were the best he'd ever tasted. Mandy said nothing, but she was secretly pleased.

The boys marched off to the fields with the lunch sack over Jack's shoulder. Mandy knew she had the day to clean and prepare a wonderful dinner.

Renewed Redemption

Again, she set herself to cleaning the kitchen. She noticed that today, she enjoyed the labor. The diligence of the prior day repeated, and she was happy to see the shine on the kitchen cookery. While she worked, she went over recipes in her head and then checked the pantry to evaluate the availability of ingredients.

Repeatedly, Mandy was reminded a trip to town to stock up on provisions was growing imminent, but she held off this trip for as long as she could—content to avoid the town.

Laundry was a big chore, and she set to it with enthusiasm. She knew all the shortcuts to swift laundry cleaning, and they stood her in good stead now. As Mandy scrubbed Brian's work shirt in the soapy water, she was reminded with satisfaction the pleased look on his face when he'd seen her that morning in the bright yellow dress from her closet. She'd taken time to clean up before going to the kitchen and even brushed her long hair thoroughly.

Mandy was adamant Brian would not find her looking like a beggar woman. She would show him she had pride in her appearance and valued cleanliness. Also, she thought, she must do the same for the boys. Brian must see she was a good mother. A hair cut for each of the boys was long overdue, she considered as she sank her hands in the hot water and scrubbed the flannel shirt.

She hung the wet laundry in the dim gray sunlight of the January day. Though winter, it was well above freezing during the noon hour. January in this San Joaquin Valley of California was not nearly as harsh as she was used to. A lingering, damp fog would sometimes hang for days, though, and occasionally it would be cold, but they rarely saw snow this far south. Nothing like the east coast weather she grew up with. Mandy smiled at the memory of blanketed snow across the Virginia farm.

As she glanced up at the towering peaks above her, the Sierra Nevada Mountains glistened with new snow. Their white-capped ridges were a constant reminder of the bitter cold snow not far from where she now stood. Glad she was to be in this secluded little valley below the high mountains. Quail Valley seemed a secret oasis in the hills where Brian's farm nestled peacefully.

The last of the laundry hung on the line, Mandy turned to walk back into the cottage. She halted abruptly, her eyes widening at the sight of an old Mexican man, keenly watching her.

He leaned comfortably against the wall of the house, both his hands resting on the top of a walking cane. Dark hair streaked with gray covered his hawk-like head, deep wrinkles lined his weathered face, and Mandy was drawn to his black eyes studying her intently. He wore a hint of a smile, an almost amused look in his frank gaze. Mandy thought she detected a twinkle in the old eyes.

Mandy learned from hard experience to be a judge of men, and she quickly decided she liked this old man. He seemed kind without even saying a word.

"Good morning, señorita," he said, his accent thick in his words. "I see you are doing Señor Brian's laundry and the laundry of small boys." He pointed with his cane to the line behind her.

Mandy glanced over her shoulder at the laundry rustling in the breeze before facing the old man once more. She nodded. "Yes. I am Mr. Dawson's housekeeper. The small clothes belong to my sons."

"Sons?" His eyes clouded. "Then you are married?"

Mandy wondered at the regret in his voice. She shook her head. "A widow. My husband passed away."

Mandy tilted her head when she noticed the old man's eyes light with interest once again.

"I am sorry to hear that, Señora." He straightened stiffly. He was no taller than Mandy. "I am Carlos Vallejo. I've worked on this land for many years." He gestured all around with a gnarled hand.

Renewed Redemption

Many years? Her curiosity piqued. Certainly, this man would know much of Brian Dawson.

She opened her mouth to ask questions when a chilled breeze blew a strand of hair across her cheeks. Mandy brushed it aside, remembering her manners.

"Perhaps, Mr. Vallejo, you would like to come inside for refreshments? Mr. Dawson would want me to welcome his guests with the same hospitality he'd offer if he were present. I have coffee and apple turnovers made fresh this morning."

Mandy opened the back door of the cottage, and the elderly man strode without hesitation down the darkened hallway. He maneuvered knowingly around the table to the sitting room where he lowered himself with a sigh into one of the side chairs.

She poured coffee, and placing a turnover on a plate, carried the refreshments to the sitting room.

His eyes glowed as he received the plate, steam rising from the mug as he rested it on the arm of the chair. He sighed again as he leaned back in the chair, sipping the coffee thoughtfully.

Mandy watched him closely as he ate the pastry with evident pleasure. Finishing the dessert, he licked his fingers and took another sip of the hot coffee. He glanced at Mandy.

"So? Brian has a housekeeper who can cook. He is a blessed man. The angels favor him." Mr. Vallejo nodded and grinned.

Mandy was pleased by his praise. "Thank you, sir." She bit her lip and twisted her hands in her apron. "You mentioned you've worked this land for many years. I was under the impression that Mr. Dawson only recently came to this farm."

The old man gestured to the couch beside him, indicating Mandy should be seated. As she moved, he spoke. "Oh, yes. Brian has only been here a couple of years. I worked for the Rogers family before Brian arrived. Old man Rogers made his money in the gold fields and built this little cottage to live out his years."

He paused to take another sip of the hot drink, and Mandy smiled at his referencing the previous owner as 'old man Rogers.' How old was Mr. Vallejo?

"When Mr. Rogers passed away," Mr. Vallejo continued, "his widow wished to return to the east coast, so she sold the land to Brian. I stayed and continued to work with the young man."

"Is Mr. Dawson a local man?" Mandy knew that Brian had said he was from Maryland, but she wanted to know how much this man knew of her employer.

Mr. Vallejo shook his head. "Oh, no, Señora. The young farmer is from the east. He only moved out here after a terrible tragedy he suffered back there."

Mr. Vallejo drained his cup, and Mandy squirmed impatiently, eager for more information.

"Tragedy?" she prompted, her eyebrows arching with curiosity. For too long, Mandy had focused on simply meeting the necessary demands of each day. Now she was free to indulge in topics of interest. She was a little surprised to find she was intrigued by Brian's history.

The old man held up his empty cup. "Please, Señora? And possibly another apple pastry?"

Mandy frowned as she took his cup and plate and swiftly returned with seconds. Seating herself again, she continued her questions.

"Mr. Vallejo? You mentioned a tragedy about Brian?" Mandy found she could hardly wait to hear the news about Brian Dawson. This was better than reading a novel.

The old man took a tentative sip of the coffee, then licked his lips appreciatively. "Yes, the young farmer was brokenhearted when I found him. Only by God's grace was I able to persuade him to come here. He is doing so much better now."

The little man ate the second turnover quickly, repeating the same action with his fingers upon completion. He sipped the coffee lovingly.

Renewed Redemption

"Broken heart?" Mandy tried again, leaning toward Mr. Vallejo. "What was he broken-hearted about?"

Did Brian have secrets about his past as Mandy did? Were there skeletons in his closet? Misery loves company, and Mandy dearly wanted to hear something sordid about the happy, handsome farmer she worked for.

Mandy squirmed excitedly and peered at Mr. Vallejo, waiting, intent on his tale of woes regarding her new boss.

"Brian lost his sweetheart. His own dear wife was taken from him, and her loss made him very sad. He suffered greatly, but the Lord has restored him. God is good and cares for the broken-hearted." The old man nodded once, satisfied.

Mandy leaned back, her desire satiated for the moment. Then she frowned and crossed her arms over her chest, considering what she'd learned. So, Brian had been married. He had lost his wife in some tragic way.

Mandy's gaze went to the ceiling, and she chewed the inside of her cheek thoughtfully. Perhaps Brian's marriage had begun promising before turning sour like her own. Maybe Mrs. Dawson was like Richard, a conniver and a liar.

Mandy's mind raced with the possibilities. Brian Dawson's smug and confident manner might be a ruse, a mask to conceal his own horrible tale of deceit and heartache.

"And you?" The unexpected question brought Mandy back to the present. She'd forgotten her guest.

She smoothed her dress before she looked at the wrinkled little man.

Mr. Vallejo leaned forward, curiosity glinting in his dark eyes. Mandy could see he wanted to know about his friend's new housekeeper.

"Me?" Mandy waved a dismissive hand. "There's not much to tell."

Mr. Vallejo chuckled at her evasive reply. "The señora has a broken heart of her own, yes? What tragedy brought you to our quiet valley?"

The old man watched her closely, his intensity pronounced. Now he interrogated her.

Relax, Mandy. Don't let him see your anxiety. Mandy smiled casually and shrugged, feigning insignificance.

"There is no tragedy," Mandy lied easily. "I'm merely a housekeeper. Mr. Dawson is my employer."

Mandy was rewarded with the look of disappointment in Mr. Vallejo's eyes.

She stood. "I'm so grateful that you dropped by, Mr. Vallejo. I've enjoyed our little chat, and I hope you will come again soon."

The old man frowned and then shrugged, a smile coming easily to his face. "All right, Señora. I will go now. I am curious why God has brought you here, but all in good time. There are no secrets in Quail Valley."

CHAPTER 10

The weathered man stood and handed her his empty cup. With a backward glance at Mandy, he moved nimbly out the front door, his walking cane in one hand.

Taking his dirty dishes to the kitchen, Mandy pondered the details of the interesting visit.

Well, now, this was news. Brian had been married before. Mandy felt sadness for him briefly at the recollection his wife had passed away, and then the feeling left her as quickly as it had appeared. Perhaps his marriage had been miserable. Maybe he was not so bothered at his loss. She certainly wasn't over hers.

She remembered then Mr. Vallejo explained Brian had been very upset when he came to California. He must've loved his wife greatly to miss her. Mandy remembered how she felt the night she found Richard in the Sacramento gutter. At first, she was mad there was now no chance he would ever help her with the boys. Then, realizing he'd never helped anyway, she felt relief he was out of the picture. She was free.

Mandy chewed her lip thoughtfully, wondering about death and why some people are missed while others aren't. After placing Mr. Vallejo's dishes in the sink, she stared out the window, her mind on that long-ago day.

Mandy remembered a lot of love in her house growing up in Virginia. Mandy's mother would never have felt free if Jack Mulligan had died. She would've been broken-hearted, truly upset as Mr. Vallejo claimed Brian was about his wife.

Mandy stood by the sink, the brown and barren hills surrounding the small valley unseen now as Mandy's mind drifted far away. She had not been broken-hearted when Richard

Renewed Redemption

died. In fact, she had briefly contemplated getting in contact with her father. With Richard gone, would Jack Mulligan take his daughter back?

She knew without a doubt her parents would take her back immediately. What had stopped her were her own harsh words when she'd left her father's farm. He told her she would always be welcome, but she had spoken in pride and ignorance. She lashed out at the man who had sacrificed for her, raised her. She could not forgive herself for the way she'd hurt him so deeply.

Mandy thought again about her father. She hadn't contacted him when Richard died, and she would not now. She knew he'd be eager to help her and her boys, even love to help them. She struggled on alone, living each day in her self-imposed exile.

Brushing the nagging memory away with the back of her hand across her brow, she quickly washed the few dishes and began preparing supper.

Mandy didn't mention the old Mexican's visit during dinner. She made a pudding that had been her father's favorite, which she served for dessert.

There were loud acclaims from the boys for such a tasty dessert, but her eyes were on Brian. He thanked her for supper in his polite way as she sat opposite him.

When they'd finished and she'd cleared the dishes from the table, she decided she'd broach the subject.

She pursed her lips, wondering how to begin. "You had a visitor today," she said casually, eyeing Brian over the spoon in her hand.

"Oh? A visitor?" He shifted, his chair scraping on the flagstones. He jabbed his spoon into his bowl, not even looking up at her words.

"Yes. A Mr. Vallejo," she went on, watching for any sign that might give some indication of Brian's true emotions.

Brian looked up and laughed. "Old Carlos? He's a good friend of mine. A dear friend. Sometimes he works for me. He's good with the bees. Did he say what he was here for?"

Mandy blinked. For the life of her, she couldn't remember if he'd said the purpose for his visit. She wrinkled her brow, trying to remember what the old man had mentioned.

She shifted in her chair. "Well, no, he didn't really come right out and say why he was here," Mandy replied, stumbling over her words. Why had he come?

Brian leaned back and eyed her suspiciously. "You mean he came to this house and spoke to you, but never said why he was here?"

Mandy shook her head. "No, he didn't rightly say."

Brian squinted at her across the table and Mandy went on, a defensive tone in her voice. "He did tell me a little about you, though."

Brian put down his spoon and stared at her.

"Me? Why would he speak of me? Were you asking about me?" He eyed her closely now, but Mandy simply shrugged.

"No. I just gave him coffee and treats, and he talked away. I can't even remember what all he said." Mandy glanced around the room, hoping she looked very bored and uninterested.

Brian frowned. "Well, I haven't seen the day when Old Carlos would *not* talk away hours over coffee and dessert," he grumbled under his breath. "He probably just dropped in to ask about the bees," Brian remarked, leaning forward again to take another scoop of pudding.

"What bees?" Mandy asked quickly, pleased to divert the topic away from her.

Jack huffed, his small eyes narrowing. "Mother, I've already told you. Brian has bees. In the spring, he'll collect honey to sell. Also, we'll eat honey. Brian says it's best on fresh bread."

Renewed Redemption

Mandy nodded. "Yes, of course. I remember now." Had they talked about bees before? She couldn't remember that either.

"There are honeybees on the farm, and they live in a honey tree, right?" Mandy rose, taking an armload of empty dessert bowls with her.

They all laughed at her. "Mother," Sam explained slowly, like he was speaking to a child. "The bees live in a box, and the honey is collected there. They are important for pollinating the fruit trees."

"What fruit trees? I thought you were going to plant alfalfa." Mandy pumped water into a pot, then set it on the stove to boil.

Sam and Jack followed her into the kitchen, eager to explain about the mysterious bees. Now they rolled their eyes at one another, astonished their mother knew nothing about the fascinating flying insects.

"The bees visit each tree when they bloom and pollinates them. Then, they make honey with the nectar they collect in the spring," Sam continued, talking like a schoolteacher. He was obviously mimicking what Brian had told them, but Mandy was impressed.

"Well, I look forward to honey in the spring, then," she added with a smile and tousled Sam's hair. She was pleased to discuss things the boys were learning.

The life they lived before coming to Brian's farm had rarely allowed for interesting conversation. They were constantly working or searching for things of value in abandoned shacks. To have leisure time to discuss interesting topics was new to Mandy and the boys. She thought of this as they helped her with the dishes.

Why would she ever consider leaving this place? Her boys were happy and learning about farming just as Mandy had enjoyed learning about farming from her father. Here, the boys were well fed and warm. She sighed contentedly and handed Sam another dish to rinse and dry.

This feeling of peace and contentment was indeed rare to Mandy. Years had passed since the last time she felt this way. In fact, she couldn't recollect the last time she felt this content and happy.

Suddenly, Jack started to sing, and the peace and contentment vanished. Jack sang not a little boy's song of nursery rhymes, but a hymn. To Mandy's amazement and horror, Sam joined in.

The song was unfamiliar to her. It was about a risen savior, Jesus by name, and he had come into the world to save us from sin.

Oh, no, Mandy thought to herself as her chest tightened and her heart began to ache. *Brian has sabotaged my happiness.*

Just as she was beginning to relax and enjoy being here, the whole God situation reared its ugly head again.

She turned toward the sitting room to vent her wrath on Brian. He was walking toward the kitchen, his voice joining the chorus coming from the boys.

"Wait! Stop!" she exploded. The singing ceased. The boys stared at her, frightened by her outburst. She scowled at Jack, hands on her hips. "Where did you learn that song?"

Jack's eyes bulged. "Brian taught it to us. We sing in the fields while we work," her youngest explained, the fear disappearing from his face as he broke into a broad smile. "Isn't it pretty, Mother? Sam and I have learned all sorts of new songs. Brian is teaching us about Jesus."

Slowly, she turned to fix her eyes on Brian. He stood, watching her, as she faced him. She eyed him coldly, like a cobra, ready to strike.

Brian held up a hand. "Mandy, maybe we should go outside and have a talk." He grabbed a coat from the hook by the door and pulled it on. Then, he grabbed a couple of mugs from the cupboard and filled them with coffee. "It'll be cold." He lifted the steaming mugs and led the way out the front door to the porch.

Mandy ground her teeth, her fingernails digging into her palms. She didn't even know where to begin. She had told him to leave the boys alone. She had made it quite clear he was not to talk about God with Sam and Jack.

She glanced at the boys. "Mother and Brian are going to have a little chat. We'll be right back," she spoke through clenched teeth. Closing the door behind her, she turned on Brian.

"How dare you?" she snarled, anger rising within her. "I specifically told you not to tell God stories to my children. You knew my feelings about this, and you ignored me," Mandy spat.

Brian had seated himself on the bench, leaning against the house, two mugs resting on his knees. He looked out into the night, surprisingly calm.

The inky twilight mirrored his manner, quiet and sedate. Not a whisper of breeze disturbed the cold dusk. Mandy didn't even feel the chill as she spoke.

"Don't pretend you can't hear me," Mandy continued, her eyes narrowing as she railed. "You know this is absolutely against what I asked you to honor. They are my boys, Brian, and I don't want them learning about Jesus and the Bible."

She inhaled sharply, finished, her voice rising as she spoke. Emotion drove Mandy and she could feel it. She was afraid she would start screaming or ranting. Richard and she had argued very loudly sometimes. She didn't want to lose control like that now.

Mandy stared at the silent Brian, seething. She needed to make her point clear and then demand Brian obey her. She blinked when he turned to face her, his eyes peaceful and kind. He was in perfect control of his feelings, and she hated him for it.

He took a sip of his coffee, watching her over the rim. "Why?"

Mandy stared and then tilted her head. "Why what?"

Brian gestured to the bench beside him and handed her a mug. Hesitating, she sat down, her knees suddenly weak.

"Why no Jesus or Bible stories?" Brian continued. Mandy was surprised how calm his voice sounded. Richard would be screaming by now.

"I know you don't want me to talk to your boys about God, but why is that? What are you afraid of?" Brian spoke in an even voice, drawing her closer to him in a sing-song way that made her trust him.

Mandy didn't want to trust him.

She hunched her shoulders, digging in her heels. "That is none of your business. You are to respect my wishes. Why I ask it, doesn't concern you," she answered, her hands tightening around the steaming cup.

He blew gently on his drink and steam wafted from the cup. "But it is my affair. You're at my house. More than that, I like your boys. They're eager to learn, and they ask many questions. They know nothing about things I'd have thought all children would know."

Her brow wrinkled at his accusation. He annoyed her, but she tried to keep her anger in check. Again, Mandy straightened her back, lifting her chin slightly. "Don't be telling me how to raise my children. I do not want them learning about Jesus, and that is final."

She was aware that she and Brian sat close together in the darkness, which made her uncomfortable. The closeness of him made her feel uneasy, and she found it difficult to concentrate.

"You haven't answered my question. Why?" Brian pressed, demanding a reply. "I don't want to hear I'm to simply respect your decision. Tell me. Explain. What purpose is there in not teaching these children about Jesus?"

Renewed Redemption

Mandy hesitated. Her shoulders suddenly sagged. She wanted to unburden herself from this weight she'd carried alone for so long but didn't know how. His persistence and kindness seemed to be working on her. Richard had never tried to communicate with her or hear her point of view. Their arguments had always ended as a shouting match, defensive and blaming.

She clenched her teeth tightly and then whispered, "I am angry with God and don't want the boys to know about him. If they learn, they might take his side and not stay with me."

Brian took a sip from his cup and looked again out into the starlit night. Mandy held her breath, wondering at his response. Would he condemn her? Would he laugh at her?

His silence made Mandy even more uneasy. Had he heard her? Why wasn't he speaking? Was he disgusted with her and her stubbornness?

"What exactly is his side?" Brian's quiet inquiry broke the uncomfortable silence.

Mandy sighed. She tried so hard to not think of these things. The memory of her parents back in Virginia and that last day at home, haunted her still. But she'd always had the discipline to stop herself from remembering all the facts before they filled her mind, consuming her with guilt and sorrow.

Now, as if Brian possessed a power to cause her to speak, she wanted to tell him.

Her head came up and she looked at him. "When I left home with my new husband, my father was very angry. He was disappointed in Richard as my husband. I was not surprised. Richard was dashing and fun. He rode in a carriage and told me how beautiful I was. He didn't have a job or a profession or money, though I thought he did. I knew he was not the kind of man my father would want me to marry."

Mandy paused. She could feel the knot forming in her throat, and she was afraid she'd begin to cry. This was the most she'd spoken about her past to anyone in ten years.

She drew a deep breath, regaining her composure. She must be strong, stay in control. *Never show weakness.*

"You said your father was disappointed, but you were not really surprised. What about your mother? How did she react?" He watched her, his brown eyes soft in the dim light.

Her hands trembled, and Mandy gripped the mug tighter. Her throat closed, she couldn't speak. To remember her mother's words hurt too deeply. She had refused that memory admittance into her mind for ten years.

The knot in her throat tightened, the floodgate burst. Not only tears, but intense sobs rolled from her, shaking her slender frame. She dropped her coffee cup from lifeless fingers and hung her head again.

Brian drew her to him. He grasped her shoulders firmly and pulled her to his chest. He stroked her hair as she buried her face in his coat, telling her over and over she would be all right. His warm breath on the top of her head made her tingle in ways she could not understand.

When was the last time she'd been held, comforted, cared for?

Sobbing, she allowed the pent-up emotion to flow, freeing her. Her shoulders quaked with the force of her powerful tears. Brian's firm hold on her felt so comforting, so warm. There'd been no one to hold her with care and concern for years, and she was overwhelmed, felt foreign. Then she tensed.

Brian had tricked her, and she'd lost control. Her strong and prickly fortification had been breached by his kindness and gentleness. Her defenses toppled, tumbling down at the gentle caress of his strong hands.

Mandy pushed fiercely against his chest and leaped to her feet. Anger, resentment, regret, and longing wrestled within her. She saw the surprise on his face as she took a step backward.

Clenching her fists, Mandy leaned forward, bracing herself for battle as she glared at the stunned man before her.

Renewed Redemption

Her voice trembled as she spoke. "I will not tell you more, Brian Dawson. It's enough that you've made me feel weak. I am Sam and Jack's mother, and I will raise them the way I see fit. You will not trick me with your gentle ways and smooth tongue. Stay away from my boys with your Bible stories and stay away from me. I've had enough of God."

Mandy watched Brian's soft, brown eyes widen at her harsh words. His face paled, but she couldn't stop herself now. Anger drove her—anger at herself, anger at her circumstances, anger at God.

She turned from Brian, needing to get away, to flee. Her heart pounded loudly with the passion of the moment, the pain of disappointment mingling with the unfamiliar desire to be honest and open with this man.

Brian stared at her as Mandy struggled with her anguish. His patience and kindness drew her like a moth to a lamp, but she resisted, telling herself again to get away.

She swiped at her tears with both hands and shot an angry scowl at the dark sky above, disappointed she'd shared more than she should.

Without another word, Mandy stumbled off the porch, shoulders sagging as she stalked into the night.

CHAPTER 11

Mandy fled into the darkness, unaware where she was going. She only knew she had to escape.

She walked rapidly, her feet crunching on the gravel as she passed the barn and headed into the road that ascended from the little valley and led to town. She needed time to get the swirling thoughts in her head sorted and back under lock and key once more.

The hard-packed dirt road shone dully in the late evening light, and she followed the track without thought of where she was headed. She only felt the need to walk, to think, to regain her composure.

She'd tried hard not to think about her parents much since leaving Virginia. In fact, she purposely told her sons very little about their grandparents. When the boys questioned her, she'd been evasive, intentionally vague, and changed the subject.

Her parents would've loved to have grandchildren around them, if not Mandy. When Sam was born, she spitefully ignored their repeated attempts at meeting their first grandchild. Denying them was one way Mandy could hurt her parents. She'd left Virginia with deep pain in her heart. Mandy kept control by not letting them see Sam, hurting them because she'd been hurt.

Her parents didn't know another son was born. Richard had chided her when she named the new baby after her father, but she ignored him. His opinion by then counted for nothing.

A rock rolled beneath her foot, her ankle bending cruelly,

but she ignored the stabbing pain, limping now as she trod the dirt road. The exertion of her swift stride and the weight of her emotions warmed her body, despite the cool night pressing in around her. The warmth rose to her cheeks when she remembered Brian's tender touch and the way he'd held her. Oh, she hated that she enjoyed his sweet embrace. It almost made her spill her secrets. But not all of them.

Shoving the disturbing memory aside, she thought of her unhappy marriage. Her father opposed the match, not wishing his Christian daughter to have anything to do with that lazy gambler, Richard Barrett.

Despite her father's warnings not to marry Richard, she had been captivated by Richard's charms. He professed his undying love and convinced her to elope. The idea had seemed romantic, forbidden. She'd agreed, and they were soon married.

Her father's response was one of disappointment, but he still tried to help, offering her dowry as required. Her mother's words at that time had turned out to be prophetic. With tears streaming down her cheeks, Mandy's mother had clung to her arm, staring intently into her daughter's eyes.

"You've been fooled by this man. He does not truly love you, and you'll find this out in time. Your stubborn heart and your desire for the pretty things in life will cause you to have nothing. Only by following the Lord can true happiness and contentment be found."

Mandy learned the truth of her mother's words. Sam was born soon after and Mandy had received a letter from her father, pleading to see his only grandson. She had thrown the letter in the fireplace at the lodging house where they lived. Within a month, they left for California, one step ahead of the law and numerous creditors.

Within two months of landing in California, Mandy and the boys found themselves destitute on the streets of San Francisco. Richard had merely been after her dowry, not her, and had burned through the money in record time. He'd turned out to be a deceiver. And, certainly, no Christian.

Mandy quickly understood that the care of her sons—both physically and monetarily—had fallen to her.

Halting suddenly, her shoes skidding in the loose gravel, she peered into the darkness on either side of the road, recognizing nothing. She'd been very ill the day she came to Brian Dawson's house and hadn't been coherent when she'd traveled this road before.

She peered into the darkness. The road was visible enough in the dim light of the stars above and she remembered it would take her to the small bridge over the Yuba River. She walked on, going over her thoughts methodically, testing each of them in turn.

She'd worked hard these past years, and her mother's words haunted her, surprised at how quickly they had come to pass. Within no time at all, Mandy and the boys were living hand-to-mouth.

Mandy kicked a rock protruding from the mud at her feet. It didn't budge. She halted and kicked more forcibly. The rock moved slightly, and Mandy kicked again, hurting her toe but unearthing the stubborn stone. She bent and hefted it, throwing it into the brush along the edge of the trail. Wiping her hands on her dress, she marched on.

Mandy had been raised in a Christian home and knew God's truth, but her own selfish desires to live with a wealthy, flashy, handsome man and her stubbornness had caused her to ignore all wisdom she found in Scripture. She'd ignored verses from Proverbs warning of the dangers of honey-tongued, wicked men and not heeding wise counsel. Not to mention the admonition for Christians to only marry other believers, spouses who would encourage and support their Christian mate in their faith.

Mandy had made her decision alone, without consulting any of the wise people she knew within her own church and family. Instead of repenting of her stiff-necked ways, she'd continued in her own way, chosen her own path, and tried to prove God wrong.

But God's truth could not be denied.

She'd had years of hard toil, and she was still intent on trying to do things her own way, but she was growing tired of failure. The boys were older now and not as easy to convince her way was best.

Mandy sighed as she plodded on the dirt road.

Keep moving. Don't slow down. Don't admit defeat.

As long as she moved forward, there was the hope of success. Or so she told herself.

Attempts had been made along the way by various strangers to include Mandy and the boys at church or invite them to Christian gatherings, but Mandy had avoided them all. She'd kept her children ignorant of God and his perfect plan for his people, plans to prosper them and not to harm them.

That is, if you did things his way.

Mandy stopped once more. The little bridge loomed in the darkness, and she could hear the roar of water from the Yuba River below. Across this bridge, the trail forked. To the right was Yuba City, and the trail to the left wound up into the hills toward the various gold camps.

She walked to the bridge, rested her elbows on the railing, and peered down into the noisy water. She glanced at the trail on her right, vaguely outlined in the dim light. That way led back to a dead-end life, working her fingers raw, doing laundry for miners and tradesmen. She even occasionally cleaned saloons but had to quit after repeated harassments and unwanted attention from drunken men.

She peered back down into the rushing water below. The river was dark and noisy, much like her troubling thoughts. Heated blood coursed through her veins. Irritably, she brushed a rebellious strand of blonde hair from her face. Was her warmth caused from the exertion or her own clouded emotions?

Abruptly, unbidden, she thought of Brian Dawson. He'd made a generous offer to a drowning woman. She and her boys hadn't lived this well since leaving Virginia.

She thought then of Brian as a person, about his kindness, his attitude of helpfulness. Mandy hadn't known a man like Brian since her father. She wanted to act angry and push that thought from her mind, but she couldn't. The memory of Brian made her feel safe, valued.

True, they disagreed on how to raise children, but he was not mean. He believed what he was doing was right and in the best interest of her boys. Sam and Jack enjoyed working with Brian. He'd been able to inspire them somehow, and they seemed to genuinely like him.

Her new employer seemed like a good man. She tilted her head, intrigued by the novel thought. Mr. Vallejo had hinted at problems in Brian's past, but Brian was a landowner and had future potential. The alfalfa crops would bring in a goodly sum from the nearby ranches and farms that needed stock feed.

Mandy straightened and hugged herself against the growing chill. She was reluctant to leave the solitude of the quiet bridge, liking the sound of the raucous flow of the river. However, tomorrow's work would soon be upon her, and she needed some rest before the new day began. It was time to go home.

Home? The word pierced her like a knife. Could she call Brian's house her home? Home came and went. However, the farm was home for now, and she and the boys were not used to that kind of permanence.

One day, she'd like to have a real home, Mandy contemplated, drumming her fingers on the rough wooden railing. If she were to have a home one day, she'd like it to be similar to Brian's small cottage, with an indoor water pump and a large stone fireplace in the sitting room.

A faint smile tugged at the corner of her lips as she considered how unimportant those nice things were compared to the peace and happiness she felt flowing freely through Brian's small house. These unfamiliar sensations would be preferable to the creature comforts she initially listed.

Mandy looked up at the few stars that hung amid the clouds. The allure of wealth and expensive things were as nothing now in comparison to the truly significant things in life. Love, warmth, security, happiness, and family were everything. She scowled. Another lesson from God?

Hadn't God and her parents tried to teach her these truths? Mandy sighed, shaking her head. Would God stop at nothing to teach her the right way of life? Would he never give up on her and simply leave her alone?

Her impulsive, stubborn, and immature heart had caused great hurt among those she loved, including herself. Her heart ached with regret and sorrow for the past, and Mandy sighed again as she turned and started the long walk back to Quail Valley.

The trip to the bridge had passed so quickly, as her mind was full of disturbing thoughts, but the walk back to the cottage seemed interminable. Mandy was very cold by the time she reached the cottage.

She paused, shivering in the darkness, and observed the house for movement. Surely no one was awake at this hour. Brian and the boys had gone to bed. She entered quietly through the front door. Bright embers glowed red on the hearth in the sitting room.

Closing the door securely behind her, she moved into the cozy room. The heat enveloped her, making her shiver more as the warmth crept into her bones. She stood before the fire, warming her chilled hands. She tossed wood on the glowing coals to help keep the fire alive until morning.

This house did feel welcoming to her, Mandy decided with a curious glance around the darkened cottage.

Crawling into her bed, wrapped in the comfort of her clean sheets, she realized how much she appreciated the place

Brian Dawson had created for her and her boys. They were safe and warm here.

∞∞∞

Awakening early the next morning, Mandy resolved to outdo herself this day. She spent extra time on her appearance, hoping Brian would notice the previous evening's events held no permanent impact on her. She was as right as rain and would work doubly hard to prove it.

Mandy smiled as she brushed her long blonde hair. She'd grown to love this practice since coming to Quail Valley and was not sure why. Pulling her hair back, she tied it with a blue ribbon she found in the closet and put on the yellow gingham dress that hung there. She wrapped another blue ribbon around her slim waist and then moved to the door.

The coffee water was just beginning to boil when she heard footsteps coming down the hall. Brian appeared in the dim light of the cooking fire. He smiled tentatively, seeming to assess her mood.

"Good morning, Mrs. Barrett. You look chipper this morning." He pumped water at the sink and washed his hands.

Brian kept his face averted, but Mandy stared at him, willing him to face her. He didn't. Instead, he busied himself around the kitchen, peering into drawers and checking pots hanging on the wall.

"Yes, I feel wonderful," she replied quickly. A little too quickly, perhaps. "I thought I would get up early and make biscuits and gravy with sausage."

He turned, his gaze intent and searching. Mandy found she couldn't look him in the eye as she'd hoped and turned away, attentive to the dough on the counter. She could feel his gaze upon her, and an uneasy feeling filled her as she leaned into the soft dough.

She kneaded the mounds and worked them vigorously, trying to keep her mind on her duties.

Renewed Redemption

"Well, I got up early myself to come out here and thank you for our conversation last evening," he said, pushing his hands suddenly into the dough, kneading it roughly.

"To thank me? I don't understand," Mandy stammered, unable to stop herself from glancing up at his face. Her hands touched his in the messy dough, and she could feel the warmth as her cheeks reddened with embarrassment.

Brian nodded. "I've been curious about you since we met, and I feel last night's conversation was informative, to say the least. Thank you for letting me get to know you a little better. I look forward to learning more about you as time goes by." He smiled, reflecting a casualness Mandy did not feel.

"You were certainly presented with more information than you bargained for." Mandy chuckled softly, her eyes dropping to the dough once more. She shifted her hands to a safe corner of the gooey mess where they wouldn't meet Brian's again. Her behavior of the previous night still annoyed her. She could only imagine what Brian's true feelings were about her.

She glanced up shyly when he didn't respond.

Brian smiled softly at her, his brown eyes full of compassion and warmth. He obviously didn't hold her outburst of last night against her. She dropped her gaze again.

He cut the prepared dough into biscuits and helped Mandy place them on a cooking tray before sliding them into the oven.

Mandy stepped back and watched him from behind, a slight frown on her face. She didn't want this man to get to know the real her. He might not like what he discovered.

Brian turned toward her. "Coffee?"

Mandy nodded, unused to having someone do things for her. Brian poured two cups and handed one to her.

"Hold on to this tightly. Last night, you couldn't seem to keep a good grip on your mug," he teased, a twinkle in his eye.

She took the mug from him, a heated retort on her lips, but when she saw he was joking, she relaxed and thanked him.

They stood for a moment, alone in the kitchen, sipping their hot drinks. The house was dark except for the muted light from the cook stove. The room felt pleasant and warm, and Mandy felt comfortable and almost happy.

Why did this man make her feel so relaxed? Mandy could feel the familiar tension leave her shoulders as she sipped the coffee, furtively glancing at Brian over the rim of her mug.

After a minute of silence, Brian lowered a pot from its hook on the wall and turned to Mandy.

"Okay. You must show me the secret to good gravy. I've tried unsuccessfully to make it, but not even Mr. Vallejo will eat my cooking."

Mandy laughed. The sound surprised her. When was the last time she had laughed—a real laugh?

She peered at Brian and watched the glow of the dim light on his chiseled features as he placed the pot on the stove top. Her laugh had gone unnoticed by him.

"It's easy." Mandy set down her cup and moved beside him, reaching for a skillet. "I'll show you."

She dumped sausage into the heated frying pan, the pork sizzling. "We'll need some sausage grease to mix with the flour, so I'll fry the sausage first," she instructed, making a show of stirring the sausage.

"Mr. Vallejo seems to be a good friend of yours," she went on, watching Brian's face closely. "He said you moved here a couple of years ago after you had some trouble."

Brian smiled sadly, wrinkles appearing around his eyes. "Yes. Carlos was important to me at a time when I desperately needed a friend. I'd recently lost my wife and was not sure which way to turn. He helped me find the right direction."

Mandy stepped back, feigning surprise. "You were married?"

It was his turn to laugh. "Don't look so shocked. Yes, I was married. Someone did tolerate me. Someone quite special, actually." Brian reached for his cup, and Mandy noticed the trace of flour on his wrist. "I still miss her. She was strong, much stronger than I."

He was silent a moment and then added, "You remind me of her somehow."

A door slammed down the hall, and Sam and Jack appeared before Mandy could respond. His comment stayed with her all morning.

CHAPTER 12

With Brian and the boys gone to work in the fields, Mandy had the house to herself. She again scoured the kitchen and cleaned the boys' room. She carried wood in and filled the wood box even though the boys were supposed to do that chore each evening.

The sun peeked through gray clouds that hung over the little valley, but Mandy was accustomed to the gloomy weather of January. She loaded her arms with logs and turned to the door just as a figure coming down the road caught her eye. Mandy squinted, discerning an attractive young woman.

Her dress was pressed neatly and fit her well, she was obviously from a good family. She carried a jar of preserves and a dubious scowl on her pretty face as she drew near to Mandy.

"And who might you be?" She eyed Mandy from head to toe, a skeptical sneer curving her thin lips.

"Good morning. I'm Mrs. Barrett, Mr. Dawson's housekeeper," Mandy replied cheerfully.

The woman's eyebrows arched. "Housekeeper? What does Brian need with a housekeeper? He lives here alone," she persisted, glaring at Mandy.

The newcomer stepped even closer, peering curiously all around as if an investigation would produce the answers she sought. Mandy was suddenly pleased she'd taken the time earlier to do her hair and put on a nice dress. She sensed the younger woman's arrogance and enjoyed unsettling her confidence.

Mandy lowered the armful of wood to the ground, disappointed she could not take the load to its place by the fire. Brushing her hands, she offered one to the young stranger.

"I didn't catch your name, miss?"

Frowning, the young woman shook Mandy's hand. "I'm Ruby Wilson. I'm neighbors with Brian. Is he here?"

Mandy pointed to the distant fields. "He's clearing land with my sons. Can I offer you a glass of water?" Mandy could sense a relationship between this woman and Brian that piqued her curiosity. She was not going to let this girl get away without learning more.

Mandy watched as Ruby looked expectantly toward the nearby pastures and hills, searching for some sign of Brian. Finding none, she pouted, her narrow face appearing pinched in the morning light.

Ruby shrugged, disappointment thick in her words. "Sure. I'm thirsty."

Mandy led her to the porch, where Ruby took a seat on the bench—the very spot she'd sat in last night with Brian. She hurried indoors and quickly returned with the promised drink.

Ruby took the glass and drank. Mandy watched the girl's slender throat as it bobbed. She decided, grudgingly, that the girl was pretty, although her eyes seemed a little too close together.

"Ma wanted me to bring these preserves over." Ruby handed the jar to Mandy.

Mandy accepted the jar, squinting at the contents. "Have you known Mr. Dawson long?"

Ruby brightened. "Oh, yes. We've been good friends for over a year. My family thinks very highly of him."

Mandy chewed the inside of her cheek, hoping the visitor would soon leave. Suddenly, her initial curiosity fled, and she didn't want to know more. *No sense in encouraging the girl with conversation*, Mandy mused sourly.

"I also came over to invite Brian to a barn raising next Saturday at the Hamilton place. He knows where it is. There'll be food and dancing. I can't wait to dance with him. He's quite good, you know," Ruby informed her, a rosy glow coming to the pale girl's cheeks. Ruby tilted her head, a wide smile creasing her thin face.

Mandy scowled and then tilted her own head. "Well, if you don't mind me saying so, I think Mr. Dawson is a bit old for you, don't you think?" The smile fled from Ruby's face, and she flushed crimson. "Mr. Dawson is only twenty-eight, scarcely ten years older than me."

Mandy was immediately reminded of the age difference between her and Richard. She nodded. "He's too old for you, trust me."

A stricken look came over Ruby's pretty face, and she leaped to her feet. She handed the empty water glass to Mandy, her eyes blazing. "I do not see that it's any of your business. You are the housekeeper." Without another word, Ruby Wilson spun on her heel and marched from the yard.

That night at supper, Brian spread the preserves on a piece of bread. Mandy watched him eye it intently. "This jam reminds me of Mrs. Wilson's preserves. She's a neighbor of mine."

Mandy was silent a moment, then said, "Yes, I forgot. You had a visitor today. A very young child named Ruby brought those preserves over and told me to tell you there will be a barn raising at the Hamilton's next Saturday."

"A barn raising?" Sam exclaimed. He turned to Brian. "Will we go?"

Brian nodded, spreading the jam liberally on the bread. "Absolutely, Sam. To help and serve each other is right in a community. We'll go and lend a hand. I daresay that your mother's cooking will make quite the impression," Brian added, smiling at Mandy.

The boys talked excitedly to each other about the upcoming event, and Brian leaned closer to Mandy.

"Ruby isn't that young," he whispered. Mandy enjoyed the doubt in his eyes. "I think she's attractive, don't you?"

Renewed Redemption

Mandy's eyes opened wide in surprise as she shrugged indifferently. "Is she? I hadn't noticed."

CHAPTER 13

The upcoming barn raising and dance were all the boys could talk about for the next few days. At first, Mandy hoped she could avoid having to personally attend the event and simply provide food and her sons.

Brian would hear none of that, though.

"Of course, you will come with me," he said, smiling wide. "You're my housekeeper and the boys' mother. You should be there."

Despite numerous appeals, Brian would brook no opposition to his original plan.

The Friday before the barn raising, Mandy spent the day baking and making her specialties, remembering old recipes from her home in Virginia.

Making the old favorites brought back a joy of cooking she hadn't felt in years. The task also brought back a flood of memories of her mother and the wonderful smells that had always surrounded the family kitchen in Virginia.

She had all she could do to keep Brian and her boys away from her platters of goodies that evening.

Saturday dawned gray and overcast like usual, and a cloud of fog hung low in the little valley. Bundled up with the dray full of the prepared dishes and necessary tools, the boys rode in back while Mandy, feeling a little self-conscious in the fancy burgundy dress, sat on the high seat beside Brian.

The boys peppered Brian with questions along the way, wondering what to expect when they arrived. Sam and Jack couldn't conceal their anticipation and excitement. They'd never been to a barn raising.

Renewed Redemption

Brian did his best to give a rough outline of how the day would progress with the walls being shaped on the ground before finally being raised and secured into position. A roof would be added as some men worked on the completion of the walls.

He glanced at Mandy when the boys were satisfied with the description of the impending activity. "Have they ever worked with neighbors on projects like harvest or digging a basement or well? Helping can vegetables for winter?" he whispered out of the corner of his mouth as he jiggled the leather reins, prodding the horse over the small bridge that spanned the Yuba River.

Mandy knew this was just another example of where she'd failed as a mother. She pursed her lips tightly, her eyes narrowing with irritation. "I was too busy to join in community affairs," she snapped, an obvious edge to her tone.

Brian glanced at her but said nothing. Mandy felt his silence condemned her.

The yard was already crowded with a variety of wheeled vehicles when Brian's dray pulled into the Hamilton place. Immediately, men called cheerily to Brian, and he became enveloped in a small crowd of burly men. Amid shouts of showing him the site for the barn, Brian turned to help Mandy dismount.

A few of the men cast appreciative, appraising glances at Mandy, and she shifted uneasily as Brian lifted her to the ground. They continued to stare at her until an impatient Brian tugged on their arms.

"Come on, Bill," Brian growled as he led the small group of men away. "Sam! Jack! Come with me," he shouted over his shoulder as he disappeared into the throng of workers.

Not bothering to ask permission from Mandy, the two small boys eagerly jumped from the wagon and chased after him.

Mandy stood alone for a minute wondering what she should do. Then, remembering similar events back in Virginia, she began carrying food to a nearby table set up under an enormous oak tree.

After three trips to the wagon, she'd deposited all the food she'd brought and began fussing over the arrangement of the dishes. Loud whispers drew her attention, and she turned at the sound.

Ruby Wilson stood with a cluster of women, looking her way. They whispered loudly, glowering boldly at Mandy.

Heat stole up her neck, and Mandy lifted a hand to her crimson cheeks as she turned away. Did they know her? Embarrassed, Mandy continued to move the dishes around the long table, wishing she could disappear. She remembered the borrowed shack on the river, and a knot formed in the pit of her stomach.

"Hello," a voice sounded at her elbow. Mandy looked up. A woman in her mid-thirties dressed in a simple cotton dress smiled at her.

Mandy ran a nervous hand over the front of her own dress, suddenly feeling pretentious in the Widow Rogers's nice clothes.

The woman gave Mandy a broad, welcoming smile and held out a hand. "I'm Mrs. Bricker. I believe you know my husband, the blacksmith?"

Mandy hesitated but detected no deceit in the woman's eyes, and her genuine sincerity put Mandy at ease. She took the woman's outstretched hand. "Indeed, I do. I did his wash until he got married. I assume you are my replacement."

"I am that," Mrs. Bricker laughed, her kind eyes dancing. "He's a good man, and I'm happy to have him. When my first husband died, I wondered what would become of me."

She paused, and Mandy blinked, a warning bell going off in her head. This woman married again? Mandy stared, stunned. What would ever induce a woman to make the same mistake twice?

Then Mandy recalled the dingy shanty on the banks of the Feather River, and she softened.

"Will you join me for lunch?" Mrs. Bricker gestured to a place under the nearby tree.

Mandy allowed herself to be led away, a small plate in her hand. Glancing over her shoulder, she saw the other women still watching her, still chattering like magpies.

The two women seated themselves and ate a little before Mrs. Bricker spoke again.

"I understand you are now Mr. Dawson's housekeeper. I hear he's hired your sons to clear land."

Mandy felt self-conscious. She hadn't been to an event like this since she was a young girl in Virginia. The men worked and women took turns taking them coffee and food while the barn rose slowly. Women stood in groups and gossiped or barked orders at playing children. The event was more than a barn raising, it was a social gathering where news was shared and relationships formed and strengthened.

"Yes." Mandy nodded slowly. "Mr. Dawson has been very kind to hire me and the boys. They love to work in the fields. I daresay they may be farmers one day."

"You have two sons, I believe," Mrs. Bricker went on. Mandy wondered if this woman was a scout for the old regime of gossips she'd seen earlier.

"Yes, Sam and Jack. They are my life."

Mandy felt like she now was one of the older women she had giggled at during the parties and dances of her youth. The old matrons would sit and chat amongst themselves, and Mandy often wondered what they had to talk about. Now she understood.

"You are not married, then?" Mrs. Bricker arched her eyebrows inquisitively.

Mandy cringed and could feel the warmth creep into her cheeks. Was this woman fishing for information or was she simply curious, wanting to enjoy a friendly conversation?

She hesitated but decided there was nothing gained in hiding the truth.

"Mr. Barrett passed away a few years ago," she replied evasively and turned to search for the boys in the crowd. Earlier, she'd watched Brian showing them the tools and taking time to instruct them in their use. Now she caught sight of Sam carrying planks that appeared too heavy for him. Mandy smiled proudly.

"I'm glad you came today, Mrs. Barrett. It's good to meet new friends," Mrs. Bricker added with a gentle hand on Mandy's arm and smiled sweetly.

Mandy wondered if she could lower her defenses to enjoy visiting with this nice woman, but she struggled to totally relax. She understood how people, especially women, maneuvered around social situations like whaling ships at sea. Always on the hunt for the big one, the one piece of gossip too juicy to keep to yourself.

Was Mrs. Bricker like that? Mandy hoped the woman was sincere. She seemed so nice and pleasant. A glance at the other women made her doubt, however.

"Thank you, Mrs. Bricker, but I am not too sure that others here would agree with you," Mandy replied. Her gaze drifted to the small group of women who were still casting annoyed glances in her direction.

Mrs. Bricker chuckled. "Don't mind them. They're good enough ladies. Only they're worried what your intentions are toward Mr. Dawson. Ruby Wilson feels she has first claim on him and sees you as a sudden competitor."

Mandy scoffed. "Nonsense. I assure you, Mrs. Bricker, I am only the housekeeper and have no such intentions. My designs on Mr. Dawson are only as employer. He has been kind enough to offer jobs to my sons and myself, and I am very grateful."

"Well, you can't blame the girls for worrying, Mrs. Barrett," the smiling woman went on. "You are a beautiful woman, after all, and Mr. Dawson is a very eligible bachelor. He would stand out in any crowd. He's not only handsome, he is a man with land and a bright future."

"Handsome?" Mandy repeated as she glanced toward the building site and watched Brian pounding nails into posts. "I hadn't noticed," she said softly, averting her eyes so Mrs. Bricker would not perceive the lie.

The afternoon passed swiftly, with Mandy taking cups of coffee and plates of food to the busy workmen. Slowly, the barn became more complete. A loud cheer went up from the crowd when the final floor plank was fitted in place. The evening's dance would take place here.

Mandy marveled to see Sam and Jack move among the crowd of workmen, delivering tools and planks. A sense of pride welled within her as she watched her young boys doing men's work. She knew she had Brian to thank for this, for he had taken the time to show them what was needed. Her boys worked so well for him and seemed to enjoy making him happy. Their young eyes shone when he praised them.

Mandy vowed to use praise more often. It seemed effective in getting the most out of her boys. It wasn't like they didn't deserve it, only she hadn't seen it used in such a way since she was a girl, and she'd forgotten how effective it could be. Certainly, Richard had been no example of one who encouraged his family members.

Mandy served coffee to a man who seemed vaguely familiar. He doffed his hat when he saw her, revealing a balding head she recognized. He smiled boldly, glancing up and down her frame.

"Good afternoon, Mrs. Barrett."

Mandy felt her chest tighten. "Oh, Mr. Stine, I didn't recognize you." He looked different not covered in horse manure. Mandy nodded at the livery man, planning her escape.

He took the cup of coffee from her. "You're looking most pretty today, Mrs. Barrett. I hope you'll save a dance for me this evening." He winked brazenly and grinned. Mandy noticed his missing tooth.

"I doubt if I'll be doing any dancing, Mr. Stine," she said over her shoulder as she turned to go. "Have a good day."

Mandy whisked away before she could hear his reply.

As she returned to the food table to fetch another plate, she smiled grimly. She would not be dancing at this event, she was sure of that. Her reputation as either laundry woman or housekeeper, in fact, would make sure of that.

She brushed her hands, laughing to herself at the thought of her dancing with any of these men. But she did recall a time when she'd loved to dance.

"Mrs. Barrett, it is good to see you again."

Mr. Ambrose stepped beside her, leaning close. His pinched face wore a serious expression. Mandy blanched, her eyes widening. Oh, why had she allowed Brian to talk her into coming today?

"I hear you've found employment again. I assume that means you'll soon be paying what you owe me." The storekeeper eyed her through lowered eyelids. Mandy hated the way he stared at her, so solemn, like he was the Lord himself.

Mandy smiled brightly, concealing her fear of this businessman. "Of course, Mr. Ambrose. Just as soon as I get paid, you'll be seeing me."

She moved quickly away, her thoughts darkening. Just when she was getting on her feet, someone showed up to take what she was making. It had been her fortune to never get ahead.

Mandy looked skyward and scowled to the clouds. "I

know it's you again. You won't leave me alone. Will I never be allowed to just be happy? Am I always to suffer?"

No answer was given to her heartfelt plea, and Mandy frowned at the silent clouds as she moved toward the food table.

CHAPTER 14

The afternoon sped by, and everyone worked either building or serving. The great structure was more than half completed when the sun dropped and construction slowed. Lanterns were lit, and some finishing tasks were completed. The roof had been almost totally nailed on, and some of the loft was firmly in place.

"Hello! Hello!" Mr. Hamilton called loudly from the center of the barn floor. A crowd gathered. "I want to thank everyone for today's work. My sons and I can finish it from here. Now it's time for the dance! Thanks also to all you women who brought food and served us all day. Now let's rest and have some fun. Let me say a blessing on this time together."

A silence filled the great building, and all activity ceased. Hats were removed, heads bowed. Mandy quickly peeked to find Brian standing near Jack and Sam, a hand resting on each boy's shoulder.

She purposely made herself think of other things as Mr. Hamilton prayed aloud. She thought of Sam and Jack and how hard they'd worked today. The catty women who snubbed her all afternoon. The smell of wood and how all the different pieces fit together to build this barn.

She owed Mr. Ambrose money. She would have to pay him back. He knew where she was and who she worked for now. Mrs. Bricker had been nice to her. She realized with a start the conversation had been pleasant. It'd been so long since a woman wanted only to talk with her, not to tell her how to wash her clothes.

Renewed Redemption

Mandy squinted at Brian, his head bowed. Those silly women thought she had plans on this unsuspecting farmer. She laughed silently to herself. Mandy was through with men. She only wanted a job to pay her a fair wage and a place where her boys could work and possibly learn a trade.

Though, as she looked at Brian standing with her boys, she decided he was quite handsome.

A tingling in her chest alerted her, and she shook her head angrily. She closed her eyes. *There will be none of that, Mandy Barrett.*

"Amen." Mr. Hamilton concluded, and an excited echo rose from the listeners. Someone lit a bonfire outside for people to warm themselves, and several coffeepots were placed on the coals.

A fiddler started to tune his instrument, his bow dragging noisily across the strings. With a whoop, men started to search for partners. Sam and Jack were suddenly by her side.

"Mother? Can we help you serve?" Jack asked with a politeness Mandy had never heard from her youngest.

Mandy was astonished they wanted to help, but she was starting to get used to this odd behavior from her boys. She tousled Jack's hair, smiling fondly at him. "I would love the help. Where's Brian?"

"He's dancing with that Ruby Wilson." Sam pointed to the whirling couple on the dance floor. "Mother, she doesn't look like a little girl to me."

Mandy saw Brian sweep past them with the young brunette in his arms. They laughed and talked like old friends, oblivious to everyone around them. An unaccountable pang struck Mandy's heart and she looked away, chewing her lip.

Pushing the boys ahead of her, she moved toward the bonfire. "Let's fetch coffee and water for folks."

Throughout the evening, Mandy worked tirelessly to serve drinks. Repeatedly, she caught sight of Brian dancing with various partners, but most consistently with Ruby Wilson.

Twice she evaded the requests of the livery owner. Each time, barely making an escape from his ardent attempts to get her on the dance floor.

The evening was far advanced when Mandy started to think they'd best be getting back. Sam and Jack had already crawled into the back of the dray where she'd covered the weary boys with blankets. They had fallen asleep at once.

She studied their still faces in the dim moonlight. They'd worked so hard. She smiled, happy to see they weren't like their father.

Mandy searched the crowd for Brian to try and advise him of the late hour. Her bones felt weary. It'd been a long day.

Suddenly, he was beside her. The fiddle player called last dance and Ruby Wilson pulled on Brian's sleeve.

"Come on, Brian. It's the last dance, and my feet are still ready for more. Dance with me," she pleaded, smiling alluringly, tugging on his arm.

Brian turned to Mandy and spoke over his shoulder. "Thank you, Ruby, but this one is reserved for Mrs. Barrett." He gently disengaged himself from the girl's clutching hands.

Without asking permission, he took Mandy's arm and guided her onto the new barn floor. Behind them, Mandy heard Ruby ask, "What about me? Who will I dance with?"

"I believe Mr. Stine is looking for a partner," Mandy called over her shoulder as she was whirled into the throng of dancers.

In a moment, she was transported back in time. The loud music and the many couples filling the wooden floor caused Mandy to recall former events. She remembered the dances and balls she'd attended in Richmond and the great fun she'd always enjoyed. True to Ruby's claim, Brian was a wonderful dancer, light on his feet. He held her hand firmly but not too tight. His other hand rested easily on her slender waist, and she felt his strength as he twirled her around the floor.

Renewed Redemption

She looked up at him, watching his kind eyes as they danced. They twinkled as he laughed, and Mandy was pleased to see him enjoying himself. A thrill ran through her, and she relaxed in his arms, not wanting to miss an instant of this unexpected pleasure. As they twirled, Mandy could feel herself melting into his tightening embrace, leaning into his muscular chest. Or was she imagining it?

For the briefest of moments, Mandy felt happy. She was not the housekeeper, nor Richard Barrett's widow. She was a happy young woman without a care in the world dancing with a very handsome man. Life was good.

The music played on, and Brian smiled down at her.

"I had no idea you were an accomplished dancer, Mrs. Barrett," he whispered in her ear. His warm breath against her neck made her blush. Mandy was sure Brian could hear her thumping heart.

She did not reply, but instead, simply allowed herself to move with the music, to be in his arms and enjoy the dance. She didn't want these moments to end.

When was the last time she'd felt anything other than disappointment and frustration? She constantly felt overwhelmed by the demands of taking care of her boys. The Lord was always making her life difficult.

Now, for this brief moment in time, Mandy let herself enjoy. She could feel her heart pound wildly in her chest. Was it from the quick, whirling dance or the wonderful sensation of being in this man's arms? Was the heat in her cheeks from the dance alone? Mandy couldn't tell. Nor did she care.

Too soon, the music finished, couples applauded and then moved wearily to the doorways. Mandy heard the music end, yet Brian held her still, his hand on her waist as they looked into each other's eyes. She held her breath, not wanting the moment to pass.

Within seconds, Ruby Wilson loomed before them, a scowl marring her thin face.

"Well, you two made a fine couple," she snarled. "Everyone agreed you were the best dancers of the night."

Brian smiled at Mandy and stepped back, still holding her hand. "Thank you, Ruby. I enjoyed this dance very much. Mrs. Barrett is a wonderful dancer."

"Better than me, I suppose you mean," she snapped, her eyes narrowing as she looked at Mandy.

If looks could kill, Mandy mused, returning Ruby's cold stare with an innocent one of her own.

"That is not what I meant, Ruby. Only that Mrs. Barrett dances like girls I remember back home," he explained, attempting to placate the younger woman.

Ruby wrinkled her nose. "That's because she's old, Brian. She's already lived her life." Her face was as dark as a thundercloud. Mandy decided Ruby Wilson suddenly did not appear pretty at all.

The brunette girl turned and disappeared into the crowd of departing dancers. Brian led Mandy out to the dray, and people milled around them, some calling goodbyes to friends and neighbors. He still held her hand, his other hand returning to the small of her back, guiding her along.

Brian helped Mandy up the tall wheel to the high wooden seat and finally released her hand. A strange feeling came over her as she realized she didn't want him to let go.

As he walked around the horse, Brian checked the harness. Mandy looked behind her, glancing at the sleeping boys in the back. They seemed peaceful. She frowned into the dark night, not understanding her own feelings of unease that now filled her.

Wagons and riders of all descriptions were leaving the Hamilton's, and their two-wheeled vehicle seemed lost in the swarm of wagons and buggies moving along the road in the moonlight. Laughter and talking died out within a few minutes of leaving the farm behind as people fell asleep or grew silent with the long drive ahead of them.

Renewed Redemption

Brian and Mandy also rode along in silence. Though cold, the night sky shone clear and starlit above. The moon brightly and plainly revealed the road ahead of them.

Brian cleared his throat. "Uh, I want to apologize for what Ruby said. You are not old. Your life is not over."

Mandy smiled sadly, not really agreeing with him. "Well, I didn't take offense. In a way, she's right. I've made my choices, and my life is what it is." Disappointment and grief were old friends of hers. She wasn't angry that Ruby pointed it out. The girl was young. She would learn in time what Mandy already understood.

"It's never too late to change," Brian countered. "You are still young enough to choose a new path, if you wanted to."

Mandy scowled. "No, Ruby was right. I am old."

"I'll bet you're my own age, and I'm not old," Brian protested with a laugh. "Ruby is just very young and hasn't lived much life yet."

"I was married and had a baby at her age," Mandy said, enjoying the time to talk to Brian. He seemed to really listen, and she appreciated his patience. Once again, she realized the peace she seemed to feel when in his presence.

Brian turned and glanced at her in the darkness. Mandy could feel his gaze on her. "I'd guess your age at roughly my own. I'm twenty-eight."

Mandy nodded. "I know. Ruby told me." She paused and then added, "I'm twenty-eight too."

Brian shifted beside her. "Well, then, we're not too old to try new things. Ruby lacks the wisdom that can only come from experience." He glanced at her in the darkness and gently flicked the reins on the back of the horse. "We've both had our share of experiences." Mandy remembered what Mr. Vallejo said about Brian's experiences. He'd had tough times too. "Don't be too harsh on Miss Wilson. I believe she's set her cap for you, twenty-eight or not," Mandy remarked, a dry chuckle escaping her. Marriage was horrible, and she wouldn't wish such difficulty on this kind man.

Brian sighed. "I guessed as much. I'm not interested, though. In her, I mean," he added hastily. "Marriage was wonderful, and my wife showed me the true meaning of love. I'll marry again, but I don't think it will be to Ruby Wilson. God has other plans for me, I think."

"God," Mandy sneered. "His plans aren't always what we wish them to be." She could feel the deep lines come to her brow. "I'd hoped my life would be different than it is, but look at me now. I'm a housekeeper for a bachelor. Marriage to Richard showed me I will never marry again. What a nightmare."

"Wait a minute." Brian laughed. "I'm that bachelor, and life hasn't been easy for me, either. But that doesn't mean God doesn't love me and doesn't want good things for me. Maybe he wants me to remarry."

Mandy laughed in turn, but hers lacked humor. "He does not want good things for me. When my mother told me I would regret my decision to marry Richard, that God had something to teach me about my stubborn heart, she surely knew. I hate to admit she was right."

Brian was silent for a moment, and Mandy wondered what he was thinking. "Well?" he finally blurted.

"Well, what?" Mandy retorted, confused by his question.

"Well, what has God taught you about your stubborn heart?"

She frowned and then chewed the inside of her cheek. The wagon wheels crunched on the gravel below, and she shivered against the night air. Somewhere, an owl hooted.

Mandy sighed, her shoulders slouching. "I've learned I have a stubborn streak a mile wide that often gets me in trouble. However, sometimes it carries me through rough situations because I'm too stubborn to quit or know I'm beaten."

There. She'd said the words out loud. The thing she'd worried about for ten years was now out in the open for her to see it for what it was. Rebellion.

Renewed Redemption

"I have a rebellious heart, I guess," Mandy continued, dropping her head as she spoke. "I think that's what God is trying to teach me. I don't want to learn it, though," she added, matter-of-fact.

"Why not?" Brian asked, surprise in his voice. "Don't you always want to know the lesson God is teaching you?"

Mandy shook her head. "No. Do you?" She spoke swiftly, not really thinking about what she said, only knowing she didn't like to consider life lessons. Especially hard ones.

They both remained silent for a long while, and Mandy wondered if their talk was over. She hoped not. But why should she be surprised if it was? Wasn't she a boring, ruined, old woman? That little snippet, Ruby Wilson, had youth and life still ahead of her. She certainly didn't have the baggage Mandy carried.

Suddenly, she felt tired. The day had been long, and she grew tired of thinking about gossipy women and the money she owed Mr. Ambrose and Brian and Ruby and life. She was weary of everything.

The clip-clop of the horse's hooves thudded rhythmically, and Mandy's eyes drooped. Brian's unexpected words startled her.

"You're right. I've had a rebellious heart too. When my wife died, I chose to run away rather than face the pain and grief. I ended up out here, and with time, I dealt with the loss of my best friend. God brought me Carlos to help guide me. With his help, I see what Jesus wanted me to learn, and I hope I've become a better person because of it."

Mandy was awake again now. "How was your wife dying a good thing?" she demanded.

"I'm not saying her death was a good thing. But I have learned good things from it. I've learned compassion, kindness toward others who are hurting. I've learned to be grateful for the time I had with her. Better to have her love and lose her than have never experienced the joy we shared. God has shown me what love is, in that he gave his son for me. Through that kind of love and sacrifice, I'm able to better understand what real love is. To serve another person, to sacrifice my desires and wants for theirs." He paused and then said quietly, "God has made me a better person through the terrible experience of losing my wife."

This man amazed her. From a terrible situation like the death of his beloved wife, this man had allowed Jesus to show him things to learn, ways to improve, ways to grow.

She fell silent, wanting desperately to understand, while at the same time not wanting to think, to ponder the pain. The strong walls she'd built around her heart were cracking a bit, and she was worried. She'd avoided this topic for so long. Realization struck, and she knew she couldn't avoid the past any longer.

Maybe it was time to think on these things.

What had God been trying to teach her about her elopement, the tragic marriage that had followed, with Richard? Were there lessons to be gleaned from that mistake?

"So … you don't think you'll ever get married again?" Brian asked quietly. Did she sense disappointment in his inquiry?

"No," she answered, shaking her head. "Once was enough for me."

He nodded slowly. "I had fun dancing with you tonight," he said, changing the subject suddenly.

"Thank you. I did too. I wish …" she began and then stopped herself.

"Don't stop. Tell me. What do you wish?" She could feel his gaze on her in the dark as he spoke.

She tossed her head defiantly and lifted her chin. Perhaps from the lively dancing or the few stars peeking through the clouds or maybe his comfortable presence beside her, but whatever it was, Mandy felt relaxed and wanted to share her feelings with him.

Renewed Redemption

"If there were dreams that came true—and I don't think there are—I wish I could do things over. I wish I still had a relationship with my folks back in Richmond. Gosh, but I'd love to hear how they're doing. I wish I could feel the happiness I felt tonight forever." Mandy paused, then continued, her voice low. "I wish my father and mother knew their grandsons. I wish Mother would hold me when I hurt, and I wish Father were there to tell me he was going to help make everything all right."

She stopped herself and pinched her eyebrows together. *Why had she said that?* She was going soft, allowing her emotions to crowd into her mind. She glanced at Brian from the corner of her eye. Why was she forever opening up to this man? He seemed to have some power to make her lower her guard and share her heart. It made her angry. Angry at him and at herself. There was no room for dreams in her world. She pushed them back like she'd done thousands of times before. Silently, she slammed the lid back on her dreams.

With a grim laugh, she waved a hand dismissively. "That's all nonsense, though. There's no going back. Mistakes or no, life rolls on and you must roll with it or get run over. Dreams are for babies and rich people. I can't afford to have dreams."

She stopped again, wishing she'd said less, revealing nothing of herself to Brian. "But I know I'll never marry again. I can be fooled once, but not twice."

∞∞∞∞∞

Brian remained silent as Mandy talked. One moment she seemed confident, brash, sure of herself, and the next, lost, abandoned, lonely. He prayed silently the whole time she spoke.

They came into the yard of the little cottage, and Brian moved the boys to their beds while Mandy carried the dirty dishes to the kitchen. He turned to Mandy before taking the wagon to the barn.

"Thank you for a wonderful day, Mrs. Barrett."

He shuffled his feet, nudging loose gravel with the toe of his boot, wondering how much to say. He paused and then rushed on, heedless of the consequences.

"Jesus has something special for you. God bless you and goodnight."

Mandy's eyes widened, but she said nothing. Brian climbed the wheel to the high seat and looked down at her, moonlight shimmering on her long blonde hair. Her eyes were dark pools, shadowed, but he knew how blue they really were. He remembered smiling when he'd seen them sparkle tonight on the dance floor, so full of life and happiness. The sight had warmed his heart.

Mandy sighed loudly and turned to walk into the cottage. Brian watched her go, praying for her still.

He put the horse in his stall and then came into the house. He lit a candle and glanced warily down the hall, making sure there was no sign anyone else was awake. He placed the candle on the desk and seated himself in the leather chair, glancing once more toward the hallway.

The house was cold, but he didn't feel it. He had something big on his mind.

He opened a drawer and took out a piece of paper. He sat for a long time, staring at the blank page before him, arranging and organizing his thoughts. Then, Brian began to write.

CHAPTER 15

Mandy slept late the next day and was not ashamed to do so. Today was Sunday after all, and Brian's habit was to rest on the Sabbath. Mandy thought this a silly practice, but she enjoyed it, nonetheless.

Lazily rolling over in her bed sheets, Mandy looked out the window. The sun was just rising over the eastern peaks. She needed to start breakfast. The boys would be hungry. Perhaps oatmeal today. Brian always liked things to be simple on Sundays, not wishing anyone to work hard today, not even the housekeeper.

Abruptly, Mandy remembered the night before. She frowned, knowing she'd let her guard down. Brian had done it again. He'd gotten her to relax and say too much. This was becoming a bad habit, she mused sourly. He was always getting her to open up more than she intended.

She'd certainly done *that* on the ride home from the dance. The dance. Oh, that had been fun. Brian knew how to hold a girl, and he danced well. Mandy hadn't had that much fun in a long time.

She smiled mischievously when she remembered what Brian had said about Ruby Wilson. He'd agreed she was too young for him, and he was not interested in her anyway.

Mandy's eyes widened in surprise, and she sat up quickly. So what? What was that to her? Why would she care who Brian Dawson was interested in? It was certainly none of her business.

Slowly, she got out of bed and dressed for the day, returning her thoughts to the dance itself. She enjoyed being with the crowds yesterday. Despite the rudeness of some of the women, it'd been good to be with people. As she fastened a ribbon around her waist, she hummed the tunes from the previous night, and an unfamiliar joy filled her.

The boys slept late also, and her chores were not completed until mid-morning. Brian had made himself scarce as well. Mumbling something about catching up on some reading, he'd poured himself coffee and disappeared behind closed doors. Leaving the boys behind in the house to read or whittle or play games, Mandy decided she would go for a walk.

Afraid Sam or Jack might see her and ask to accompany her, she snuck out the back door and slipped into the line of trees along the river, wanting to be alone.

Quail Valley was not warm, but the little basin seemed to be protected from the dampness and harsher weather of the greater San Joaquin Valley that lay over the hills to the west. Somehow, Quail Valley felt unusually secluded and isolated.

Mandy walked along the riverbanks upstream, watching the dark pools and noticing the deep ripples as water tumbled over rocks. The water was brown but clear, easy to see even to the deeper depths.

The naked trees that lined the banks rubbed bare limbs together in the cool breeze. Occasionally, a gust of wind off the mountains above sent a chill down her back, but mostly the weather was ideal for walking.

Mandy reached the point of the farm where the boys had cleared land. Piles of stone lined the borders of the field, and only an occasional boulder too large to be moved protruded from the dirt.

She surveyed the ground critically, studying it with a farmer's eye, which she'd learned from her father. So, this is where Brian hoped to plant his alfalfa? Mandy turned and looked at the river, searching for signs where Brian planned to build his dam to irrigate the crop. The plan sounded clever, and she was impressed. Her father would've thought of things like this, she decided.

Would her father have liked Brian? Yes, of course, he surely would've. Brian was a farmer and a Christian, the exact type of man of which Jack Mulligan would approve.

Mandy smiled, thinking of her father sitting on Brian's porch with a cup of coffee, talking crops and soil and yield and weather. They would get along nicely, she believed.

"Mrs. Barrett," a voice interrupted her. "It is good to see you, Señora."

Carlos Vallejo stepped from the trees, appearing as if by magic.

Mandy lifted a hand to her throat. "Oh, Mr. Vallejo, you startled me. I didn't think anyone would be out here today."

The old man nodded, a wide smile creasing his leathery face. "I must check on my bees. Not only are they important to the fruit trees, they will be important to the alfalfa." He gestured to a weathered box under an oak tree near the river. Mandy had walked past it without taking notice.

"I didn't realize that was a beehive." She laughed, joining the old Mexican in his inspection of the box.

"I chased a swarm years ago and watched where they built their hive. Then, I started harvesting their honey. Brian had the idea to move them into a box and bring them close to his fields. It has worked beautifully these past few years."

Mandy stared hard at the wooden box and noticed a couple of bees flying around it. "Oh, there are bees now." She pointed to the sluggish, clumsy bees.

"Yes. They are starting to move about. These few are scouts, reporting on the outside weather to the rest of the hive. Soon, they will begin pollinating the trees. Maybe in the next two weeks. Perhaps three." The old man moved back from the box and walked toward the house. Mandy glanced ahead, not seeing any movement in the distant cottage.

Mandy felt reluctant to end her walk so soon, but she wanted to talk with the old beekeeper.

Renewed Redemption

"Mr. Vallejo," Mandy began, matching his pace. "You say you knew Mr. Dawson when he first came to California from Maryland? He says he owes you a great debt. He says you were responsible in helping him settle here."

Mandy abruptly sat on a large boulder, causing the Mexican man to stop and stand beside her. She didn't want to reach the house before she'd gathered some answers.

"No, no," he said, shaking his head. "Brian gives me too much credit. It is I who told him about this farm for sale. That is all. I worked for the Rogers family, and when Mr. Rogers died, Mrs. Rogers wanted to return east and Brian bought the farm. That is all I did."

Mandy persisted. "But Mr. Dawson says you showed him the right direction to take when he came here with his broken heart."

Was there hope for her broken heart? If Brian could get on with life, perhaps she could too. Mandy felt it was worth a try.

"Oh. Now I see what you are asking." He rubbed his hands together. "Brian was hurting after the loss of his young wife and fled to California to escape the memories and the pain. I simply showed him Christ."

Mandy frowned. This was not going in the direction she'd hoped for. "Jesus?" she said, hoping there might be another option.

"Of course. He is the Great Physician. He is who wants to heal our wounds." He paused and looked out over the tiny valley. Then he spoke, not looking at Mandy. "You have come here seeking the Great Physician too, Señora. I can see that your heart needs to be healed as Brian's did."

Mandy shook her head. "No, no. You are mistaken. I have come here for a job. I need the money. I was only curious about Mr. Dawson, that's all."

Any talk of Jesus was too much talk.

Mr. Vallejo turned to her, and he smiled again, his white teeth flashing in the cool sunlight. "Your words say no, but your eyes say yes. You need Jesus, Señora. He is eager to help you heal. Let him come back into your heart. I know he used to live there."

"How do you know that?" she whispered, her eyes widening.

He shrugged. "I can tell. You were raised knowing our Savior, yes? But something happened, and now you are reluctant to open your heart to him again. He forgives all, Mrs. Barrett."

Mandy noticed the title he used for her, and it cut into her, making her wince. Richard Barrett had always told her God was a waste of time, a myth for the simple-minded.

Mandy scowled. "I did know Jesus, but I've turned my back on him."

Mr. Vallejo chuckled and held up a finger. "Ah, but he has not turned his back on you." He paused, his dark eyes twinkling. "He is calling to you."

She turned her face to look at the trees along the river. "I did know Jesus when I was younger," she admitted. Her voice was low, almost a whisper. "My parents taught me about him." She hesitated and then chuckled bitterly. "He only wants to break my heart more. If Jesus brought me here, I can blame him for all my tears. I've cried more in the last few months than in the entire decade before."

Mr. Vallejo nodded. "Good. He is working on your walls. He is breaking them down. It is a good sign."

Mandy squinted, her brow wrinkling from the unexpected response.

She pursed her lips, steeling herself, and continued. "I have wronged him, Mr. Vallejo. Why would Jesus want me back? I have wronged my family. I have hurt them deeply. I wanted to show them they were wrong. That I could do things on my own. But my best was a total mess, a disaster."

Renewed Redemption

Mandy paused again, a lump forming in her throat, waiting for the old man to say something, but he did not interrupt. Slowly, Mandy went on.

"I used to have love and security. I lived in a warm house and had food to eat. I've placed my sons in dangerous situations because of my pride and my stubborn heart. I have made terrible decisions, and I believe it's too late to go back."

Why was she telling this complete stranger all about herself? Why did she feel safe with him? She couldn't understand but felt compelled to go on, to tell him all.

"I knew Richard was a mistake, but I refused to ask for help. I needed to show my folks they were wrong about him. I wanted to make things work on my own."

The old Mexican had turned and gazed at the river, but now he looked again at Mandy. He arched his eyebrows, an amused glint in his old eyes. "And how did that work out for you?"

She smiled sadly. "Terribly. I'm not able to keep things together. I know I need help, but I don't know where to turn."

She felt as if she were drowning and needed to be saved from her own unsuccessful plans. Somehow, this man drew her like a sunflower to the light. She couldn't resist being transparent, sharing her life with him. Perhaps he would be her lifeline.

"Jesus is the answer, Señora. He is able to help you heal and be restored. Trust Jesus," the old man said quietly, a gentle smile on his lined face.

She clenched her fists. *No. It is too late for me. I have broken my parents' hearts. I have sinned against them and God. I am getting exactly what I deserve. Pain. Grief. Hardship.*

She could feel the tears well in her eyes, and a lump formed in her throat, threatening to burst. Mandy swallowed hard, forcing it back down. Crying never solved anything, she well knew. Hadn't these past ten years taught her that?

She shook her head. "Mr. Vallejo, I thank you for your kindness, but it's not for me. I've made my choices, and I must live with the consequences." Mandy stood, ready now to return to the house.

"Wait, Señora," he said, placing a firm hand on her arm. "Think of the children. They are innocent. Teach them about Jesus. Let them have a chance to know peace and a relationship with their creator. Do not punish them for what you believe you deserve."

He was right, of course. Mandy saw clearly then. Sam and Jack deserved every opportunity she could provide for them. They were innocent, not to be punished for what she'd done. Perhaps they would choose better than she had when temptation came upon them.

Memories of her early childhood swept over her, reminding her of the security and love she'd felt when she was young and in her parents' home. She'd had no responsibility except to love and learn. Her parents had taught her about life and about God. Looking back, Mandy knew those were the happiest days of her life.

Didn't Sam and Jack deserve similar memories?

Perhaps it was too late for the boys to experience the comforts Mandy had been blessed with back in Richmond, comforts she had taken for granted. But maybe it was not too late to allow them to know Jesus. He had been Mandy's constant companion back when life was good.

Mandy had been given the chance to choose, and her choices had caused pain and misery. She deserved the consequences, but the boys did not. Maybe learning about Christ would help them become wiser, stronger than she was when Richard hissed his lies in her ear.

Mandy nodded, sniffling. "You're right, Mr. Vallejo. The boys deserve a chance. I'll let them learn about God. It's the right thing to do." She spoke as she started for the house. "I must tell Brian."

The old man squeezed her arm, not releasing her. "Remember, Señora. Redemption is forever. Jesus doesn't give up on us even when we give up on him."

Mandy narrowed her eyes but said nothing. His hand fell from her arm and she started walking.

Mr. Vallejo moved in step with her, speaking as they strode. "Brian is aware of this, Señora. It is why the Lord has brought you here. Brian will share Jesus with your sons."

They walked on in silence, the house not far now. She'd hardened her heart against the Lord and was not ready to open it again to him. She didn't feel she could after her stubborn rebellion. But the boys, they would hear about Christ, know what it meant to know God and the plan of redemption God has for every person. Mandy knew it was the right thing to do.

Brian sat on the porch, a book across his lap. He saw them coming and waved, snapping the book closed as he stood.

"Hello, Carlos. What brings you out here today?" He shook hands with the old Mexican and glanced curiously at Mandy.

"I needed to tend the bees. They are starting to move about some," Carlos announced, lowering himself slowly to the bench.

"I will get you something to drink. What would you like?" Mandy moved past Brian quickly before he could discern too much. She was still unsettled by her conversation with Mr. Vallejo and did not want Brian to see her unease. Not yet.

"If you have any coffee and maybe some of those sweet things you make?" Carlos answered as Mandy went inside. There, she found Sam reading to Jack.

"Hello, Mother," the smaller boy quipped. "Sam is reading to me."

Mandy halted in her tracks. She hadn't seen Sam read aloud in a long while, but it was the look in his eyes that worried her. Sheepishly, he glanced at her, his eyes widening.

Sam looked away as Mandy took a step nearer. He seemed guilty. His eyes darted to and fro, and he quickly closed the book on his lap. He stood and shifted on his heels.

Mandy frowned and rested her hands on her hips. She'd been a mother long enough to recognize the signs.

"Sam? What's wrong? What are you reading?" She glanced at the thick book, recognizing it immediately.

The older boy hesitated, not speaking, freckles standing out on his pale face.

Mandy picked up the book, and a knot formed in her gut as she glared at the leather binding.

"I'm sorry, Mother. I know you don't like Brian talking to us about God, but I didn't know if you'd let us read about Jesus on our own," Sam sputtered quickly, his words tumbling over one another.

Mandy felt empty, as if she'd intentionally withheld something good from her sons. *Mothers are not to keep good things from their children.*

She reached for Sam, resting her hands on his shoulders, and pulled him to her. Mandy stared deeply into his worried, frightened eyes. "Oh, Sam, Mother was wrong," she began, a lump coming thickly to her throat. She had a hard time continuing, but she pushed on, needing to get the words out.

"I realized today that it's good for you to read about God and learn. His truth will guide you through life. Obey God and walk with him always. Don't get impatient and jump ahead of God's plan for you. Wait on the Lord."

The lump shifted, and Mandy paused, fighting back the tears that threatened. She hoped her son would heed her warning better than she had listened to her father's.

Renewed Redemption

She glanced at Jack and then, back at Sam. Both boys stared at her, watching her closely. She read disbelief and doubt in their young eyes and she scowled, suddenly angry at keeping her sons from the Lord.

Mandy smiled weakly and released Sam. She strode to the kitchen, opening and shutting cupboard doors, pretending to fuss over coffee and sweet cakes as the tears flowed freely down her cheeks. Mandy cried bitterly as she waited for the water to boil.

If she could go back. If only she was seventeen again and could choose to do things over.

She wept. The hot, salty tears touched her lips.

Her boys deserved a chance. Perhaps they would be wiser and more patient than she'd been. With all her heart, Mandy hoped they would.

The water boiled, and she dropped the ground coffee into the steaming pot. Wiping her wet face with her sleeve, Mandy put a tray together of sweet rolls and coffee.

Carlos smiled encouragingly at her as Mandy handed him his cup. Brian seemed oblivious, averting his eyes from her own when she served him his pastries. He didn't even look up when she gave him his coffee, the cup rattling noisily on its saucer.

She went back inside then, wishing to be alone. She promised herself to talk to Brian when the opportunity arose. But not now, not when she couldn't even control her emotions.

Again, Mandy wiped her wet eyes. She frowned suddenly, curious about something nagging at her. Was she crying for herself or for the boys? Were the trials of the past years filling her with regret and sadness, or was she hopeful that the boys would not repeat her mistakes?

Confused, Mandy wept harder. Today was Sunday and she could be alone. She retired early to her room, telling the boys she didn't feel well, as she wrestled with her demons.

CHAPTER 16

The next morning, Brian entered the kitchen while it was still dark. He yawned and then halted, his eyes widening when he saw Mandy working at the stove.

She smiled at him as she deftly flipped flap jacks. "Breakfast will be ready in a minute. Grab a mug. Coffee's ready."

He stared at her and shuffled to the cupboard, returning with a cup.

She hefted the pot, steam rising thickly as she filled his cup. He averted his gaze and mumbled his thanks as he lumbered to the living room.

She frowned as she watched him go. He sat on the couch and stared into the fire, not opening the Bible, as was his usual daily practice.

Mandy wanted to tell him about her change of heart. Brian would be pleased to hear her news regarding the boys and the Bible lessons, but he seemed quiet, distant, oddly out of sorts this morning.

She decided she would wait until he was in a more receptive mood.

"I'll get the boys started in the new field, but then, I must make a quick trip to town," Brian called from the living room, not taking his eyes from the fire.

Mandy scrambled eggs at the stove, thinking of Mr. Ambrose and the debt she owed him. "Let me run your errand. I'd like a trip to town too. I can do anything you need doing."

Renewed Redemption

"No," he snapped. Mandy turned at his harsh tone. Brian glanced over his shoulder. "I'm sorry, but I need to run this errand myself."

Mandy pursed her lips. Maybe it had something to do with Ruby Wilson. She squinted at the pieces of bacon sizzling in the skillet and shoved them roughly with her fork.

Brian stood and moved beside her, watching her work. "No, thank you," he said, his tone softening considerably. "This is something I must do. I can run any errand you need, though."

Mandy squirmed. She didn't want to tell Brian about the bill she had at Mr. Ambrose's store. "Uh, that's quite all right. It'll keep. You run your errand, and I'll check on the boys today, if you like."

Brian nodded. "Fine. That sounds great," he said, his false enthusiasm ringing hollow. "Have Sam start on the place above where we've already cleared. He knows the spot, and he knows what to do. I'll be home as quickly as I can."

Mandy placed a plate before him and tidied the kitchen as he ate in silence. When he'd finished, she removed his empty plate while he retrieved an envelope from his desk. Without another word to her, he left the house.

Mandy watched him drive the dray from the yard on the road to town. What had been the hurry?

She brushed nagging thoughts about Brian and his odd life from her mind and turned back to the kitchen. She had her own issues to worry about. She was eager to share her news with Sam and Jack about studying Scripture but was also anxious about the debt at the general store. She hoped Mr. Ambrose wouldn't say anything to Brian if the two men met in town.

After serving Sam and Jack their breakfast, she explained Brian's instructions for their day.

"Sam," Jack whispered, bouncing a bit in his chair. "This is a test. Brian wants to see if we work hard when he isn't watching us. When only God is watching. We must do our best. Brian would want us to work hard even without him there."

"Jack, I'll bet you're right," Sam replied, his eyes shining with responsibility. "We'll do our best, and Brian will be impressed. We're not children anymore that need to be babysat. He'll see that and know we're men."

With their decision set, they eagerly trooped out to the fields, their young faces set with determination.

Mandy watched them go, her heart full of a mother's pride. They were good boys and anxious to please Brian. *And God,* Mandy mused.

She cleaned the kitchen and started laundry. As she worked, she began to formulate a plan on how to tell Brian he could now instruct the boys in Bible teaching. By the time he'd returned from town, she'd prepared her speech.

Mandy stood by the window watching his arrival. He drove straight to the barn without a glance her way. He seemed lost in thought. She met him at the front door, pulling it open as he reached for the handle. Startled, he jumped in fright at sight of her.

"Oh, Mandy, I forgot you were here," he stammered. She noticed he'd used her first name.

"Where else would I be?" She eyed him curiously, then dismissed the thought, wanting to get right to the point.

Brian shifted nervously. "Well, uh, I mean, maybe I should get right out to the fields and check on the boys." He turned to go, not even asking about lunch.

"Wait," Mandy ordered, gripping his arm. "I have a sandwich for you. You can eat on the way. I have something I want to talk to you about." She wondered at his responses but quickly moved on to her own business.

Releasing his arm, she raced into the kitchen. Mandy grabbed his lunch and hurried back out the front door. Brian had already begun to walk, and she hurried to match his stride.

Renewed Redemption

He walked as if pursued by something he feared, wearing a frown, which was unusual for him.

"So? Did you do it?" she inquired as they walked up the trail.

His head jerked as he skidded to a halt, and he turned to stare at her, eyes wide. "Do what?" he squeaked.

"Your errand, silly. What are you talking about?" She eyed him suspiciously. Brian never acted like this. He always carried himself with confidence, so sure of himself.

He exhaled deeply. "Nothing, nothing. Yes, I did my errand," he said, his voice more relaxed. He resumed walking.

She had to hurry to catch up with him. "Good. I want to talk to you about the boys learning about Jesus. I've decided that even though I do not believe God wants good things for me, I want the boys to know him and learn about his ways." She watched his face while she spoke, eager to see his response at her words.

Now he seemed to be suspicious. "Why the sudden turnabout?" he demanded, his eyes narrowing. Mandy noticed his pace did not slow.

"Well, I've been thinking, and I want the boys to have every opportunity to be blessed and walk with the Lord. I've made my decisions and they have consequences, but the boys shouldn't have to suffer for something I did. They'll be old enough soon to make their own decisions, and I want them to make good ones, ones that please the Lord." She finished her rehearsed speech, happy she'd gotten the words out.

Maybe God would be good to her boys, she thought to herself. The Lord certainly was hard on her, but she deserved it. Perhaps Sam and Jack would make better decisions than she did if they had sound teaching. Mandy knew she was taught the way of God from her family, but her wicked heart wanted what it wanted. Refusing to take God's guidelines seriously, Mandy had listened to Richard Barrett instead and regretted his counsel ever since.

Brian was quiet for a minute and then nodded. "All right," he agreed, his pace never slackening.

She halted, allowing him to continue up the trail alone. She watched him go. This man would instruct her boys about Jesus. He could be counted on to take the responsibility seriously. Smiling, Mandy returned to the house.

∞∞∞∞∞

The weeks passed, every day filled with work. Though not properly spring yet, the fruit trees blossomed, and the bees were busy. Mandy was fascinated to see the small winged insects flying clumsily like tiny barrels, carrying the precious pollen from tree to tree.

On some days, she would open the windows, at least for a few hours. Each day that passed, she'd extend the time she'd leave them open. The cool air that blew through the house carried a chilly tinge of snow from the mountains above, mingled with the pungent tang of pine.

The days grew longer. Slowly, the days passed, and winter retreated from the lower elevations. White-capped mountains still shimmered above Quail Valley, but spring was definitely in the air. Barely discernable, a hint of green could be detected among the trees bordering the river.

For the past three Sundays in a row, Ruby Wilson had ridden over to enjoy afternoon tea with Brian. Mandy had reluctantly served them, having to endure the younger girl's forced laughter and silly chatter. Mandy was amazed how polite and patient Brian was to this infernal attack of immaturity. He listened attentively and even asked occasional questions of the pretty girl. Mandy later asked him why he encouraged her so.

"I am a man of God. I don't see the visits as encouraging her. I'm being a gentleman as the Lord would have me do. I will show Miss Wilson as much respect and kindness as I would show anyone," Brian explained.

Renewed Redemption

Mandy sometimes wondered at Brian's attentions to her. Were they more than kindness? She had wondered, and now she knew. Brian Dawson was not any more interested in her than he was in Ruby Wilson. He was simply being courteous.

Somehow this rankled her for a few days until she realized the implication. Was she hoping for something more with Brian? He was strong, handsome, a man of property. He could provide for her and the boys. But, clearly, he was not interested. He was just a kind man, kind to everyone. She tilted her head, chewed her lip, and frowned. Did she hope she was special to Brian Dawson? She smiled to herself and laughed, heat rising to her cheeks. Absolutely not. She had vowed to never marry again. What business was it of hers if Brian was attracted to Ruby Wilson?

"You are far too old to be thinking childish fairytale dreams, Mandy Barrett," she chided herself and resolved to not consider these silly thoughts anymore.

One Sunday in early March, Ruby appeared on the porch while Brian was yet walking the level fields he had prepared for planting. The boys had disappeared, no doubt exploring along the river or reading in their room.

"Mr. Dawson is due back at any minute, Miss Wilson. You may wait inside or out, whichever is comfortable to you," Mandy spoke, trying to keep the bite from her words. No matter how hard she tried, she couldn't make herself like Ruby Wilson.

The slender brunette lifted her chin. "You may bring my tea to the front porch, Mrs. Barrett." She offered Mandy a thin smile on her narrow face.

Mandy mumbled under her breath as she fetched the tea. Handing the empty cup and saucer to the girl, Mandy added, "I thought the man was supposed to do the calling." She could not hide the intended sarcastic stab.

The young woman smiled without humor, her eyes giving Mandy a disdainful glance before looking up the trail for Brian's arrival. "Maybe in the old days that is how it was done,"

Ruby purred. China clinked as she accepted the proffered cup. "Mother says a girl today must go after what she wants." She lifted the steaming cup to her thin lips, swallowed a sip, and then said, "Things are done differently out here in California. Times are changing, Mrs. Barrett."

For a moment, Mandy stood over the girl, contemplating dropping the tea kettle on her head. Instead, she spun on her heel and went indoors.

The afternoon passed in tedium as Mandy served the laughing, merry couple more tea and cakes than a body had a right to eat. Ruby Wilson talked, teased, and turned her pretty head this way and that, making her dark hair bounce. Her lively eyes opened wide with interest at every word Brian uttered, and Mandy had to keep from rolling her eyes every time Ruby said she was "amazed" at "how strong and smart" Brian seemed.

At last, she departed, and Mandy came out onto the porch to stand next to the waving Mr. Dawson as Ruby disappeared down the road.

He sighed and turned to Mandy. "That was a pleasant visit. She has promised to come next Sunday as well."

"Is that a threat?" Mandy muttered as she returned inside to begin supper.

Brian remained on the porch as Mandy stomped to the kitchen, her anger mounting. The unfamiliar tumult within her made her wonder and she tilted her head, examining her feelings. Was she jealous of Ruby Wilson? Why? Brian Dawson was nothing to her.

She pursed her lips as she worked, almost cutting off her finger as she peeled potatoes. They had no relationship other than boss and worker and had both acted respectfully in every capacity. What reason would she have to dislike Miss Wilson?

∞∞∞∞∞

Miss Wilson had departed, and Brian walked to the barn. After filling the manger with hay, he patted the big horse's neck as he ate. Brian had never been any good at understanding women. His wife and he had married young, before he realized how ignorant and clumsy he was around females.

He hadn't thought of another wife, but he could not ignore the advances of Miss Wilson forever. She was pretty in a way, though her character mattered more to Brian. She was spiritually immature and that concerned him. Her spiritual development was far more important to him than her good looks.

Ruby was young, vibrant, and energetic but lacked the wisdom that could only come with time. He treated her politely, listening attentively to her numerous tales of neighborhood gossip, but her anecdotes did not interest him. He preferred conversation with more depth.

No, he decided, Ruby Wilson was not for him. He wasn't interested in spending time with her or, for that matter, a lifetime. But how to tell her? He did not want to hurt her feelings.

He patted the big horse once more and moved toward the house. He would have to pray about it. He knew the Lord would give him guidance and wisdom.

The delicious aroma of dinner assailed him as he opened the door. Mandy was a good cook, he thought to himself, smiling. *She will make a good wife for someone someday.* His eyes widened unexpectedly as the force of his thoughts struck him. *Mandy would make a good wife for someone? Where had that come from?*

He took a seat at the table and shook his head. Better to erase his mind of those thoughts before he said something he'd regret. "Mandy, I've been thinking."

She halted, laying the basket of freshly baked bread on the table. Sunshine shone through the open window and rested upon her golden head, making her blonde hair glisten like a wheat field in July. A loose strand draped across her cheek, and he had to squelch the sudden impulse to push it back into place.

Brian found himself staring and he paused, suddenly forgetting what he was going to say.

"Thinking about what?" she asked, her eyes intent upon him.

He could feel the blush rise up his neck, making him feel awkward and silly, like a schoolboy. He felt embarrassed, but he couldn't say why.

"I'm ready to begin planting the alfalfa," he stammered. He swallowed hard and tried again. "But I need help. The boys are wonderful, but I need someone taller with a good reach who can spread seed," he finished, reaching for the warm bread.

∞∞∞∞∞

Mandy stared at him, one hand on her hip. "You want me to spread seed?" Not that she was against such a proposition, she was just reminded so much of how she used to help her father on their family farm. She had always worked with him in the fields. Her mother used to get angry that Mandy wouldn't wear shoes but preferred walking barefoot in the rich Virginia soil. Mother had said such behavior was not ladylike, but there had always been a twinkle in her eyes when she'd scolded.

"Let the girl be, Mother," Father would say, sticking up for Mandy. The farmer loved to work in the fields with his daughter. "She enjoys the land, like the good Lord intended," he would say, laying a dirty hand on Mandy's shoulder.

Mandy could almost feel the warm sun on her back and the dirt between her toes. The earthy smell of rich soil filled her nose again, and for a split second, Mandy was back in Virginia.

"Come on, Mother," Jack pleaded as he and Sam seated themselves at the table. "Work with us in the fields. Having you with us will be fun."

"Do it, Mother. I'll help you," Sam joined in.

Mandy took her seat at the table, thinking. All eyes were on her as she considered the idea. Over the last number of weeks, the boys had developed into a well-operating team, and now they invited her to be a part. She couldn't deny the honor she felt. She wanted to work with them. And Brian.

Mandy smiled. "I would love to."

CHAPTER 17

For the next week, Mandy walked the fields in parallel paths to Brian, casting seeds from the bag slung around her neck. They would walk slowly, evenly throwing the seeds a little at a time. Mandy found the task a welcome diversion from her household chores. More importantly, she enjoyed being outside with her boys.

Mandy remembered those warm, pleasant summers in Virginia when she'd walked the fields with her father on their small farm. He had talked to her of the land and the goodness of God. Now, here in California, she thought of those days with fondness. For the first time in years, she eagerly sought those memories. Forbidden for so long, she now allowed herself to bask in the glow of the joy and peace she'd experienced there.

Brian encouraged their progress. As they completed one pass on the field, he would call to her, "Great. That was wonderful. You're a natural at this. Now, let's turn and go diagonally to our previous pass to make sure we lay a good covering."

Mandy was unaccustomed to such positive remarks and soon blossomed under his leadership, seeing clearly why her boys loved to work with Brian. He was kind and made working for him a real joy.

Often the boys and Brian would sing praise songs. Mandy tried hard to learn them, liking the tune and the words. She didn't sing out loud but recited them silently to herself.

By the end of the fourth day, dark clouds had formed over the mountains to the east.

Renewed Redemption

"Looks like we're in for a storm. Perfect timing." Brian rubbed his hands as he looked up at the growing darkness above them. "This rain is an answer to prayer. It'll moisten the seeds and cause germination. Soon, we'll flood the fields to irrigate them."

By time they arrived at the house, large raindrops splattered their heads. Laughing, the quartet of farmers raced the short remaining distance to the front porch. The four of them gathered together under the protective roof of the porch, the pelting rain drumming powerfully above them.

As they stood and watched the rain fall, thunder rolled and echoed around their small valley, reverberating loudly.

Chilled from the sudden downpour, they entered the house. Inside was warm and snug. Mandy added wood to the nearly dead fire.

"I'll take only a few minutes to put on a soup. Be patient and I'll throw something together," Mandy promised as she moved toward the kitchen, wiping the bark off her hands.

"Not tonight," Brian interjected, overtaking her. "Tonight, you rest. The boys and I will make you dinner. You've helped me tremendously this week, and it's not fair that you work outside with us and then come in to make us dinner."

Smiling, he passed Mandy and motioned to the boys to follow him into the kitchen. They rushed to join him, eager to assist in the dinner preparations.

"Sam, Jack, what do you suggest? What's something three bachelors can make for a lady?" Brian asked as he strode into the kitchen.

"Pancakes," Jack offered as he lifted a mixing bowl from the sideboard.

"Yes, pancakes with bacon," Sam added.

Brian glanced over at Mandy, her insides turning somersaults as she looked into his soft, brown eyes. She stared, too stunned to move. He was so thoughtful, so kind. Richard would never have thought of her like this.

"Go sit by the fire in the sitting room, and I'll bring you a cup of tea. You deserve a break," Brian encouraged with a smile.

Still skeptical, Mandy turned slowly from the kitchen, disbelief churning within her. She walked to the big couch in front of the fireplace and seated herself.

Not for years had anyone made her dinner, except when she was sick and had first arrived at Quail Valley. For the next half hour, she listened to Brian and the boys moving around the kitchen, chatting and teasing one another while making her dinner. Occasional peals of laughter filled the small cottage.

Mandy sipped her tea and stared into the fire, not sure how to feel.

Finally called to the table, Mandy found it set with plates and cups. A heaping stack of steaming pancakes were there next to a plate of hot bacon. Sitting before her empty plate, she waited patiently for the others to find their seats. She knew the routine. Brian would begin with prayer. She looked at him to say the words that started every meal. But tonight, he surprised her.

"Jack, would you like to say the blessing tonight?"

"Yes, thank you, Brian," the small boy replied as if he'd done this a hundred times before. He clasped his hands and solemnly lowered his head.

Mandy followed suit, one eye still on her youngest son. Concealing her surprise proved difficult as she listened to Jack pray openly. But Mandy felt a mixture of pride and jealously at how easily and comfortably Jack spoke to the God of the universe.

"Thank you, Lord, for this food, and thanks for having Mother join us in the fields. It was fun to be with her. Amen."

Mandy smiled. Pancakes and bacon for supper was certainly not the usual fare, but she appreciated she hadn't had to cook this evening. Also, she appreciated the fact the boys wanted to make her dinner.

Renewed Redemption

Mandy glanced covertly at Brian as she passed the plate of pancakes to Sam. Brian had initiated these incredible changes in her small family. She observed him speaking to Jack, praising the young boy for his prayer.

Her former annoyance at the stubbornness of this farmer was now replaced by gratitude. Grudgingly, Mandy admitted Brian Dawson had been the best thing to happen to her young boys in their entire lives.

She turned her gaze, watching her sons closely while they ate. They were happy, healthy, and clean. Things had never been this good for this long. She loved that they were growing closer together as a family.

She glanced at Brian again. Because of this man, they were doing so well. He'd brought them to this point and well she knew it. She was grateful to him for all he'd done. Their wonderful situation had certainly been worth her boys learning about God.

Brian looked up suddenly and caught Mandy's stare. She blushed, embarrassed at being caught. Smiling quickly, she shifted her gaze away, feeling the color rise to her cheeks. For the remainder of the meal, she made sure not to be caught staring again.

"Tomorrow will be a day off," Brian remarked, glancing out the kitchen window at the steadily falling rain. "This rain will continue, God willing, and give us an excuse to enjoy a day of rest."

His excited brown eyes turned to the boys once more. "We've worked hard and should take the time. Besides," he added slyly, "it'll be a good opportunity to discuss salvation."

"Salvation?" Sam asked, turning to look at Brian.

"Yes. Salvation is when you've learned to recognize the sacrifice Jesus has performed for you by dying on the cross for your sins. And you, in response, accept that salvation and choose to live for him. To ask forgiveness for your sins and choose to follow Christ. With Jesus in your heart, you are able to forgive others, have mercy on people, be kind, generous, be a servant. Jesus is the example you try to follow, knowing you will not do it as perfectly as he did, since he was sinless and never made mistakes. But beginning each day with a new desire to be like Christ, our king and God."

Mandy felt Jack's eyes on her, watching her, to see her response to Brian's words. She turned to him and smiled. "Brian is right, Jack. God wants you to be like his Son, Jesus. And when you make a mistake and mess up, ask for forgiveness and he is faithful to forgive you."

Abruptly, a muscle twitched in her jaw, and she squinted. Her own words struck her hard, and Mandy realized suddenly what she had said. She glanced swiftly at Brian to see if he'd noticed. He stared at her, a tentative smile on his lips.

She had allowed truth to penetrate her thick skull as she spoke to Jack, and it made her uneasy. Could she speak thus to the boys and not listen to her own words? What a hypocrite.

Her happy and relaxed mood fled. Mandy stood, gripping the edge of the table. She looked at each of them and turned, walking quickly from the room, her words trailing behind her as she called over her shoulder. "I don't feel well. Please clean the dishes for me?"

In the solitude of her room, Mandy undressed and hung her dress in the closet. Then, instead, she dropped the soiled garment to the floor, reminding herself that she'd worked in the fields today. She would wash the dress the next time she did laundry.

Pulling on her nightgown, she crawled into the soft bed. Her comment to Jack haunted her. She could tell God was urging her to open herself to accept his forgiveness, but she resisted, not wanting to give up the heavy burden she had carried for so long. The load was all hers, the weight had become part of her. Her guilt and anger, the frustration she bore daily, had become second nature, an automatic response to everything. No, more than that. The burden had become her, what she was made of.

Renewed Redemption

Mandy clung to the bitterness, which had taken root in her heart and was all she knew. To release the emotion would leave her exposed, vulnerable. Her troubles had become her fortress, the high walls protecting her from future pain.

She stared up at the dark ceiling above her, barely able to discern an occasional word from the kitchen down the hall. Her boys were with Brian, and she trusted him with her sons. He'd proven to be a good man, something Richard could have never found within himself. Mandy knew Brian was a better parent than she, as well, although he was not properly the boys' father.

Brian Dawson. His strong, smooth face filled her mind. Kind, generous, helpful, encouraging, a servant.

She realized then he was like Jesus. Brian tried hard to be like Jesus, and that effort had made an impact on her family.

She lay there in the darkness, a hot tear sliding slowly down her cheek, striking the pillow under her head. She had failed her boys. She had worked so hard to be a good mother, but she had wanted to do so without God. Mandy wanted to be a good mother, but her sons had a bad father. She was forced to work alone. She knew it was not the way God had intended.

God now tugged at her heart. She saw clearly no accident had led her to this little cottage in Quail Valley. God had met her here.

Again, her stubborn resolution rose within her and she reached for it like a warrior's sword, comforting and familiar in her grasp. "No, God," she whispered aloud. "I am not worthy of forgiveness. I made my choice, and I will live with it. I deserve what happens to me. Only, please be kind to Sam and Jack. They are so innocent. Be good to them. Thank you they have Brian to look up to. Thank you, God, for Brian Dawson."

She rolled onto her side, curled into a tight ball, and squeezed her eyes shut, attempting in vain to stem the flow of tears. She buried her face in her pillow to stifle the sobs wracking her body, making her shoulders shake with their force.

CHAPTER 18

Mandy rose with the dull gray of dawn. Rain fell all night and hadn't let up with the coming of the new day.

Brushing her long hair and braiding it with nimble fingers, Mandy donned the gray travel dress from the closet. She stole a quick glance into the small mirror mounted on her wall, irritated she even cared what Brian thought of her appearance. Then, she strode into the kitchen.

Brian sat on the couch in front of a cheery fire, his Bible on his lap. He looked up when she entered.

"Good morning, Mrs. Barrett. You are up early for a day off," he greeted her, his brown eyes curious.

She glowered at him, hoping he didn't notice the red-rimmed eyes she'd seen in her mirror.

Mandy took a deep breath. "I know you and the boys are going to have some interesting talks today, and I don't care to hear them," she snapped in way of response. She spoke a little sharper than intended, but she was not about to apologize. This man held a peace and goodness that infuriated her, a constant reminder of her own deficiencies as a parent and an individual.

He looked at her, his eyes gentle. "All right." He nodded slowly. "Anything I can do for you?"

She felt he pitied her, and the thought made her angrier. Hadn't she spent the greater part of the night pitying herself? She did not need more pity from this man. "Brian, I know you're doing a good thing with Sam and Jack, but I'm having a hard time with it. Please leave me alone."

She turned to grab a chunk of bread from the box and took a raincoat from the hook by the door.

Renewed Redemption

"I have business in town with Mr. Ambrose. I will return later," she explained, a hand going to the front door. Mandy allowed her gaze to rest upon the surprised man sitting before the fire. His Bible still lay open on his lap. She frowned at him. "Much later," she added curtly and turned the knob. "But it's raining, Mrs. Barrett. Don't walk all the way to town today," he implored, rising to his feet and taking a step toward her.

Mandy held the bread up between them like a shield. "Don't come near me. I will be back later." She opened the door and stepped onto the porch.

Halting at the steps, she pulled the hood over her head and stepped down onto the wet ground and started to walk.

The rain cast only a fine mist, and the ground was not muddy despite the rain of the previous night. The ground had absorbed this moisture, and few puddles formed on the road ahead. She walked swiftly, enjoying the exertion. Munching on the piece of bread, she rehearsed her speech for Mr. Ambrose.

"I've been far too busy to come to town and inquire how much I owe you."

She thought about the excuse for a moment, mulling it over. She nodded. Her words didn't matter anyway. The storekeeper had known for weeks she stayed at the Dawson farm and could have come for the money but hadn't. Yet the constant battles with Mr. Ambrose had developed a preparedness for war Mandy understood and accepted. It was part of how she had operated for years. Everything was a fight.

A twinge of guilt assailed her as her thoughts shifted back to Brian. Mandy had cried most of the night. Mostly for herself but some for Sam and Jack. Guilt, remorse, and frustration swept over her anew and with perfect precision born of years of experience. She parried the blow, maneuvering the troubling thoughts to their rightful place deep in the darkest corner of her mind. She would not think of these things now.

Forcing herself to consider other things, Mandy wondered again what she might encounter in town. She could only imagine what rumors were flying around the community about her. Did the rumors include Brian? She hoped not, she realized suddenly, and her mood changed abruptly toward the kind farmer. He'd been nothing but nice to her and her family. He did not deserve her sharp tongue.

I'll bet that little Ruby Wilson has had a thing or two to say about me, Mandy fumed, remembering the young girl who often visited on Sundays. No matter. There was nothing inappropriate between her and her employer.

Mandy smiled smugly to herself then, knowing Brian had no interest in Miss Wilson.

She walked on, letting her arms swing freely in the too-big raincoat. The rain was still barely above a heavy drizzle and had no effect on her journey. She would see Mr. Ambrose, arrange to repay her debt to him, and then return to the house. By then, she hoped, Brian and the boys would be through with their in-depth spiritual discussions.

What if the boys accepted Christ as their savior? Mandy stopped in her tracks. That was, of course, what Brian would discuss today. She had recognized the foundation he was building in his talk of the previous day.

Surprised at her reaction, she hoped they would. She started walking again, slowly, thinking about being a Christian. She knew it was truth and the right guide for life. Jesus offered wisdom, support, love, forgiveness. Also, she surmised with a smile, eternal life. She remembered a verse her father once taught her: "No one comes to the Father except through me." Jesus was the way to heaven.

Her feet clattered onto the wet wooden beams of the little bridge that crossed the Yuba River. She was surprised how quickly she'd walked here.

Mandy turned right in the trail to town and followed the path downhill toward Yuba City. She was near town now and did not allow her mind to wander further. Instead, she gazed about, amazed at how much the town had changed in her short absence.

Where before there had been open places along the river, shanties and canvas tents now stood. She also observed more businesses along the main street. More saloons, for sure, she thought grimly.

She espied Mr. Bricker at his forge, and he waved when he looked up and saw Mandy pass. She also saw Mr. Stine at the livery but jumped behind a wagon before he caught sight of her.

Mandy leaped nimbly over a puddle of water at the base of the steps leading into Mr. Ambrose's general store. She halted briefly to shake the rain from her coat before entering and then grasped the doorknob firmly and steeled herself for battle.

Here we go again.

Pushing the door open with her shoulder, Mandy entered. The bells on the door announced her presence, and none other than Mr. Ambrose himself saw her first. Mandy cringed as he approached.

"Good morning, Mrs. Barrett. A wet day to be out in, eh?" He held out his hand and she shook it, surprised by his congenial manner.

Mandy rallied her spirits and put on a broad smile. His pretense of kindness would not fool her. "Good day, Mr. Ambrose. You are looking well. I am here to settle my account. I know I left town with a small matter still on the books, but, as you are well aware, I have been employed by Mr. Dawson. I've been much too busy to come to town before this, but I am here now and would like to know the balance on my tab."

Mr. Ambrose cocked his head to one side, his eyes clouded. "I don't understand, Mrs. Barrett. I am somewhat confused. I was under the impression you sent Mr. Dawson to settle your account. He paid it weeks ago. The day I mailed that letter of his in Sacramento, the one for the Pony Express. That was a pricey one, to be sure. All the way to Virginia."

Mandy barely heard anything the shopkeeper had said after the statement that Brian had paid her debt. She was as confused as Mr. Ambrose.

"Brian paid the balance due on my account?" she asked, not able to comprehend it. She tilted her head, forcing him to repeat his previous claim.

Mr. Ambrose's eyes arched curiously at Mandy's use of Brian's first name, but he nodded his head. "Yes, it was the day after the Hamilton barn raising, I believe. No, that was on a Saturday, and I'm closed on Sundays, so it must've been that Monday next."

Mandy frowned. She had come prepared for war, but there was no war to fight. She looked at the storekeeper once more. "So, I don't owe you anything?"

Mr. Ambrose shook his head slowly. "No, nothing at all. But if you're heading back out to the Dawson place, I'd be much obliged if you'd take this letter to Mr. Dawson. Arrived only yesterday." He hurried behind the counter and leafed through a stack of mail.

He handed Mandy a thin letter, and she barely noticed the Pony Express stamp on the white envelope as she hastily thrust it into the pocket of the big raincoat.

"Mr. Ambrose, I want to thank you for your kindness when you extended credit to me and my boys. Many a time, we ate only because of your generosity. Thank you again and have a good day."

Mandy turned to walk from the store but not before noticing the shocked look on Mr. Ambrose's face. Her courteous remark had caught the shopkeeper completely unprepared.

Had Brian's influence made her wish to thank Mr. Ambrose? Certainly, Mandy would never have dreamed of being kind to the rotten old skin flint before. Perhaps Brian was having more of an impact on her than she wished to realize.

The thought bothered her, making her wrinkle her brow in irritation. Before she had the time to ponder further, Mandy had closed the door behind her and bumped into someone on the porch.

"Watch where you're going, you clumsy ox," snarled a voice Mandy recognized.

"Why, hello, Miss Wilson. I'm sorry I bumped into you. Please forgive me," Mandy purred, happy she'd almost knocked the young woman from the stoop. A wicked image of the pretty girl sprawled in the mud puddle at the foot of the stairs filled Mandy's mind.

Ruby Wilson stared at her with icy eyes. "Oh, it's you," she said, her tone condescending.

"Yes, it is me. Mr. Dawson's housekeeper," Mandy countered and attempted to step past the thin brunette.

"Wait, Mrs. Barrett," the young girl called. "Ma sells her famous jam in Mr. Ambrose's store, but I would appreciate if you'd deliver one to Mr. Dawson. Tell him I will see him this Sunday, if you would."

Ruby pulled a jar of the preserves from a basket under her arm and handed it to Mandy. A taunting smile played at the corner of Ruby's thin mouth, a gleam of victory glinting in her eyes.

Mandy scowled but accepted the jar. Putting the jam with the letter in her pocket, she then pulled up her hood and muttered, "Have a good day."

She plunged off the porch before the young girl could respond and hurried from town, taking the trail back up the Yuba River.

She was both glad and angry as she walked, trying to make sense of the events behind her. Brian had paid her debt at the store. Why?

And little miss snobby girl with the fruit preserves. Mandy gritted her teeth. Ruby Wilson irritated her through and through. She wanted to throw the jar away and pretend she'd never received it.

An evil plan formed in her heart, and Mandy smiled a mean smile to herself. She would throw the preserves into the river when she crossed the little bridge and tell Brian it had been an accident.

She shook her head, clearing the thought from her mind. *No, that was wrong.* The gift was not intended for her, and she should deliver it as she promised.

Mandy narrowed her eyes and pursed her lips. But she hadn't really promised to deliver the preserves, had she?

She went back and forth, wanting to do right and wanting to throw the preserves away until she came suddenly to the small bridge. Here, the trail branched toward Quail Valley. She halted abruptly and leaned against the railing, watching the gentle rain striking the surface of the rapidly flowing river below. She could see the swollen water churning madly, white caps leaping with each wave that crashed around submerged boulders, rolling over rocks in its path.

The water below matched her turbulent emotions within. Mandy felt angry and irritated at Ruby Wilson. Why did the young girl get to have a nice husband? Who cares? Mandy reprimanded herself harshly. She didn't want a husband anyway, did she?

Mandy frowned again, wishing she wouldn't allow herself to think of Brian. He was none of her business. But why had he paid her debt at the general store? She was irritated with him too. Confused, she glanced skyward, letting the rain strike her face, water streamed down her cheeks.

"It's you again, isn't it?" she whispered, her heart aching with the grief and pain that always assailed her when she spoke to God. He was a constant reminder of all her mistakes. And there were so many to consider.

The gray sky overhead was silent. She gritted her teeth and looked down again, realizing at this very moment Brian was telling her sons of God's forgiveness and the free gift of grace. Hadn't she been told the very same thing when she'd been young back in Virginia?

A sudden chill ran down her back and she trembled.

Was God's forgiveness for her? Again? Hadn't she knowingly turned her back on his way, the way her parents had lovingly instructed her?

Her eyes narrowed, the quiet gray clouds peering down at her. "Forget it," she mumbled as she glanced at the river again. She would not allow herself to wrestle with this question again. She had made her bed, now she would lie in it.

Leaning on the bridge railing, the slight drizzle falling on her hooded head, Mandy contemplated again the thought to destroy the preserves. The anger and frustration she felt within her burned like a red-hot ember, driving her to action.

Her teeth still gritted, her jaw tense, Mandy could feel the intense heat in her belly as she thought again of her life. The incredible heartache, the impossible demands placed on her by Richard's negligence and absence, the unutterable grief at missing her parents. These old, familiar aches flooded over her like unwelcome companions. Companions that made her sick, but ones she knew she was meant to hold close forever.

Mandy could feel the hot tears welling up in her eyes, and she roughly wiped them away with the back of her hand. She would not cry. Pushing the disturbing thoughts from her, she allowed the space to be filled with the more accustomed, comfortable feeling of anger. Mandy decided the young brunette deserved nothing else than to have her gift thrown into the torrent below. Hadn't she always been rude to Mandy?

Finally, she gave in to the darker side of her mind and she reached into her pocket to extract the jar. She would do it. She would throw the jar from the bridge.

As she pulled the container from her pocket, the letter from Mr. Ambrose came with the preserves and fell to the ground. Reaching quickly to retrieve the envelope before it got wet, Mandy saw the writing on the cover.

Andrew Roth

The stamp of a Pony Express letter was bold across the front of the envelope. Also, the return address was very clear, written in a strong hand Mandy immediately recognized.

Her heart leaped to her throat, and her blood chilled in her veins as she read the address: Jack Mulligan of Richmond, Virginia.

CHAPTER 19

Startled, Mandy absentmindedly returned the ill-fated jar of preserves to her pocket. She stared hard at the envelope, not fully comprehending its implication.

The letter was from her father. But how? How could he have known where she was?

Then the truth struck her like an axe. The letter was addressed to Brian. Brian had written her family in Virginia. She had stayed hidden for ten years, too ashamed to tell her parents they had been right all along. She'd suffered because of her stubbornness and God had punished her cruelly for it. Now, with one letter, Brian Dawson had unraveled all her secrets.

Mandy saw the fine rain falling on the envelope in her hands and realized it was getting wet. She cared not, but she was spurred to action, nonetheless. She tore open the letter, her hands trembling.

Scanning the letter, she noticed it was simple, one page, and contained only a few paragraphs. She steadied herself against the wooden railing and read the letter slowly.

Dear Sir,

It is with much joy and gladness I write this note. You have no idea how long my wife and I have prayed for this day. To receive word, any word, about our beloved daughter gives us great cause to rejoice and praise our God and Savior. Thank you for your thoughtfulness to inform us of Mandy's location and welfare.

Renewed Redemption

We are encouraged to hear she is doing well. That you have provided employment to her truly reflects your kindness. Any financial hardships you procure because of your aid to my daughter will be immediately compensated by me. Have no fear on that score.

We were surprised to learn that Mandy has two sons. She had only Samuel when she departed from Virginia, and we are genuinely interested in any information you can provide regarding our grandchildren.

We are terribly sorry to hear of the demise of Richard Barrett. Although a scoundrel, to be sure, I wished him no ill will.

Please write back promptly and let us know if there is anything we can do to improve Mandy's situation in California. We love her dearly and have missed her mightily. We eagerly await further communication from you.

Yours respectfully, Jack Mulligan.

Mandy read the letter a second time, trying to digest all the information at once.

Her parents knew she was here. Brian had written them. They missed her and were glad to hear about her. Nothing had been said about her disobedience or disappointment to them.

Folding the note carefully, she returned it to its damp envelope. She stared blankly out over the river, not seeing. The rain continued to fall, unheeded by Mandy. A miner marched by her on the Yuba City trail, and he glanced curiously at her, but she paid him no mind.

For almost ten years, she'd stayed hidden from her parents, too embarrassed with her life to contact them. Now all was known.

Or was it? How much had Brian Dawson mentioned in his letter to her father? Had he informed her father of the shanty Brian had discovered her in or the debt he had paid for her at the local market? Mandy shuddered, recalling the numerous dwelling places she had inhabited these past years. Most of them were disreputable, dirty, bug-infested.

Her eyes widened in fear. What had Brian shared with her parents? How much did they now know of her horrible existence? They would certainly reprove her for the life she'd given her children, their grandchildren.

She spun suddenly and started up the trail toward the little cottage, stuffing the letter once more into her pocket. She must see Brian, ask him what he'd told her parents. It was of utmost importance.

That she stay in control of her emotions was equally important, as well. Her iron will was needed now. She'd always been a master at controlling herself, never letting any situation or person get the better of her. She'd driven Richard crazy that he couldn't nettle her. She had always held a strong fortress around her heart.

Mandy marched now with purpose. The rain forgotten, she hurried to the farm in Quail Valley. This was the most important thing she had done in years. She must know what he had said.

She stalked into the yard just as the rain ceased, a tinge of blue peeking from between gray clouds. Stepping onto the porch, Mandy was startled to hear laughter from within. Yes, the boys were here. Mandy had forgotten them in her haste to confront Brian. They must not know of the letter from their grandfather.

She drew a deep breath and opened the door slowly. Jack called to her. "Mother, we've learned about Jesus and his dying on the cross for our sins. I've been forgiven. I have accepted Jesus into my heart."

Her young son ran to her and hugged her, squeezing

her with all his might. The letter temporarily forgotten, Mandy knelt in front of Jack and held him at arm's length.

"Jack, you have done right to accept Christ. Good for you. I am grateful that you have become a Christian. Live your life for Jesus and always obey him."

"I will, Mother. I love God," he responded and hugged her again.

Sam approached her then with a sheepish grin. "I accepted Christ two weeks ago, Mother, but was afraid to tell you. Is it all right we love God?"

Ashamed, Mandy stared at her oldest son. His innocent words tore at her heart, making her feel wicked and deceptive, like she'd kept a special treasure from her beloved children all their life.

"Of course, Sam," she finally said, looking deeply into his clear eyes. "It is right to love God and serve him always. Don't do as I have done. Walk with the Lord all your days."

Mandy hugged both boys to her then, the feeling of complete joy at her children being saved from their sins and gaining eternal life overwhelming her. A twinge of jealousy came over her as she felt left out of their happiness. She quickly pushed the feeling aside, happy for Sam and Jack.

They were now children of God. They had been adopted into a new family, the family of God. Her family was full of secrets and heartache, but now her boys were part of a victorious family, one that lived for the Lord.

Mandy felt her chest tighten, and she wondered how this would affect her.

Then anger returned. She felt angry at the lost and wasted years, multiplied in its power and intensity. Overwhelmed with remorse, she hugged her boys more fiercely.

"Oh, Sam, Jack, I wish I could be forgiven for my sins. I have wronged God and my family. I'm glad you've made this decision today."

"But Mother, Brian says it is never too late to be forgiven," Jack said, stepping back from her. "Brian says God is always ready to forgive."

Suddenly, all came back to her then. The letter. Mandy looked up at Brian, standing by the fireplace, a wide grin on his handsome face. "Brian says that, does he?" Mandy said as she stood, releasing the boys. She could feel her eyes narrow as she studied Brian. "Well, Mother needs to talk to Brian alone for a while. Will you two excuse us as we chat?"

Sam and Jack kissed her lightly on the cheek and went to their room. They each gave one last look at Brian as they left. He nodded encouragement at them, a warm smile on his face.

Mandy waited until she heard the boys' door close behind them. Then, taking the preserves from her pocket, she thrust them at Brian.

"These are from your little girlfriend. I ran into her at the store. I also found out from Mr. Ambrose that my debt at his store has been paid by you."

Brian eyes widened, and he shifted on his feet. "She's not my girlfriend," he mumbled as he took the preserves from her.

"I don't care if she is," Mandy growled, her voice rising. She paused, glancing nervously down the hall toward the boys' room. She looked back at Brian and continued. "What about the debt you paid? Why did you do that?"

Mandy could feel her anger rising. She took a deep breath, remembering the coaching she'd given herself on the walk home. *Stay in control, Mandy, stay in control.*

He shrugged, apparently unconcerned. "I paid the money owed because you're an employee of mine. Your debt to Mr. Ambrose reflected on me. It is done. It wasn't much anyway."

Mandy stared, squinting at him. Not much? Mandy had lost sleep worrying about how she would ever repay the shopkeeper, and Brian casually says it's done?

Renewed Redemption

She bristled and dug into her pocket once more. She flung the letter at him, her voice starting to rise again. "What about this? You wrote my father? How dare you take it upon yourself to interfere in my personal affairs?"

Brian's eyes flew wide at sight of the letter. He bent and picked it up from the floor, glancing briefly at the address before replying. "I interfered because you told me to," he said in an even tone.

"I told you to?" she almost screamed at him. "I did no such thing!"

"You did," he quickly countered. "The night of the dance. You said you wished you still had a relationship with your parents. I took it upon myself to write them because of what you said."

Mandy quaked, her shoulders shaking with emotion. Her hands, clenched tightly into fists, hurt. She forced herself to relax them. She flexed her hands a couple of times, making herself regain her composure.

"Brian, I was talking figuratively that night," Mandy spoke, her voice calm and steady once again. "I did not want you to write my father. Now, I must be going. The boys and I will be leaving. I do not want to hear from my parents again. I know I've disappointed them, and I will not hear it told to me again."

She hesitated then, letting her words sink in. Brian looked like she'd struck him with a block of wood. He stared at her, dazed, his eyes glassy and uncomprehending. Mandy could read the hurt in them.

"I would like my pay now, Mr. Dawson."

"No," he said simply.

Her brow puckered in confusion. "You owe me for weeks of work. I would like you to pay me now." Mandy could feel her hands clenching again.

Brian shook his head. "You have no money coming to you. I gave it to Mr. Ambrose," he explained, walking toward her. "Mandy, it was God who brought you here. Let him work. Your boys have come to know the Lord, and God wants you to heal. That was a long time ago, and you need to let it go."

He was close to her now, and she found herself liking his nearness. He reached out and gently grasped her shoulders. She hated that she liked his touch.

"Trust God, Mandy," Brian continued, his voice soothing and warm. He looked deeply into her eyes, and she could see the sincerity and kindness there. "Forgive yourself and be healed. I'll bet your parents have forgiven you. Stop punishing yourself for something you did years ago. Let God's mercy be upon you. He wants to draw you back to himself."

Mandy could feel herself weakening. The words of her father's note came back to her. Her parents still loved her. They wanted to know her again.

Stubbornly, she shook her head. "No, I am wicked. I have broken my father's heart, I cannot be forgiven," she mumbled. She could feel herself softening, and she was worried. Her resolve had been all she'd had for so long. Her determination had helped her succeed.

Yet, she realized with bitterness, she had not succeeded at all. She had only run from God, keeping him at a distance as she struggled and stumbled year after year. She could feel him now, calling to her, reaching lovingly for her, wanting to hold her in an embrace as Brian now did.

"We have all broken the Father's heart, and he still forgives us," Brian continued, never taking his eyes from Mandy. "It's called grace. He loved us even while we were sinners. He gave his only Son for us, so we could have eternal life. Accept his forgiveness, Mandy. Jesus wants you to feel his love and forgiveness."

Renewed Redemption

Mandy rallied for one final battle and shook her head. "No, Brian, you don't understand. I cannot ever go back."

He shook her gently, his brown eyes pleading. "Your stubborn heart is what got you in trouble in the first place. Stop it. Stop being stubborn and let God in."

She had no more words to argue with, and she melted. He was right, of course, she knew. She had always known. But her rebellious heart wanted to make things right without help, without her parents, without God. Her way had not worked.

Brian pulled her to him and held her gently as she leaned into him, letting God's grace and mercy wash over her. She was forgiven, she knew. Jesus had been knocking for ten years, and she had kept him out. Now, with the door open to him, Mandy felt his perfect love and peace, coursing through her entire body like a warm river, filling her with an incredible and complete joy.

The heavy weight she'd carried slipped away as she allowed Jesus to touch her, to heal her. Mandy choked as she suddenly realized his forgiveness was not what filled her. Jesus had always forgiven her. She had finally forgiven herself and accepted his free gift. Her own stubborn, hard heart had kept her from the love of the Redeemer.

For the first time in a long time, she let her guard down. She would no longer need to be ready for battle. God would fight for her now.

Peace washed over her like a wave. She remembered her mother saying, "Take up his yoke, his burden is light."

Suddenly, Mandy felt her arms go around Brian. She hugged him hard, not wanting him to let her go. "Thank you, Brian. Thank you for everything," she whispered hoarsely into his shoulder.

She felt so good to be in his arms. Mandy could feel the forgiveness God presented to her and something else she could not identify. Something to do with Brian.

"You're welcome, Mandy," he replied, his warm breath teasing her hair as he held her close. "But God deserves the glory. Thank him, Mandy."

He was right again. God had brought her to the end of her rope in that dingy shack in Yuba City, and God was who had provided Brian Dawson. A stranger on the trail had been used by the Most High God to bring one of his sheep back into the flock.

She released Brian and gave him a brave smile. Moving around the couch, she made her way to the seclusion of her room and quietly closed the door behind her. Mandy wanted to spend time with God alone, time that was long overdue.

God's redemption was forever, like Mr. Vallejo told her. God provided new mercies every day, even when mistakes were made and wrong paths chosen. God's forgiveness was an ever-flowing well of living water that never runs dry. Mandy knew this and felt renewed.

That night, dinner was a festive and fun time. Mandy said the prayer for the meal, and the boys sat wide-eyed, watching their mother's heartfelt talk with God.

Brian was cheery, asking Sam and Jack numerous questions about the Bible, leading discussions about its history and message.

After dinner, Mandy washed the dishes as Jack and Sam cleared the table. Brian stood with a towel, drying each plate as Mandy handed them to him. As the boys moved to fetch firewood for the wood box, Brian quickly whispered, "I read the letter. What should I do now? Am I to reply to his inquiries?"

Mandy chewed on her lip, thinking rapidly. She handed him a soup bowl, glancing after the boys before she replied. "Don't do anything right away. Let me think. I'll tell you what to do in a day or two."

The next day was Sunday, and as was Ruby Wilson's wont, she appeared that afternoon in a red and white checked dress.

Renewed Redemption

"Do you like it?" Ruby asked, smoothing the material with her hands. She whirled and swayed before Mandy's critical, sour scrutiny. "Mother made it for me. She said a man would have to be blind to not see how well this dress fits me," she smiled tauntingly.

Mandy poured the visitor a cup of tea and bit her tongue. How badly she wanted to retort, to say hurtful things. Why, the girl looked like a tablecloth.

Instead, Mandy smiled at Ruby and nodded politely. "Mr. Dawson certainly isn't blind, and I'm sure he will admire your new dress, Miss Wilson."

Pleased with her kind remark, Mandy retreated to her room for the remainder of the afternoon, letting Brian fetch more tea and bread.

Mandy had secretly hoped that Ruby Wilson would make an appearance today as Mandy eagerly wanted to spend time in Scripture. With a pounding heart, Mandy closed her bedroom door and lay across her bed, resting on her elbows. She held Brian's Bible in her hands.

Gazing in awe at its black leather cover, she opened the book, her hands turning the pages with old familiarity. She'd not searched Scripture for a long time, but the habit was not forgotten.

Mandy started reading the Book of Matthew, the first book of the New Testament. There she read about Jesus's burden being light. Next, she leafed through the Book of John, where she saw that Jesus had been sent into the world to forgive sins.

Next, she turned eagerly to the Book of Romans. Here she read that we are saved by grace, a free gift from God. Following this, she found in the Book of Jeremiah that God has a plan for us, not to harm us but to prosper us.

Finally, with the light outside of the window beginning to fade, Mandy read in the Book of John where those who accept Jesus as their savior are called children of God.

Mandy closed the Bible slowly, lovingly, and ran a hand over the leather cover. She was a child of God. She had accepted Christ as her savior and would live for him. She was forgiven. Again and forever.

Mandy lay there, pondering the many days she had foolishly wasted rejecting God's forgiveness. Everyone made mistakes—look at King David, she mused. But God forgives. He does not want us to continue in our sins but to repent and allow the Holy Spirit to guide us through difficult situations.

Mandy realized then God had been trying to reach her for some time, but she'd not been sensitive to the Spirit's call. She saw everything clearly now. Brian had been sent to draw her to the Lord. More than that, he had been instrumental in leading her children to Christ.

With the room darkening around her, Mandy rose with stiff joints. She had lain in the same position for hours. She realized she owed Brian more than she could ever repay.

Walking back to the sitting room, Mandy was in time to catch sight of the departing Miss Wilson.

"It was good to see you again, Miss Wilson. Thank your mother for her delicious preserves. Have a good day," Mandy said as Ruby Wilson stepped from the porch into the hard-packed dirt of the yard. Her face reflected her surprise at Mandy's kind words.

"Well, I will, Mrs. Barrett," she stammered. Her tone held suspicion. "Have a good day," she added, her eyes full of uncertainty.

With a final glance at Brian, the young girl turned and walked from the yard.

Mandy stood beside Brian, watching her go. "Isn't that a pretty dress Ruby is wearing, Mr. Dawson?"

Without looking at Mandy, Brian nodded. "A little snug, I think."

∞∞∞∞∞

Renewed Redemption

Mandy was amazed how fast the alfalfa grew, showing green shoots through the dirt. Within two weeks after planting, a thin, jade colored carpet of new plants stretched across the fields the boys had cleared.

"Mother," Sam said to her, "We've taken the rocks out of the way so the hay could be easily mowed. If we irrigate correctly, we should get a number of crops from this field this year." The young man beamed proudly at his knowledge.

Mandy was proud of him too. Brian had taught the boys many things about farming, and now she ventured to add to their growing knowledge. She was reminded of how her own father had taught her when she was younger.

"Sam, the soil is the key. Always make sure your soil is healthy. That includes the proper amount of moisture so the crop gets enough water for proper growth. The better the growth, the better the yield."

Sam stared at her, astonished. "Mother, do you know a lot about farming? Like Brian does?" He tilted his head, his young eyes shining.

Mandy laughed and tousled the boy's hair. "Probably not as much as Brian, but I know a thing or two."

"Did you learn it back in Virginia? Did your family have a farm?" Sam persisted, his eyes searching hers for answers.

Mandy hesitated. How much should she share? She had masterfully avoided these types of conversations for many years. What about now?

Just then, Jack called to his older brother and pointed to a squirrel near Sam's feet. Sam leaped at the unprepared animal and almost caught the little gray creature by his tail. The boys gave chase and Sam's questions were forgotten.

But Mandy had been giving much thought to the future conversations to come. How much should she say about the grandparents back in Virginia? Her father had written that they very much would appreciate news about the two small boys, one of whom bore the grandfather's name.

Andrew Roth

Brian had asked about writing back to her parents, but she had put it off. What was she waiting for?

CHAPTER 20

The mild spring days were filled with the buzzing of bees. Every afternoon, Mandy found excuses for going outdoors, needing to be in the open. She watched the bees as they traveled from the new shoots of the alfalfa and the fruit trees to the wooden boxes Mr. Vallejo had built. Everywhere, spring was in the air, which she loved. These moments reminded her again of how she used to wander in the fields with her father, checking the blossoms and talking over the promise of a good crop to come.

She walked to the alfalfa fields she'd helped plant to the mounds of earth where Brian had planted the fruit trees. A sense of pride welled within her as she gazed lovingly at the fields her family played a part in creating. Here, she moved among the granite boulders to the various orchards, closely scrutinizing the bright blossoms.

There were cherry blossoms, red and white and pink. Each one as different as snowflakes. She watched the cumbersome bees, their barrel-shaped bodies flying slowly among the branches of new leaves, alighting gently on the blossoms. They wandered over the fragrant flowers, their tiny legs moving awkwardly as their little arms quickly rolled and gathered the desired nectar. Mandy knew pollen was distributed by the insect landing on each blossom. The nectar would then be taken back to the hive, used in making honey.

Peach blossoms, orange with red splashes across the fold of the trumpet around each pistil, drew the bees like a waving banner draws a bull. The apple blossoms with their delicate white and amber colors fusing together with no clear distinction between each individual color amazed Mandy with their profusion.

Brian had planted all these trees when he first came, and now they were being pollinated for a crop. This would be his first harvest since arriving in California. Also, the newly planted alfalfa would bring numerous cuttings, and Brian hoped for a busy year of constant harvesting, provided the bees did their duty.

Brian had sold honey in Yuba City the last two years while he waited for the trees to mature. Also, Mr. Vallejo had pointed out clusters of wild grapes growing near the river Brian hoped Mandy could utilize.

She looked at the young grapes now and thought of what her mother would've done. Jams? Pies? Wine?

It was still early spring, and Mandy decided she had time to figure out what to do as she turned away from the young vines. Eagerly, she strode to where the boys were preparing to dam the river.

Brian stood in the river, stripped to the waist, moving large boulders into place. Sam worked beside him, his shirt thrown on the river bank next to Brian's. Though the water was freezing cold from snow melt farther up the mountain, the boys didn't want their shirts to get wet or torn.

Mandy watched as Brian and Sam wrestled the heavy stones into place, carefully positioning each rock in such a way as to allow little water to get past.

Jack wandered along the bank, gathering firewood to deliver to the house. He wanted to help the other two but had discovered the cold water was more than he could endure. Brian assigned him to firewood duty instead, keeping the small boy busy.

"Hello, Mother," Jack called when he saw Mandy approach.

Mandy ignored Jack's call, her attention riveted on the grown man in the river. Brian's chest heaved with the exertion of moving the large stones, and his muscles flexed white, rippling and rolling in the warm sun as he strained to move the giant rocks. His slender waist twisted easily as he turned and grasped new members of the dam, patiently fitting them snugly into the wall he constructed.

Brian and Sam stopped as Mandy approached. Brian placed his hands on his waist and smiled at her. Her heart gave an unexpected leap, and a rush of warm blood coursed through her veins as she realized he made a very handsome dam builder.

Her thoughts startled her. She'd not thought of a man like this in years. As a young girl, she noted handsome men and even discussed them in length with her girlfriends, but she hadn't wanted anything to do with men for a long time. Her sudden observation of her employer with his shirt off made her feel uneasy, as if she was seeing something she shouldn't. Blushing, Mandy averted her gaze.

"Good afternoon, Mandy," Brian called. Mandy was forced to look at him again, noticing despite the cold water, his smile was warm as his brown eyes. "You're just in time to witness the final stages of the wall. Sam has been a tremendous help in preparing the dam, and now we're ready to place the gate, which will effectively close the dam and force the water to back up, flooding over its banks and watering my alfalfa."

His muscular torso heaved again, and he lunged from the water to the nearest bank. Sam followed him out of the frigid water. Brian picked up the three-foot-wide gate made of oak planks that lay on the bank.

Wading into the water once more, he slowly made his way to the last opening in the dam where the water rushed through in torrents. Here, Brian lowered the gate and blocked the escaping water.

Renewed Redemption

Lashing the gate securely into position, Brian retreated again from the river.

Retrieving his shirt, he pulled it on, leaving the buttons undone. Jack came to stand near the trio as they watched the trapped water slowly rise and begin to back up the little river. The young boy looked up at Mandy.

"Your face is so red, Mother," he observed. "Are you all right?"

All eyes turned to stare at her. If possible, the uncomfortable attention caused her to redden more.

"Am I?" she questioned, her hands rising to her heated cheeks. Oh, she hoped Brian could not guess what she was thinking about. She glanced at him, eager to gauge his response to her crimson face. Did he suspect her hidden thoughts?

But Brian only peered at her with curiosity, a concerned gleam in his deep brown eyes. Surely, he was oblivious to her confusing feelings. She was not interested in a man, any man, let alone her employer, Mandy told herself. Swiftly, she turned her attention back to the rising river, forcefully pushing everything but the dam from her troubled mind.

The height of the water rose imperceptibly for a while, and Mandy spoke before it breached its banks and flowed into the nearby fields. "I have to go to town tomorrow for supplies. Is there anything in particular I should take with me or pick up while I'm there?"

She kept her eyes fixed on the rising river water behind the dam. The large pond that was forming seemed a safer target for her gaze.

"Licorice, gum balls, maybe some chocolate," Sam suggested, grinning at his mother. Mandy noticed how tall he was getting. He was becoming a young man.

She grabbed Sam and pulled him close to her, hugging him tightly and tousling his hair with affection. "Oh, you are cold, Sam. Put your shirt on before you freeze," Mandy instructed, releasing the laughing boy.

She watched him reach for his shirt, marveling at how comfortable she'd become at showing her love to Sam and Jack. Since coming to the farm, Mandy had grown more accustomed to hugging and holding her children. They, in turn, seemed to love the attention.

Sam bent to pick up his shirt, and Jack moved quickly beside his mother and held her hand. Mandy glanced down at her youngest and smiled. She loved the extra affection too.

"Carlos has put some jars of honey on the front porch. Could you please take them in to Mr. Ambrose's? He knows how to put them on my account," Brian said, watching the river rise.

"Sure." Mandy turned and headed toward the cottage. Suddenly, she was eager to leave Brian's presence.

"Mandy?" Brian's call halted her.

She glanced over her shoulder. Part of her wished to escape quickly, and part of her wished to never leave.

"Yes?" She chewed her lip. Despite her best efforts to control her eyes, her gaze once again scanned his lithe, strong form. Oh, she hated her own weakness.

Brian glanced quickly at the boys. "Are you mailing something?" he asked in low tones.

"Yes." Mandy nodded and then turned hastily away. She needed to move from this place, or she'd be in danger of staring. She hurried on.

Mandy pushed the haunting memory of Brian from her mind as she strode to the cottage. She knew to what he referred. She'd been thinking and praying about it for a long time. She was right to reply to her father's letter.

Brian had given the note to her, and she'd read the words over and over. Thoughts of home had been working in her now for weeks, and she decided now was the time to acquaint her parents of her new identity, for she was truly a new creation in Christ.

Renewed Redemption

Although Mandy had accepted Christ's sacrifice when she was a little girl, she had not accepted him as Lord of her life. That decision had been made in Brian's living room.

She'd written a brief letter explaining a few facts of her current life. The age of her boys, their names, her duties at Brian's house, and her change into a Christian. She knew her parents would be most interested in that fact.

That night at dinner, Sam reported the success of the dam and the progress of the water as it poured into the young alfalfa fields. The irrigation would create better growth and promised a bigger yield.

Brian informed the group he would have to watch the fields closely. When he determined enough water had been pushed onto the thirsty crops, he'd open the gate in the dam and release the water, draining the flooded fields.

"Depending on rain," he explained, "the gate should only have to be placed a couple of times a month. That should ensure proper irrigation, and we should have our first cutting in a few weeks." Brian beamed, his plans for the alfalfa coming true before his very eyes.

"I've been working on this for the last couple of years, and only with your help has it come to pass. Your help and, of course, God's," he remarked, letting his eyes rest on each of the young boys.

Sam and Jack glowed under Brian's praise, and again Mandy noticed how much her boys revered this farmer. Her thoughts also seemed to always be with Brian. She rose to fetch more coffee when he spoke again.

"Mandy," he said, glancing her way. "If you should see Ruby Wilson tomorrow while you're in town, let her know I will be making a visit to her home this Sunday."

Mandy blinked. Had she heard him right? Wasn't he the one who'd said he was not interested in the young brunette girl? What had changed?

Mandy merely shrugged and nodded to him. Inwardly, she cringed. She could feel the color drain from her face at his unexpected words. Was Brian really interested in courting that annoying girl? Mandy found Miss Wilson too immature and petty. Her constant prattling about stupid things drove Mandy crazy every time the girl visited. But she had to admit, Ruby was pretty. And, after all, Mandy did not have to like her.

She scowled as she moved toward the stove. Fetching the coffeepot, she realized she was who was acting petty. She prayed for forgiveness. If Brian liked Ruby Wilson, who was she to say naught? Mandy certainly had no intentions of ever getting married again, she'd said as much to Brian. Maybe Brian was tired of being alone. He'd said he would remarry, that his previous wife had shown him how wonderful marriage could be, even though that had not been Mandy's experience. Married life was not for her.

She chewed the inside of her cheek, pondering. What would it be like to be happily married? Mandy had heard of such things. Certainly, her own parents seemed very happy with one another.

She returned to the table. Steam rose as Mandy poured Brian a fresh cup of coffee and then one for herself. She was about to return to the kitchen and start cleaning up dinner dishes when Brian interjected.

"Sam, Jack, do you mind doing the dishes tonight? I think your mother deserves a break."

Sam rose first with Jack a close second. "Mother, Brian is right. Sit down and rest while we do the dishes." Sam began picking up dishes and stacking them. Jack moved alongside his brother and took another armload to the kitchen.

Mandy watched her boys move to the work, neither of them voicing a complaint. She marveled at how the boys had grown and changed with Jesus in their lives. Now they understood love meant service, and they seemed eager for opportunities to serve Mandy.

Renewed Redemption

She picked up her mug and followed Brian to the sitting room. He tossed another log on the fire and seated himself on the couch next to her, both staring into the dancing flames. Spring had come to California, but it still grew chilly in the evenings. Soon, after-dinner fires would be unnecessary.

Mandy sipped her coffee, fighting to not say what was on her mind. It was not any of her business, she knew. Brian was an adult. He could make his own choices. But Ruby Wilson? She was not right for Brian. He needed someone who … someone like …

The confusing thoughts angered Mandy, but she could not say why. Agitated, she narrowed her eyes and pursed her lips. A glance at Brian from the corner of her eye made her belly burn. He was so good. Ruby Wilson didn't deserve him.

She frowned and then blurted, "So, you're going to Miss Wilson's on Sunday?" She found keeping the iciness from her words impossible. "I didn't think you were interested in her. In fact, I recall you thinking she was too young."

She dropped her gaze so Brian wouldn't see the jealousy in her eyes. She'd tried to not say anything about Ruby, but the impulse to ask proved too difficult for Mandy. She simply couldn't contain her burning curiosity.

Brian stared into the fire, watching the flames leap up and around the log, both hands holding his cup. He sighed. "Well, I've made it no secret that I wish to remarry. She seems to be the only girl interested in me," he said at last.

He paused, perhaps waiting for a response from Mandy, but she gave none. The quiet chatter of the boys sounded behind them as Sam and Jack washed the dishes.

"I've worked hard these past few years, and I'm not getting any younger," he chuckled without humor, his eyes still fixed on the blaze before him. "I've made a good farm, and I believe it'll begin to pay this year. I need to get on with the business of living." He took a deep breath and then sighed again.

"Ruby Wilson is young. But she is also strong and not afraid of hard work. God will guide me as I pray about this. It's in his hands," Brian concluded.

Quiet reigned between them as the fire crackled on the hearth, and Brian sipped his coffee.

Mandy clenched her teeth and said nothing. She'd decided she was wrong in saying anything in the first place and would now leave the matter with the Lord. If Brian was to marry Ruby Wilson, so be it. If God's will was they marry, then nothing Mandy did or said would have any impact.

Besides, she wanted nothing to do with another marriage. Her intent had been to merely warn him, to protect him, nothing more.

However, she realized suddenly—and the thought gave her an abrupt sense of utter panic—if Brian remarried, she and the boys would be thrown out of the cottage with nowhere to go. Ruby Wilson certainly wouldn't allow Mandy and her family to stay under the same roof with her. Mandy would have to consider this as a real probability. Of course, she now believed the Lord would provide.

Mandy said nothing of these sudden fears out loud. Sipping her own hot drink, she forced herself to relax and simply enjoy Brian's company. The fire was pleasant, and the nearness of this man made her feel warm and content.

But how long could this last? Hadn't she been living a fantasy for the last few months? Mandy and her boys had not enjoyed such peace and security in years.

An unexpected sadness filled her at the thought of leaving Quail Valley. This small cottage was the closest thing to a home she and the boys had experienced since she left Virginia. Mandy knew it couldn't last forever. She took another sip of coffee and glanced at Brian from the corner of her eye. He'd been good to her and her boys. She would miss him.

CHAPTER 21

The next morning, Mandy left for town with ten dollars in her pocket from the little box in Brian's desk. She also carried a basket full of jars of golden honey and with no real hurry in her step. She felt good to be moving and out of doors.

The gray days of winter had retreated and allowed for more days with blue skies. The air warmed a bit more as each day passed. Today, puffy white clouds skittered across the sky, and birds sang to her as she walked. The road was even dry and without mud to impede her travel in any way.

Mandy noted the little bridge over the Yuba River when she came to it and halted abruptly. She rested the basket on the railing and looked at the water below. As she stared at the rushing, noisy river, her thoughts were far from this peaceful place. She thought of the letter she'd read here only a few weeks ago, and the memory reminded her of the return note she now carried in her pocket.

Mandy straightened and joined the trail to Yuba City.

The road here was busy, more so now that the weather had warmed and mountain streams had released their winter stores of moisture. The new waters from snow melt would release more gold from its hiding places in the rivers and would wash down to the eager miners who awaited this annual spring thaw.

Mandy joined her stride with a few others going into town while most of the men on the trail passed her going the other way, up into the mountains to the various gold camps.

She watched the miners as they passed, noting individual characteristics of each man. This one had a dirty face, his salt-

and-pepper beard streaked with tobacco juice. This one carried a shovel and a heavy pack. Another touched the brim of his hat when he passed her.

Since coming to Brian's and wearing nicer clothes, men seemed more respectful to her. Certainly, this miner was not the only man she'd seen this day to glance her way in admiration. Some of the men were down-right rude in how they brazenly stared.

Mandy entered the bustling town and noted how different she felt on this trip than the last. She felt relaxed, at ease. She did not sense the need to prepare for battle. She owed nothing to Mr. Ambrose, and God's peace was upon her.

The bell tinkled musically as she entered the general store, and she waited patiently until Mr. Ambrose was available. Within moments, he caught her eye and motioned her to him.

"Ah, Mrs. Barrett. I am glad to see you. What can I do for you?" He eyed her basket with a curious glint in his eye. He smelled business.

"Mr. Dawson sent me to town to fetch supplies and drop off this honey. He said you'd know how to credit his account." She rested the heavy basket on the counter.

"Indeed, I do," the shopkeeper exclaimed as he reached eagerly for the amber jars. "Take care of your shopping, and I'll attend to this."

Mandy moved around the store and filled her arms with various items she needed for the kitchen. Then she returned to the counter and had the clerk fill a few requests for candy and smaller essentials.

As she shopped, she repeatedly touched the letter in her pocket, fearful to pull it out. Now, as her requests dwindled, she silently said a prayer and then handed the letter to the clerk.

"Can you please send this on? Let me know what I owe for postage," she commented, acting casual while butterflies fluttered inside of her. She was surprised to feel so excited.

"Yes, ma'am," the young clerk replied, taking the letter from her.

"It is true, I tell you," a loud voice sounded behind Mandy as a burly man entered the store. His partner trailed behind him, shaking his head.

"What are you talking about now, Pete?" Mr. Ambrose called good-naturedly to the big miner.

Pete turned toward Mr. Ambrose, and his voice carried with excitement. "Ambrose, the South has pulled out of the Union. It's called secession. They've formed their own government with their own president, a senator named Davis from Mississippi."

Mandy stared, aware that the entire store had grown quiet. "Where did you hear such a thing?" Mr. Ambrose demanded, walking from behind the long counter.

"I heard it from a gent I know in Sacramento. He told me the southern states' new nation is called the Confederate States of America," Pete continued, looking around the crowded store, thumbs hooked into his suspenders. He rocked on his heels and nodded once before speaking again. "I had to practice that name a couple of times before I got it right, that's how I know it so well."

"Well, what is Mr. Lincoln going to do about it?" Mr. Ambrose crossed his arms over his apron.

"He says he won't tolerate it. He says the South must rejoin the Union or else," Pete said.

"Or else what?" the impatient shopkeeper questioned.

"Or else it could mean civil war," Pete explained.

Mandy heard a low moan go up from the crowd. Immediately, many people who'd been busy shopping just a few minutes before, hurriedly left the shop with the troubling news. Some customers clustered around and began to whisper among their group.

Mandy felt deeply bothered by this information too. Virginia, she knew, would be at the heart of this calamity.

Renewed Redemption

Long had the issue of slavery been a sore subject on the border between the northern and southern states. Her father had never owned slaves but had always defended the idea of each state making their own laws regarding slavery.

"It's the Constitution we must look to, or we'll be like other countries with no legal direction," Mandy's father had argued. "The law permits slavery in some states. If a man does not like that, he is free in this country to move somewhere else or to work hard to change the laws where he lives. That is the basis of freedom," her father had often commented. "This is Virginia, and I live in Virginia. I do not like slavery, but I obey the laws."

Pushing thoughts of her father aside, Mandy gathered her purchases and stowed them inside her basket. Turning to the door, she sighted Ruby Wilson entering. So preoccupied with her own thoughts, Mandy almost forgot the message she carried for the young girl.

She rushed forward to the pretty brunette.

"Miss Wilson, forgive me, but I've just heard the most disturbing news. The South has left the Union. I need to hurry home to acquaint Mr. Dawson with this information. But first, I am to relay a request Mr. Dawson has of you," Mandy spoke hurriedly, trying to quickly take her leave.

Was she in such a hurry because Virginia was in danger? Because her family might well be in harm's way? Or was she anxious to leave because the information Brian was now openly courting this young girl so disturbed Mandy? She could not easily discern.

At first, Ruby eyed Mandy with disdain, but at the mention of Mr. Dawson, the young girl gave her full attention.

"A request of me? How thrilling," the girl pealed with delight.

Mandy thought again how this girl's eyes seemed awfully close together and her lips so thin and tight. *None of my business,* she reminded herself.

"Mr. Dawson asked me to inform you of his intentions to visit you this Sunday and wanted to know if that would be all right?"

Ruby eyed Mandy suspiciously for a moment and then visibly relaxed, a bitter smile tugging on her lips. "Well, Mrs. Barrett, I must say I am somewhat surprised. I had almost believed you were interested in Mr. Dawson for yourself."

Mandy laughed. "Not at all, I assure you. I have no interest in marrying again. Marriage is not the bed of roses one is led to believe when one is young. But it is better for everyone to discover that for themselves, I guess. Fairy tales are simply that, fairy tales. Good luck, Miss Wilson. I hope you find what you're looking for."

Mandy turned from the young girl, who stood fixed in place with a stricken look on her pale face, and left the store, fairly leaping from the stoop to the ground.

She waved at Mrs. Bricker as she passed the blacksmith shop and ignored the welcoming look from her. Mandy moved swiftly now, taking the trail from town with great strides, her legs pounding the hard-packed dirt.

She walked on, her mind consumed with Miss Wilson and the political turmoil brewing on the east coast. The little brunette got under her skin, and Mandy didn't understand why, but the unrest along the Atlantic Seaboard frightened her. Her family was there.

Suddenly aware that her jaw hurt, Mandy opened her mouth, prying her clenched teeth apart. Her shoulders ached too, as she walked painfully hunched.

Mandy stopped at the little bridge for the turnoff to Brian's farm. She relaxed her shoulders and swapped the heavy basket she carried to the opposite arm. Mandy worked her jaw open and closed a couple of times, feeling the tension dissolve.

She was, of course, upset by the potential war of the east. But she couldn't do anything about it. She chewed her lip and lowered the heavy basket to the ground, then leaned on the railing and stewed again about Ruby. The river surged beneath her, leaping and racing downstream to join the Feather River at Yuba City, the tumultuous water mirroring her own emotions. Restlessly, she tried to pray.

"God, the conflict is worsening back home, isn't it? I don't wish any harm on my parent's farm. Protect them, Lord. Keep my parents safe."

She paused, wringing her hands as the turmoil simmered within her. "I don't understand why I'm so upset. Could it be because of Ruby? Is it merely concern for Brian? I don't think this Miss Wilson is for him, but it's none of my affair. Why am I so bothered? Do I want to protect him from what my marriage had been? Forgive me for my attitude of worry. I'm not supposed to worry, I know. I am to cast my anxieties on you. You are sovereign and in control, if I will only get out of your way. Let me trust that you have a purpose here with Brian and Ruby. Your will be done, not my will."

Mandy finished her prayer and felt the gentle reminder she had only to obey God and he would guide her. Brian was in God's hands too, and he would watch out for the naïve farmer, Mandy was sure.

She sighed, not certain her prayer was for her parents or Brian or for herself. Oh, why did Ruby Wilson bother her so? The young girl came from a good family, and she was a hard worker like Brian said. Why was Mandy so concerned?

Scowling, she hefted the basket anew and trudged on at a less frantic gait, but her thoughts remained troubled.

CHAPTER 22

Mandy returned to the farm with her emotions in chaos. She was upset about the possible war coming between the states and the implication this had for her parents located in Virginia. They were right in the path of the impending storm over states' rights.

She found Jack in the kitchen busy putting food in a sack for lunch when she entered the house.

"Brian and Sam are very dirty," the boy explained with a giggle. "They've been working all morning in the mud and are covered from head to foot. Brian told me to fetch something to eat."

Mandy placed her heavy basket on the counter and inspected the boy's sack. In it she found cookies, a block of cheese, and some cold muffins from breakfast.

"Jack, these are goodies or snacks. The men will need some meat or something that will carry them until dinner time." She took the cookies from the sack. "Let me help you."

She made three sandwiches with thick slices of ham and liberally smeared mustard on each. Also, she boiled water for coffee, and soon she and Jack trooped back to where the men worked.

"Ah, we've been watching for you, haven't we, Sam?" Brian greeted them as they approached. "And you've brought coffee. Oh, you know me well, Mandy."

That was probably true, she mused, thinking of this man's particular likes and dislikes. She knew he enjoyed his potatoes thoroughly cooked, did not like cabbage nor radishes. Brian claimed to not enjoy desserts but loved Mandy's butter cookies and was often pestering her to bake them.

I know this man a lot better than Miss Wilson does, she reflected with a sour taste in her mouth.

She laid the sack on the ground near a fallen log she could use as a serving table. Pulling items out of the sack, she lined them up on the log. Then she poured two cups of coffee.

Sam and Brian moved swiftly to her side and took the proffered sandwiches with dirty hands. Mandy handed Brian a steaming mug of coffee and then gave both a close scrutiny. Jack was right, they were both filthy.

"I've been so hungry, Mother," Sam announced with his mouth full of sandwich.

Brian swallowed a bite and then gestured to the dam construction with his tin cup. "We dammed the river, and it's working well, but little escaping rivers have cropped up that must be stopped so the water will settle on the alfalfa fields," Brian explained with a grin that competed with mud for space on his face.

Mandy turned and looked at the young alfalfa field behind her. Water from the dammed river had indeed covered large parts of the green field.

"It looks like the dam worked," Mandy commented, lifting her own cup to her lips.

Brian was quick to confirm her observation. "Oh, yes, it has, thanks to these young men. I couldn't have done it without them," he said, nodding his head at both young boys. Then he tilted his head and narrowed his eyes. "I wonder what I would've done without you two. You've made such a difference on the farm and in my life. I had no idea how much I enjoyed children."

Mandy eyed Brian carefully, not liking the odd inflection in his voice. Had he told them about his intentions with Miss Wilson?

"I saw Miss Wilson in town and informed her of your plan to visit her on Sunday," Mandy blurted. No reason to keep the impending relationship from the boys, she thought. Sam and Jack would learn of it soon enough. Might as well have it out in the open.

The happy grin vanished from Brian's muddy face. He turned from the boys to face her. "You did, did you? What did she say?"

Mandy nodded, pleased at his sudden discomfort. "She said she was most eager for the visit. She is a nice young lady, is she not?" Mandy cocked her head to one side, trying her best to look innocent. "She will make someone a good wife someday." She tried to keep sarcasm from her voice.

"I think she is very pretty, Brian," Sam said, as he finished his sandwich and brushed his hands on his dirty pants. "What do you think?"

Brian gulped and then began to gag. Sam patted him on the back until the clog cleared.

Brian cleared his throat and said, "Miss Wilson is a young lady, and I agree with your mother. She will make someone a good wife someday." With a quick look over at Mandy, he added, "Maybe sooner than she knows."

Mandy felt a sharp kick in the pit of her stomach. So, there it was. Brian was telling her it was coming soon.

With a toss of her long blonde hair, Mandy turned to walk from the trio. Then she stopped, remembering the news of the seceding states. "Brian, I also heard men talking about the South withdrawing from the Union. They thought it might lead to war. Will it have an effect on those in Virginia?"

Brian nodded. "I was afraid of this when Lincoln got elected. He said if he were made president, he would stop the expansion of slavery into the western lands. It is unconstitutional to limit where a man can take his property."

Renewed Redemption

"Property!" Mandy scoffed. "Men and women are not to be thought of as property." Her anger burned. She had felt she'd been Richard's property, and it hadn't been pleasant. Well, she was free now and was determined never to belong to another man as long as she lived.

"I agree," Brian said with a nod. "But the Supreme Court has decided that slaves are property and belong to their masters. They are protected by the government. It'll cause a ruckus back east, I daresay."

Sam and Jack—who had been chasing a frog—now returned to stand by Brian. Without looking at the boys, the farmer reached for them, pulling them close, before placing a rough hand on each boy's shoulder.

Mandy realized her boys had really grown close to Brian. They would be greatly upset to be parted from him.

Not wanting to think further on that subject, she turned away again and started for the house. "I'll have supper ready when you get home," she called over her shoulder.

∞∞∞∞∞

That Sunday, Brian departed for Ruby Wilson's farm.

Mandy stayed in her room until he was gone. Then, moving to the living room, she elected to enjoy her Bible reading on the couch before the stone fireplace. She found this to be the best location for reading in the house.

The afternoon sped by as she read many Bible stories she remembered fondly from her youth. She'd not read of Noah, Samson, Elijah, David, and Moses for a long time. These old Bible characters had come to life in her house back in Richmond, and now she read about them like old friends, enjoying getting reacquainted.

Sam and Jack had built small wooden ships and were out floating them on the trapped river water. Brian had promised to open the floodgate on the dam on the morrow, and both boys knew that soon their flooded field would be dry again.

When Mandy saw them returning in the late afternoon, she closed the thick book on her lap and rested her hand fondly on the smooth leather cover. She sighed and realized with a start how much she'd missed the Word.

Sending a thankful prayer skyward, Mandy moved to open the front door.

Mr. Vallejo stood with the boys, and he carried a heavy wooden box, his walking cane tucked under one arm. Mandy saw the boys also were loaded down with heavy canvas sacks.

"Good afternoon, Mr. Vallejo." She frowned as she addressed the boys. "Sam, Jack, you two look like a pair of drowned cats. Go around back and take off those dirty clothes. Wash off and put on clean clothes before supper."

The two boys deposited the canvas bags on the porch and ran around back to comply with Mandy's orders.

"They are good boys, Señora Barrett," Mr. Vallejo commented, resting his own load on the porch before sinking onto the bench. He sighed dramatically as he relaxed.

"They are indeed, thank the Lord," she smiled, watching the two boys disappear around the corner. "Can I get you something to drink? And would you like to join us for supper? We're only having soup, it being Sunday and all. I usually don't do a big meal on Sunday," she remarked, noting the old man's obvious pleasure at her invitation.

His dark eyes twinkled as he nodded. "I would love to stay for dinner. Thank you. And I would dearly enjoy a cup of coffee, if you have it."

Mandy walked into the kitchen to fetch two cups of coffee. She glanced out the back window at the washing boys and then returned to the front porch.

"Oh, thank you kindly, Señora," Mr. Vallejo said as he accepted the steaming cup. He sipped his drink gratefully while Mandy curiously nudged the sack at her feet, the sound of glass tinkled from within.

Noticing her gesture, the old man smiled. "Honey. I gathered some jars today and was hoping to leave them here."

"Of course. Whatever you think is best," Mandy replied and sat down next to him on the bench.

They were quiet then, enjoying the late afternoon shadows stretching across the yard. Suddenly, the old man spoke, breaking the comfortable silence.

"Brian, he is a good man."

She glanced slowly at her neighbor, her eyes narrowing with suspicion. "Yes, he is. Today he is visiting Miss Wilson." Mandy could not pretend she didn't hear the bitterness in her words. She hoped Mr. Vallejo hadn't noticed.

The old Mexican drew a deep breath and looked off over the fields. "I remember when he first came to Yuba City," the old man began, politely ignoring Mandy's rude tone. "He had only recently lost his wife back east, and he'd sold everything to come to California. He thought he would spend time searching for gold in the hills, but I persuaded him to buy this farm instead. He got a good deal too. My former boss was eager to sell and get out."

Mr. Vallejo took another drink from his cup as Mandy tapped her foot. "It sounds like you didn't even know Mr. Dawson well when you told him of this farm for sale," she mused quietly, trying not to show her interest. Brian Dawson was none of her business, and soon she and her boys would be out on their backsides, seeking new lodgings. She thought of Ruby Wilson moving into this warm, snug cottage, and she gritted her teeth.

"I met him that very day," the old man continued. "Brian was buying supplies in Yuba City when I first saw him. I told him of this farm, and he came out here and bought it that same day."

Mandy scowled and turned to look at the little man. "How did you know to approach Brian? If you'd never met before, what prompted you to talk to him in the first place?"

Mr. Vallejo turned to face her, a mischievous smile creasing his weathered face. "The Holy Spirit," he whispered. "I'd been praying God would reveal to me who would buy this farm and be my new boss. The Lord showed me Brian, and I knew my prayer had been answered. Brian was grieving and hurting, but the Spirit had guided him to me. He knew it too. We have spoken of it many times. This place has helped Brian heal."

Mandy snorted. "He has healed, all right. He's over at Ruby Wilson's right now, courting her to marry. Soon, if I don't miss my guess," she added with a disdain she couldn't conceal.

The old man shook his head. "No, you are mistaken, Señora. It is not Miss Wilson that Brian is to marry."

Mandy blinked. Again, she eyed the old man with misgiving. Could he be right? "How do you know who Brian is to marry? Did the Holy Spirit tell you this?" she asked, wanting to know the man's spiritual insight.

The old man chuckled. "No, it is not the Holy Spirit. I know Brian will not marry the young miss, because he is in love with another woman, only he is not sure what to do about it."

"Another woman?" Mandy echoed, shocked again. Had there been someone before she arrived at this farm? Brian hadn't mentioned it, but Mandy had only been here a few months. It could be possible there was someone else.

She was about to question the old man further when she caught sight of Brian walking down the road. The pair on the porch watched his approach, neither saying anything more.

Mandy studied Brian closely. He wore an uncharacteristic frown on his handsome face, and Mandy thrilled, pleased to see he wasn't happy after his Sunday visit to the Wilson farm.

He stopped before them, his fists deep in his trouser pockets and rested one foot on the lowest step. "Is supper ready?"

Mandy glanced at Mr. Vallejo before she stood and opened the front door. "Soup is simmering. I'll have dinner ready in two shakes of a lamb's tail."

She glided into the kitchen, listening to catch the boys talking in their room down the hall. After moving the soup kettle closer to the flame, Mandy stirred, unable to keep the sly smile from her lips. She desperately wanted to ask about Brian's visit to Ruby Wilson's house, eager to learn what had agitated him so.

Soon, she called everyone to dinner and served soup and fresh cornbread. The boys chattered merrily of their boat races in the alfalfa field, and Mr. Vallejo discussed the proper way to smoke bees to safely acquire the honey from their hive.

"The bees will flee from smoke, and no one need get stung," he explained to his listeners.

Brian sat silent, his face set with a stern expression.

Mandy shifted in her seat. "I read the Bible today." She began slowly with some hesitation, but as she watched the faces of the boys as she spoke, she gained confidence and spoke with more assurance and enthusiasm. She shared about Samson, Noah, and Moses.

Sam and Jack listened attentively, and occasionally Mr. Vallejo added interesting details. Through all of this, Brian said nothing. He sat as if alone, not contributing in the conversation or asking questions.

After supper, he excused himself, mumbling something about being tired, and retreated to his bedroom.

Mandy watched him trudge slowly down the hallway as she cleared the table. Mr. Vallejo stopped near her, his arms loaded with dirty dishes. He whispered, "He is not happy. When a bee is searching for honey, it is best to not look for it on a thistle." He winked at Mandy, his dark eyes twinkling, and shuffled to the sink.

Mandy arched an eyebrow at the little man and glanced once more down the hallway where Brian had disappeared.

Now what was that all about?

CHAPTER 23

Three weeks later, Mandy was washing laundry, her arms in the soapy water up to her elbows, when her thoughts drifted again to Brian. He'd been courting Ruby for weeks now and seemed no happier. Each time he left, he'd taken a little longer leaving the cottage and was dark as a thundercloud each time he returned. Quietly, he would eat Sunday dinner and then hurriedly retire to his room.

She could not understand this man. Wasn't this what he wanted? Brian had made clear he was courting young Ruby, and yet the longer he saw her, the worse his demeanor. Mandy grinned and plunged Sam's shirt into the steaming bucket again.

She chalked Brian's bad attitude up to the effect of relationships as a rule. She recalled how Richard and she had quarreled and said mean things to each other on more than one occasion. It must simply be how it was when you spent time with someone, she figured.

Too bad people couldn't just be friends like Brian and I, Mandy thought to herself. Seemed like marriage complicated things. She paused, recalling how contented her parents seemed. They never argued like Richard and she did and always enjoyed serving one another.

Mandy thought about how she and Brian didn't argue, either—not much anyway—and enjoyed being together. He wasn't boring to her, nor did he act disinterested in her. He didn't spend all his money on gambling or wandering. Unlike Richard, Brian seemed stable and kind, even to the boys who weren't his own children.

Renewed Redemption

That was another thing, Mandy thought as she scowled into the soapy water. She and the boys would have to leave and find employment elsewhere soon enough. Once Brian was married to Ruby, there wouldn't be any need for her to be working around the farm.

You can handle it, Mandy told herself and lifted her chin defiantly.

She tossed the wet shirt into the bucket and hung her head. But she didn't want to handle it anymore. Not alone. It'd been so nice having someone to help carry the load.

Mandy sighed deeply. Brian was getting married, and she would have to move on. Just like she'd done a hundred times before.

Picking up and working a new job was normal to Mandy and somewhat expected. But the boys would take it hard. They'd come to really love being here, and they respected and admired Brian. He was strong, thoughtful, and fun. He took time to teach the boys different skills, and they enjoyed learning from him. They would not be happy to leave Quail Valley.

Would she? The thought made her pause in her washing. It didn't matter to her in the long run, did it? True, she liked living here as well as the boys did. Brian was always nice to her, and she enjoyed talking to him and spending time together.

More than that, she truly loved having a comfortable bed to sleep in, her own room, clean clothes, and the facilities to keep her and the boys warm and well taken care of. That had not often been the case, she reminded herself with a tinge of sadness.

She enjoyed being here too much, Mandy confessed secretly to herself. She couldn't say when it had begun, but she soon realized she'd often caught herself waiting for Brian to appear. Sometimes she'd even hurried to awaken in the morning, knowing he would be sitting on the couch in the sitting room. On more than one occasion, she'd interrupted his studies there to simply be near him.

Mandy didn't like to admit these emotions, not even to herself. It reflected a weakness she didn't like or understand. He was simply a nice employer, and she wasn't used to that. But something still haunted her, she knew not what.

The creaking of wagons drew her attention, and Mandy looked up as three farm wagons rolled into the yard. Drying her hands on her apron, she walked to the front porch and stood there watching as three men climbed stiffly down from their high seats. Slowly, they approached her, all three quickly removing their hats.

The man in the lead was obviously the boss. He wore dark pants tucked into boots and a flannel shirt with the sleeves rolled up, revealing powerful tanned forearms. He drew himself up tall as he glanced over Mandy, and she felt herself blush.

He nodded politely as he pushed his hair from his eyes, a little gray showing at the temples. "Howdy, ma'am," the man began, a warm smile coming easily to his brown face. "I'm Pruitt, and I run a ranch over south of here. Dawson stayed at my house after Christmas and told me he was going to grow alfalfa. I heard in Yuba City that he done it. I come up here to buy some hay."

The rancher eyed Mandy again, his gaze traveling over her slender form. "Ma'am? They said in town that Dawson got himself a right handsome housekeeper. They weren't lying, ma'am."

Mandy frowned and shifted on her feet. She wasn't used to compliments. "Well, thank you, sir. I'll fetch Mr. Dawson for you. He and my boys cut tons of hay just last week and it's fresh."

She untied her apron, threw it on the bench and hurried to the fields, aware the three men watched her go. She'd been surprised the night of the dance that men had paid her attention, and now, again, their compliments caught her by surprise. Shocked by the unwanted attention, she was reminded of the admiration she'd craved as a young girl in Richmond. Grimly, she was grateful those days were long gone.

She found Brian checking the crop and repairing drainage ditches. She never tired of looking at him. He was not only handsome, but confident, easy in his movements, a gentleman.

She informed him of the rancher. "He said his name was Mr. Pruitt. Says he knows you," Mandy said, turning to match Brian's stride as he started for the house.

"I do, indeed." Brian brushed his hands on his pants, hurrying toward the front yard. Mandy was hard put to keep up. "I stayed the night at his place after I bought the seed in Sacramento."

He glanced at Mandy as he walked. "That was right before I met you," he grinned, his eyes softening.

Mandy said nothing, her heart heavy in her chest. She would be leaving Quail Valley soon, and she was not excited about the prospect.

They strolled into the yard, and Mandy moved to one side as the men began their haggling over hay prices. Brian showed the rancher his stacks of hay, and they walked around them many times before they agreed on a price.

They loaded the three wagons and then lined up to caravan home. Before the wagons departed, Mr. Pruitt pulled on the reins, his wagon rolling to a halt next to Mandy. Smiling, he climbed nimbly down from his seat and approached her.

Once more he took his hat in his hands. "I'll be going now, ma'am, but I wanted to let you know that if ever you're in need of a job, one awaits you at my ranch." His unexpected words struck at Mandy's sharp brain. This man might provide the security she would lose when she left Brian's farm.

"I have two small sons who would be coming with me," she replied swiftly.

"They would be welcome. Maybe I could find work for them too," Mr. Pruitt added, smiling broadly. He turned to climb the wagon wheel and then seated himself, one boot resting on the footboard. With a nod to Mandy, he waved merrily to Brian. The rancher whipped the reins, and his team moved off. Slowly, the wagons behind him started forward, heavily laden with fresh hay.

With the wheels crunching the gravel in the narrow road, the wagons soon rolled from sight. Watching them depart, Brian cast a sidelong, glance at Mandy. "Are you thinking of taking a job with this man?"

Mandy turned to face him and smiled weakly. "Well, I figured once you got married to Ruby Wilson, you'd have no need for me here. She certainly wouldn't like another woman on the place. I figure to have a job waiting for me when you give me my walking papers."

"That's not going to be any time soon, I promise you," Brian retorted quickly and turned.

Mandy reached for his shoulder, stopping him. "Wait, Brian. Why not? I thought you and Ruby were courting. Aren't you going to get hitched real soon?"

Her voice held a note of teasing, but she was very serious now. Had something changed? Was this kind farmer to marry Ruby Wilson or not? She could feel her pulse race as she waited for his reply.

Brian's face was stern when he finally spoke. "I realize what I told you before and it still holds. I do plan on getting married again. But Ruby is young, and if I have to spend too many Sundays with her, I'm likely to strangle her. If I can get to the point where I can tolerate her prattle about dresses and babies, maybe I'll marry her. But not until then," he growled. He turned then and moved toward the kitchen.

Mandy sighed, her lungs releasing slowly. She was exceedingly relieved to hear this news from Brian, and she yet didn't know why. Only she was glad to know she wouldn't soon be leaving Quail Valley.

Renewed Redemption

A sly smile tugged at the corner of her lips. Neither would Brian soon be married to Ruby. Mandy had complete faith in Miss Wilson's immaturity and silliness.

CHAPTER 24

The next two weeks passed in a blur. The boys worked the alfalfa, and Mandy was hard pressed to keep them fed and wearing clean clothes. Today, Brian and the boys had elected to clear a pool below the small waterfall that tumbled over the boulders below the dam. Brian insisted it would make an ideal bathing pool.

At first, Mandy scoffed at the idea of bathing in the river, but if it meant she didn't have to boil water for baths, she would support the venture wholeheartedly.

With the floodgate in place, the water level had dropped significantly in the pool below the small waterfall to allow Brian and the boys to clear its depths.

While they did this, Mandy decided to take an unexpected trip to town to check the mail. She found the walk into Yuba City an opportunity to pray and seek God's guidance. In a little over an hour, she could make the short journey from the farm to the general store, and the time seemed to fly by as she reflected on life and spiritual matters.

She knew there hadn't been enough time for a turnabout on the letter she'd mailed to her parents, but her eagerness was such that she wanted to ask in town as often as opportunity afforded.

Brian had paid the extra high fee to utilize the Pony Express out of Sacramento, but she hadn't had sufficient funds to do likewise. Hence, she'd paid for regular postage, which meant her mail might travel by slow wagon east or by ship around the horn of South America. Either way, it would take months to receive and expect a response.

Renewed Redemption

Nonetheless, Mandy went to town as often as she could with hopeful expectations that one day a letter would be waiting for her from her father and mother. Perhaps they hadn't waited for another letter to write to her again. Their initial letter had traveled by Pony Express. Maybe they'd send another in the same way.

She passed over the little bridge crossing the Yuba River. The spot never ceased to excite her as it was here she first heard again from her father.

She stepped into the wider, more traveled trail along the river that led into Yuba City. Miners and animals passed her, forcing her from the narrow road.

Besides, the bothersome mud of winter and spring was rapidly being replaced by a layer of thick, annoying dust that rose in clouds when anything passed. By walking slightly off to the side of the road, she found she could sometimes evade the stifling dust.

Mandy mused how quickly, once again, the trip into town had sped by. Praising God for salvation that had come to her and her boys while at Quail Valley seemed to take quite a bit of time. Reflecting on how far she'd come from abject poverty and constant struggle seemed to occupy her thoughts and made the trip faster. Growth in faith and her understanding of Jesus's teaching were now uppermost in her mind, and these last thoughts carried her easily into the bustle of Yuba City.

The small city was abuzz with activity. Wagons and buggies clogged the long main street. Horses lined the hitching rails, tied in front of businesses, most common being the numerous saloons the town boasted.

Mandy passed The Queen of China, a disreputable building with bright, gaudy paintings on its large front window. She'd worked there a month, desperate for a job. The memory of the drunken men with rude and gruff talk disturbed and frightened her now. Most of the bearded, booted men simply ignored her, though some harassed her, and occasionally she received impromptu proposals of marriage.

She wrinkled her nose and quickened her pace past the saloon.

Mrs. Bricker at the blacksmith shop waved at Mandy, and she promised herself she would stop and say hello on her way out of town. First, she must check the mail.

Skipping lightly onto the wide steps of the general store, Mandy pulled on the door handle and stepped into the crowded store. The tinkling doorbell sounded above her as she inhaled the smell of familiar merchandise. Licorice, tobacco, pickles, coffee, and leather.

She smiled, grateful to enter the store without having to worry or brace herself for combat as she once had. God was good.

Mandy worked her way around large boxes and stacks of dry goods, all the time recalling the worrisome battles she used to prepare for when she would visit this store before meeting Brian. Everything had changed since meeting Brian.

Mr. Ambrose sighted Mandy at once but was unable to get to her before a young clerk waited on her. His boyish face looked uncomfortable being serious as a businessman should. A black tie peeked above his clean apron, and his hair was slicked down.

"Yes, ma'am, how can I help you?" the boy asked, his gaze traveling up and down her trim figure. Mandy noticed and ignored his bold glance. Men of the gold fields didn't have the same sense of propriety she'd experienced in Virginia. Richmond was known far and wide for its correct attitude and manners toward women. Always courteous, never familiar. California seemed to have none of these graceful, more refined social practices. Where was the subtle, more respectful gentlemanly behavior of the old days?

Mandy sighed and asked the clerk for the mail.

Renewed Redemption

The young man moved toward the mailboxes arranged on the back wall and made a show of looking carefully in each one. Finally, he returned empty-handed, feigning disappointment.

"Sorry, ma'am, but there is no mail for a Mandy Barrett." He eyed her intently, then glanced at Mr. Ambrose. The young clerk leaned forward and lowered his voice. "Perhaps I could show you around town when I get off work. I'll be finished here soon."

Mandy lifted her chin and narrowed her eyes. "You are certainly finished now, as far as I am concerned."

She moved away from the grinning clerk and headed for the door, not wanting to take more time in the crowded aisles of the general store. She yanked the door open with undue force and stalked out onto the boardwalk.

People shuffled past her and quickly took her place in the busy store. She walked farther down the street before leaning against a porch post.

Men stared at her and Mandy turned away, surprised. She'd rarely drawn men's attention before coming to Quail Valley. She'd lost her youthful bloom over the years to hard work and deplorable living conditions. Also, her constant exposure to harsh weather and malnutrition had made her thin and sickly these past few years.

Now, with good food and proper rest, she'd regained some of the vitality of her youth, she had to admit she felt good.

Regular baths and a daily change of clothes had not hurt things either, she mused, grinning to herself. Truly, coming to Brian's farm had not only affected her spiritually, but in every way imaginable.

Disappointed at not receiving a letter but not wholly surprised, she left the boardwalk and headed back toward the trail. Mandy wended her way slowly through the horses and wagons on the street to cross over to the blacksmith shop.

Not really interested in idle gossip, she was more resolved in showing kindness to someone who had reached out to her. The manner of Mrs. Bricker at the dance had made an impression on Mandy, and she wished to return the courtesy.

Mandy found the woman behind the shop, hanging laundry.

"Good morning, Mrs. Bricker. I was in town and thought I'd stop by and say hello."

She noticed how slowly the other woman pinned the clothes on the line. She must not have to move quickly, Mandy mused, remembering other times. She was tempted to take the wet clothes from the woman and show her how it was done.

The blacksmith's wife looked flushed from her work, a layer of sweat beaded her brow, but she fixed Mandy with a broad smile. "Why, good morning to you, Mrs. Barrett. I've heard so much about you lately," was the woman's greeting.

Mandy frowned slightly, taken aback by Mrs. Bricker's disconcerting words. This is not what she had expected. "Me?" she said in sudden surprise, and then her eyes narrowed suspiciously. "What have you heard?"

Mrs. Bricker laughed easily at Mandy's stern countenance. "Nothing bad, I assure you. I've been informed by a clerk in the store that Mr. Pruitt, the rancher down toward Sacramento, has offered you a nice job. They say he was quite taken with you when he picked up his hay at Mr. Dawson's farm. Also, everyone's noticed how you've blossomed since becoming a housekeeper. Some of the men in town are reporting you are a handsome girl, and some man needs to sweep you up and marry you."

Mandy relaxed at this inconsequential news and laughed with relief. She seemed to be in for idle gossip after all. But she put no stock in such chatter and decided she needed to go. She had stopped to say hello, and that done, was not interested in the wagging of town tongues.

"Well, I have no intention of getting remarried," Mandy said and took another step. "I've been down that road and do not hope to travel it again."

Renewed Redemption

Mrs. Bricker's hands froze, and she arched an eyebrow. "Oh?" Mrs. Bricker crossed her arms over her chest. "I have found marriage so enjoyable and rewarding. It's good not to be alone anymore, and Mr. Bricker is a kindly, intelligent man. I've been pleased to be his wife."

Mandy nodded agreeably, not wishing to offend, but what did this woman know of marriage? She wanted to tell her to just wait and see. She took a step backward, ready to flee. "I didn't mean to suggest that all marriages are bad, but I confess mine was," Mandy conceded. "I went against the wishes of my parents when I eloped, and my husband proved to be a terrible scoundrel. I am sure Mr. Bricker is nothing of the sort."

"Indeed, he is not," Mrs. Bricker said, sticking out her chin.

Mandy shrugged. "Well, I've made my mistakes, no getting around that. But I hope I've learned my lesson."

Mrs. Bricker visibly relaxed then, the smile returning to her face. "I am sorry to hear your experience was so disastrous, Mrs. Barrett, but, praise God, you've learned a valuable lesson."

"Indeed, I have, Mrs. Bricker. If the good Lord ever wants me to remarry, he'll have to perform quite a miracle on my damaged heart. I'm not open to any such notion, I can promise you." Mandy crossed her heart with her index finger and then turned to go. "Have a nice day," she called over her shoulder, eager to be away.

"Wait!" the blacksmith's wife called, pushing laundry from her path as she followed Mandy toward the street beyond. "I almost forgot to tell you, Ruby Wilson has a cold and is worried to have Mr. Dawson see her with a swollen nose. She asked me to tell you if I saw you to inform Mr. Dawson that perhaps he should wait a week before he visits her again."

Mandy wondered how Brian would react to this news but was quick to reassure Mrs. Bricker. "I promise to inform Mr. Dawson of Miss Wilson's request. Goodbye, now," Mandy said again and walked hurriedly into the traffic flow of miners and wagons on the road.

Would Brian be disappointed about Ruby? The thought of Ruby's swollen, red nose made Mandy giggle. Reproachfully, she composed herself once more, determined to think only good things about the young neighbor girl. Besides, she was to be Brian's wife eventually, Mandy reminded herself. She should make every effort to like who Brian would marry.

He deserved that, at least. Hadn't Brian been so good to her and the boys?

Not wishing to ponder further on Ruby Wilson or her cold, Mandy thought of other things on her way home. She had been sincere when she reported she was not interested in marriage again. The thought of being wed again made her cringe. Richard had been enough nightmare for one lifetime.

Instead, Mandy occupied her mind with thoughts of Sam and Jack. The boys were much on her mind lately, and she recognized the reason immediately. Before coming to Quail Valley, she had been forced to focus wholeheartedly on providing the boys with enough food and supplies to survive. There had been little time for anything more, other than the occasional chance opportunity to read. But now with the basic needs taken care of, Mandy enjoyed thinking of ways to occupy the boys' time. Now she encouraged them to simply play, develop their imaginations. Sometimes she even helped them construct blanket tents in their room or forts from rocks and debris along the riverbanks.

Of course, she always oversaw their studies, enhancing their abilities with reading and sums. These they would need when they sought work for themselves. But developing their imaginations had become a paramount concern to Mandy. She desperately wanted her children to have a real childhood.

A warm memory came to her about how Brian had been instrumental in this process. She smiled. He was constantly teaching the boys as they worked together. Lessons covering tool usage and work skills were common, and Sam and Jack had learned a great deal in a short period of time. But more than this, Brian had wanted the boys to have fun.

Mandy had been confused at first until he reminded her that she, too, had enjoyed a fun childhood.

"Didn't your father teach you to ride horses or to fish or how to build things? Didn't your mother teach you important things about kitchen work, including cookies and desserts?" he teased her with a twinkle in his brown eyes. "A little fun now and again is good for all children," he had informed her.

One day, Mandy had walked to the fields with lunch for the boys when she'd discovered the three of them fishing. Work forgotten, they sat on the bank of the river with long poles, lines dangling in the water.

At first, she'd been angry. "What is this? There is work to be done, and I find you sitting in the shade with fishing poles," she scolded, her boys squirming under her harsh words.

Brian had merely laughed. "They told me they'd never been fishing. All boys should learn how to fish. This is today's work, Mandy."

She walked on, remembering the way the boys had brightened after Brian defended them from her attack. They loved him, she worried, but had no answer to that dilemma. The day would come when she and the boys would have to leave Quail Valley and would no longer see Brian Dawson.

The thought made her sad as she turned from the main trail, crossed the little bridge, and continued toward the farm. Her mood darkened as she considered leaving Brian's farm, knowing the boys would miss it too.

The cottage in sight, Mandy hastened her step and arrived to find the house empty. Not surprised, she worked around the little house, opening windows to allow the pleasant spring breeze to enter. It'd been too chilly this morning to open windows, but now sunlight streamed into the little valley and warmed the cool of the cottage.

Leaving the house once again, Mandy walked toward the waterfall where the boys worked on the bathing pool. She saw at a distance where Sam and Jack were lifting buckets of water from the forced lake covering the alfalfa field and were busy watering the fruit trees.

She waved to them, and Jack waved in return, a wide grin on his face. Mandy could feel her heart swell proudly as she saw her boys working hard. Brian had taught them well.

Mandy saw the river water roaring noisily over the fall into the pool below. Brian had obviously opened the floodgate to allow the irrigation water to recede from the flooded fields. It would only take a couple of days for the water to absorb, allowing the fields to dry once again.

As she approached the bank of the narrow channel, Mandy saw Brian standing down below, hands resting on his lean hips as he watched the water cascading onto the rocks at his feet. A bubbling river gurgled merrily in the pool, and Mandy carefully made her way down to it. A path had been cut into the bank and some foliage trimmed to allow passage down into the small basin where the pool nestled among large granite boulders.

Mandy dropped below the rim of the bank, and the boys were lost to her view.

The noisy waterfall made hearing difficult, but she waved to Brian, finally catching his eye. A smile sprang quickly to his smooth face at sight of her, and again she was struck at how handsome he was, tall and broad-shouldered. Her heart fluttered, and Mandy tried to ignore the unexpected sensation. Why did Brian affect her in this way? Her brow creased with irritation at the thought.

With a gesture, he encouraged her to come closer. Cautiously, Mandy stepped on the smooth, wet rocks to the pool's edge where Brian stood.

"How was your walk to town," Brian called, his mouth close to her ear to be heard above the roar. His warm breath startled her, and she almost pulled back, but then didn't, drinking in his nearness.

"Good. No letter from Virginia, though. Too soon, I guess," she replied, her loud voice muffled by the falling water.

They stood a moment then, surveying the wide, frothing pool before them.

"We've made a path down here and cleaned a lot of boulders and old trees from the water. This will make a nice bathing spot now," Brian explained, placing a firm hand on her shoulder as he leaned close to Mandy, indicating the rocks taken from the riverbed.

Mandy nodded with interest, but she could feel her heart throbbing violently at his touch. She couldn't even consider the various stones he pointed at, her thoughts too focused on his firm grip on her shoulder.

"I saw Mrs. Bricker, and she wanted you to know Miss Wilson has a cold and will be unable to receive visitors tomorrow," Mandy blurted, wishful to keep her attention from Brian's disturbing nearness. She peered closely at him, eager to see his response to her information.

A wide grin spread across his face, and his brown eyes danced. But then, just as quickly, he pursed his lips and narrowed his eyes. "That's too bad," he remarked, waving a dismissive hand in the air, but not before Mandy heard the relief in his voice.

She almost giggled, but then choked, a hand going to her mouth. Abruptly, she stepped onto a rock in the swift current, trying to conceal her laughter at his feigned regret.

"Be careful, Mandy. Those rocks are wet and slippery," he warned.

Mandy's shoe slipped on the slick surface, and she almost fell headlong into the pool. Brian reached and caught her around her waist, pulling her backward. Together, they tumbled on the riverbank, Mandy sprawling in his arms.

She laughed nervously as she glanced at Brian over her shoulder. He lay beneath her, her head resting on his chest, blonde hair spilling across his face. At the look of surprise in his eyes, she froze. She saw something else there, something she didn't recognize. She squirmed to escape his hold, to flee the awkward situation.

Then she saw Brian smile. Not his playful, teasing grin she was used to, but a victorious grin, one of success. His embrace tightened around her waist, and Mandy gasped in astonishment as his face lifted toward hers. Too late, she realized what he intended.

Brian bent his face forward, his lips fiercely pressing against her own.

Complete shock overwhelmed Mandy as she felt the heat steal up her neck and burn her cheeks. For an instant, she was transported, soaring, giddy. Something fluttered in her belly and she thrilled, hungrily returning the passionate kiss.

Tiny lights flashed in her brain, and Mandy shoved with all her might to wrestle free and scramble to her feet. Horrified, she stared down at Brian. He still lay on the grassy bank, a shocked look on his face.

Mandy glared at him, unable to speak. She clenched her fists, wanting to shout at him. No words would come.

Angry, she whirled and fled up the path.

CHAPTER 25

Mandy raced up the narrow path, her face burning. Anger rose in her chest as she recalled Brian's face drawing near to her own and the sudden glint in his soft eyes. *Oh, the deceptive man*, she fumed.

Scowling, she propelled up the steep path, her legs churning madly as she left the dense foliage along the river. She almost collided into Jack. The young boy broke into a happy smile at sight of her.

Mandy skidded to a halt at his greeting.

"Hello, Mother. I was helping Sam and Brian water the trees," he informed her with a look of importance. He glanced past her and down the path toward the pool. "What were you doing down there?" he asked, looking back at Mandy.

Mandy felt the blush on her cheeks recede quickly. What had the young boy seen? She could feel her eyes widen in panic and shame. Her hands shot out and grabbed Jack roughly by his shoulders, drawing him to her. "What did you see?" she demanded, shaking him.

A startled face looked back at her as fear sprang to Jack's eyes. "Huh? Nothing, why? Was I supposed to see something?" Jack asked, turning to look down the path again.

She released the scared boy and hurried to the house, unmindful of Sam's cheerful call from across the sodden field. She could not stop and talk to him, afraid he might detect her embarrassing secret.

Mandy stormed on, her mind unable to focus or understand exactly what had just occurred. She knew something horrible had just happened, but she determined not to think about it further. She would push the event aside and think on other things.

Despite her resolve, however, Mandy couldn't help but remember Brian's warm lips pressing eagerly onto her own. And she had returned the unwanted kiss!

Again, she attempted to push the vexing memory from her mind, but she found the kiss consumed her instead. Like a flood she could not hold back, the picture played over and over in her head. All she could think of was Brian Dawson's handsome face coming closer to her own and his gentle kiss.

Gentle? Mandy shook her head, recalling the way his heated lips brushed her own, then crushed them hungrily. Yes, his touch had been gentle at first but had burned her cool lips, igniting something powerful within her. She did not want to explore the meaning.

Again, stubbornly, she tried to push these conflicting thoughts aside but to no avail. The memory would not leave her alone, rolling over and over in her mind, refusing to be ignored.

Mandy burst through the front door, leaving it open behind her. She rushed to her bedroom, a new and more perplexing thought crowding into her mind, astonishing Mandy to her core.

She had liked that kiss.

There it was, out in the open. The disturbing concept sharpened in clarity as she mulled it over and over. She had enjoyed Brian's tender touch. The feel of his mouth on hers had awakened a realization she could not deny. This feeling was completely unexpected, unwanted.

Brian's kiss had made her happy.

She felt like she could think on that simple truth and not go crazy, so she did. What was going to happen next, she wouldn't dwell on now. That would come later, she guessed. For now, she would remember his touch and how good the feeling was.

Mandy closed her bedroom door and threw herself onto the bed. Reaching for her pillow, she pulled it close and hugged it tightly. Staring up at the ceiling, Mandy smiled. She had enjoyed his kiss, and Jack had not seen them, she was sure. It would've been terrible if her youngest son had seen her kissing her boss.

Mandy was sincere when she'd spoken to people of her resolve to never remarry—the idea made her feel sick to her stomach. She had no desire to ever be with another man after the debacle she had endured with Richard. The mere thought of being close to a man had disgusted her.

But Brian's sudden and unexpected kiss had touched her in a way she would never have believed. She liked his firm lips upon her own. She remembered the event again, and this time she winced.

Time to move on now and explore repair options. Something would have to be said, and she wouldn't allow her odd sensation at being kissed to destroy everything she'd worked so hard to create. She didn't want to leave Quail Valley yet. She was not ready for the move.

Mandy thought first of simply ignoring the kiss, acting as if it never happened. Would Brian follow her lead?

She squeezed her eyes closed and wrinkled her nose. *This could get complicated.*

Maybe she could say it was an accident, that when she fell, her mouth pushed up against his face, unintentionally touching his lips.

She smiled ruefully to herself, remembering those strong lips against her own, sending chills down her spine. No, it had been no accident, she knew. Brian had purposely forced his lips to hers.

Her face burned anew at the thought of her kissing Brian in return. What had prompted her to such an unexpected response?

She shook her head. It was Brian's fault, not hers.

Renewed Redemption

Mandy leaped suddenly to her feet, flinging the pillow back onto the bed. That's right, he had purposely kissed her, and Brian had initiated the move, not her.

She started to pace, her shoes clicking loudly upon the flagstone floor. What had he been thinking? He was courting Ruby Wilson, not her. And what of that other woman Mr. Vallejo had mentioned? Was Brian playing fast and loose with numerous women at once?

She shook her head again. No, Mandy couldn't believe that. He'd always been such a gentleman toward her.

Perhaps he was not interested in Ruby Wilson? Mandy dismissed this notion too. Brian was indeed intentional in his pursuit of the young brunette. He'd made it clear that he wished to marry again.

Then why had he kissed her? Mandy's confusion grew and whirled around in her head. There was no explanation.

Later that evening, Jack knocked upon her door.

"Mother? Are you okay?" His hesitant voice reminded Mandy how roughly she'd accosted the small boy. She felt remorse now.

"I don't feel well, Jack," Mandy spoke quietly through her door. She still wished to be alone with her disturbing thoughts.

"Are you going to join us for dinner? Sam and I have made cookies and bread with butter. Do you want to join us?" His young voice held a note of concern.

"I'm tired, Jack. Go on without me. I'll be all right," Mandy assured her youngest son. She would not be fit company tonight, she surmised. And besides, Brian would be present. Mandy would be horrified to see him right now. What would she say to him? What would he say to her?

She heard Jack's steps retreat from her door, and again she was bombarded with nagging thoughts. A headache began to throb at her temples.

What to do now? If Brian kissed her on purpose, what was her proper course? Mandy did not wish to leave the cottage but couldn't stay if Brian persisted in his attention toward her. He was spoken for by another woman, possibly two.

The idea came to her suddenly. Carlos Vallejo. The Mexican was Brian's oldest friend in the region. He would know what to do, what she should do. She decided to see the old beekeeper on the morrow. Beyond that, she couldn't make herself think. Too many conflicting and confusing thoughts banged against each other in her crowded mind. She couldn't sort them out.

Sighing, Mandy stopped trying. She would see Mr. Vallejo and seek direction. He might have an idea.

Kneeling next to her bed like she used to when she was a young girl, Mandy bowed her head to pray. It had been a long time since she'd done this, but somehow she felt this posture seemed more humble. She needed all the help she could get.

"Dear God in heaven, forgive me. I don't know what happened today, but I confess I liked it. I hope I haven't sinned. Nor do I want Brian to sin. I know he is going to marry Ruby Wilson, or at least I think he is. Mr. Vallejo said Brian wasn't going to marry her, but I don't know. All I know is I'm confused and need your discernment. What should I do, Lord?"

She continued to pour her heart out to the Lord until, late at night, she crawled wearily and fully dressed into bed.

That night, Mandy slept restlessly, her dreams plagued with haunting memories of Brian Dawson, Richard, and Ruby Wilson. Once, she even saw her father, standing in his freshly plowed fields back in Virginia. Mandy desperately wanted to ask her father about Brian. But he was across the field, far from her, and she couldn't get near him.

For some reason, she needed to know what her father thought of Brian. The thought tormented her, drove her mad. In her dream, she shouted across the bare fields, begging him for guidance and advice.

She slept terribly.

CHAPTER 26

The next morning, Mandy rose early and left the house by the back door. She could barely discern the dim light in the sitting room, but she avoided that direction and slipped outdoors, quiet and unseen.

Holding her shawl close around her, Mandy walked through the rapidly brightening dawn toward the beehives near the alfalfa fields. She looked the other way when she passed the path leading down to the bathing pool but felt a blush come to her cheeks, nonetheless. Her mind wanted to race to that intoxicating and enjoyable memory of yesterday, but she did not allow herself to go there. She needed to talk to Mr. Vallejo.

Mandy found the old Mexican man tending the bee boxes just as she hoped he would be. He wore a canvas hood with eye slits cut for him that he pulled off when he saw her approach.

"Señora? You are up early this fine day," the old beekeeper greeted her warmly, his dark eyes shining in the morning sun.

"Good morning, Mr. Vallejo. I hoped I would find you here," Mandy began, keeping her distance from the whirring bees.

"Yes, Señora, I received a feeling you wanted to talk to me about Brian."

Surprised, Mandy tilted her head. "Yes, um, I need to ask you something," she replied, taking another step nearer.

The old man placed a tin can on the hive before approaching Mandy. Waiting, she glanced at the high peaks above the little valley. The morning sun warmed the chill from her shoulders. Mandy felt safe here, as if the towering

Renewed Redemption

Sierra Nevada Mountains held this tiny valley in its protective embrace, just for her. This place was special to her. She drank in the beauty, the fresh, cool morning air filling her lungs. She loved being here. Quail Valley had become her home, and she didn't want to leave.

Mandy sighed, watching the old man move from the beehive. He gestured to a place farther from the bees, and Mandy followed, wondering how to begin.

They sat on the newly erected stone fence, the field of alfalfa already showing signs of needing another cutting.

"Now, Señora," the old man began after finding a comfortable seat. "What can I do for you?"

Mandy hesitated, looking at the stones intricately stacked beside her. Brian had fitted them so cleverly. Then, remembering her question, she turned to the old man.

"You mentioned once about a woman Brian loved. Was that before I came to Quail Valley?"

The old Mexican smiled at her, his teeth flashing brightly against his bronzed face. "No, Señora," he replied with a shake of his head. Mandy thought she detected a twinkle in his dark eyes.

She considered the old man's response, not sure where to go from here. If there'd not been another woman before her, who then?

Mr. Vallejo rested a gnarled hand gently on Mandy's. "It is you, Señora Barrett. I have seen how Brian looks at you. He loves you."

Mandy smiled sadly. "You must be mistaken, Mr. Vallejo. Mr. Dawson is going to marry Miss Wilson. He has told me so himself."

She was saddened Mr. Vallejo had no real answers for her, but she would try and be patient with the obviously confused man.

"No, he is not," the old Mexican repeated, shaking his head again. "He does not know yet, but he will marry you. He loves you, and you love him."

Mandy laughed out loud at this. "You are really mistaken now," she said, regaining her composure before going on. "I have no desire to ever marry again."

"You might have no desire, but maybe God has a desire. Don't you feel something in your heart for Brian? I have seen the feelings growing these past months. Also, I think Sam and Jack love Brian too. Will you separate them from him? He is like their father now," Mr. Vallejo said, a calm countenance on his face.

Mandy decided the man was old, and she should be compliant with him. "Mr. Vallejo," she started again, attempting to reason with him. "I am not in love with Mr. Dawson, and I am sure he is not in love with me. We're just friends and I'll be leaving this farm soon when he marries. He will quickly forget me, I am sure."

Mr. Vallejo returned her patient look. "You are going to marry Mr. Dawson, I know this. I have seen it in your eyes. It is the right thing to do, and God will bless your marriage, I know this too."

Mandy frowned. This conversation was going nowhere, and she was weary of trying. Obviously, there was no information to get from Mr. Vallejo. Mandy rose to her feet.

"Thank you. It is good to talk to you. Have a good day," Mandy said and turned to go. Desperately she'd hoped this old man would have some answers, a direction, some information that would help her choose a course. Now, Mandy would return to the house, as confused as before.

"Señora Barrett, wait," the old man placed a gentle hand on her arm, halting Mandy's retreat. "Look me in the eyes and tell me you have no feelings or thoughts about Brian."

Her eyes widened in surprise at his insightful question. Could he see into her soul? Mandy shrugged. "I've been confused. It all happened so fast. I am sure it was an accident. Nothing more."

"Ah? See? I am right," he said, pointing a finger at her and smiling. "I knew I could not be wrong. Tell me, what did he do? Did he kiss you?"

The embarrassed look on Mandy's face answered for her.

"So! He kissed you." He smiled and slapped his knee. "It's about time. I worried he waited too long. I thought he'd do so before this." The old man rubbed his hands together.

Mandy's eyes narrowed at the little man. "You expected this?"

"But of course. I saw it long ago," Carlos replied confidently. "I knew it was only a matter of time before he tried to show you his true feelings. You were confusing him with all that talk of never getting married again. It scared him."

Mandy crossed her arms over her chest before she spoke. "But I'm serious. I don't want to ever marry again."

The Mexican man laughed in her face and drew his hand from her arm. "You mean you never want to marry a man again you don't love."

Mandy gasped, and her hand flew to her throat, astonished by the old man's assertion. Was that what she meant? Certainly, her immature infatuation with Richard Barrett had never sprung into real love. And he'd never loved Mandy, either. Was her heart merely waiting for true love? The kind of love she'd never experienced? Still confused, she peered intently at the little Mexican man.

"Don't look so surprised. You were never in love with that other man. You were a young girl, in love with the idea of being in love. He was a scoundrel, was he not?" Carlos demanded.

Mandy nodded, unable to speak, her full attention riveted on the insightful man before her.

"Well, now you have fallen in love with a real man. He is a follower of Jesus, he is patient, a hard worker, a servant to all around him. And he is in love with you. It is as God would have it," Carlos explained with a warm smile on his leathery face.

Mr. Vallejo finished and turned to pick up his canvas hood and tools. Mandy stood rooted in place, her mind struggling to understand what he had said. Then his words hit her with the full impact, and she knew he had gauged her correctly. It was as if this man had seen into her very soul and knew the progression of her feelings.

Slowly, day by day, Mandy had become more drawn to Brian, learning his likes and dislikes, his habits, and his patterns of behavior. She had eagerly watched for him, anxious to be near him. Without trying, they had developed a comfortable friendship and truly enjoyed each other's company.

From the beginning, Brian had been kind and attentive to her. She'd thought these were merely the traits of a Christian man, but then they'd increased, and now she saw them for what Carlos said they were, the actions of a man in love.

Mandy had been so against the idea of love that she hadn't even recognized it when it happened. Where her infatuation for Richard had been for all the wrong reasons, stubbornness, rebellion, impatience, greed, she saw her feelings for Brian in a different light. She loved Brian Dawson for all the right reasons.

Now she wanted to serve, be kind, work with him to make him happy. Before, it was all about her and making her happy. Now, Mandy was eager to work for the benefit of others. For starters, her two young sons and the man she loved.

Mandy looked at Mr. Vallejo, her eyes widening as she smiled, finally comprehending. Her confusion melted away as Mandy understood at last. She'd never loved a man before, and the new sensation was foreign to her.

"You're right. I didn't realize it until now. I love Brian."

The old man smiled in return and started walking toward the house. "Come. I am hungry."

She fell into step beside him, silent now as her jumbled thoughts fell completely into their proper place, sorting themselves out one by one. Suddenly things seemed much clearer. All except one.

"What about Ruby Wilson?" Mandy demanded, panic starting to rise within her at the thought of the snippy young brunette. "She'll be furious. What about the folks in town? Their tongues will surely wag at this news."

Mandy moaned and covered her face with her hands.

"Don't worry about it," the old man said, patting her shoulder. "God is in control. Just obey him with a humble heart, and he will work everything out." Mr. Vallejo stopped for a moment and then added, "Besides, do not worry about what others think of you, worry about what God thinks of you. You have accepted Jesus as your Savior, you have committed yourself to follow him, and you are walking in his ways. Continue to do so. Let God guide the events—you just be obedient and allow him to work in your life."

They continued walking the short distance to the cottage, and Mandy saw the home with new eyes. Could this be where she would live forever? She'd always wanted to live in a house but never thought it would be possible again. The thought of living here with Brian made her feel a sense of joy and security she didn't believe could happen to her.

They stepped onto the front porch, and Mandy opened the door. She held it for the older man, as a homeowner would hold the door open for a guest, and then she entered. Brian was there, sitting on the couch with his Bible open on his lap.

Her heart leaped at the sight of him. Mandy realized she'd not seen him since he'd kissed her. The memory brought a fresh blush to her face. She calmed herself and looked directly at him.

It was time to be honest. With Brian and with herself.

Chapter 27

"I love you," she said and waited for a response.

"Is coffee on?" Carlos asked.

"What?" Brian asked, staring at Mandy with wide eyes.

"I asked if coffee was on," Carlos repeated.

"Did you say you loved me?" Brian whispered, closing his Bible and laying the thick book aside. Slowly, he rose to his feet, his gaze intent on Mandy.

She watched him stand, studying him closely, and Mandy could feel herself tremble as he stepped nearer. This was the man she loved. It seemed so natural, so comfortable to love Brian Dawson. So right.

Mandy nodded, tears forming in her eyes as she smiled with quivering lips. She could feel God's hand upon her as she looked at Brian. This was not a silly, selfish desire like the one she and Richard shared so many years ago. This was love, blessed by God. Finally, Mandy understood the good things that God wanted for her. She only needed to be patient, obedient, humble.

Carlos threw up his hands and strode to the kitchen.

Brian edged closer to Mandy, his arms by his side. His eyes were warm, expectant, excited.

"I do love you, Mandy. I've known it for quite a while, but I thought it best to stay away from you, you were so against love."

She smiled as a tear rolled down her cheek. "You've taught me a lot about God's love, Brian, and I've seen it demonstrated in you," Mandy explained, taking a tentative step toward him. "Your kindness and service to both me and my boys has spoken volumes to my heart. I love God first, Brian, but I love you, also."

He smiled at her. "I'd have it no other way, Mandy." His eyes sparkled, and she knew he felt the same way she did.

He bridged the remaining steps between them and swept her into his arms, picking her up and twirling her around. She buried her face in his shoulder as he hugged her and then placed her on her feet.

Mandy drew back from Brian and looked up at him, her eyes warm with wetness, her hands resting on his shoulders. "Brian, I love you so much. God has taught me how to love and has forgiven my hard heart. Now he's brought me to you. I thank God for you."

Brian looked down at her, his arms still locked around her slim waist. "Mandy, you are a gift from the Lord to me. I, too, thank God for you. It'll be good to begin a new chapter in my life with a Christian woman by my side."

Mandy laughed, remembering Sam and Jack. "And Christian sons, don't forget."

Brian returned her laugh. "I've not forgotten. I'm proud to be their father. A man couldn't ask for two finer sons. I dearly love them too."

"Most of that is because of your teaching. I've been grateful for the way you've influenced them. Thank you for being so good to my boys. Our boys," Mandy corrected with a chuckle.

"As for me and my house, we will serve the Lord," Brian quoted and then hugged Mandy to him again.

He drew back then, and she saw the mischievous gleam in his eye. "You know, Mandy, you kissed me yesterday."

Mandy gasped and looked over her shoulder to where Mr. Vallejo stood out of earshot in the kitchen. She lowered her voice. "You kissed me, Brian. I had no idea you would do that. I was taken by surprise."

His eyebrows arched. "Me, too, but I think you liked that kiss."

Mandy felt the heat burn her cheeks, and she buried her face in his chest, unable to speak.

Brian lifted her chin with a strong hand and looked deeply into her eyes. He smiled, and Mandy felt the warmth and love sweep over her like a tidal wave of goodness. God was so good. Why hadn't she waited for God to provide for her when she was younger? Why had she impatiently tried to find direction and love on her own? *But God knew what I needed, in his perfect timing, not mine.*

Now Brian smiled at her, and she smiled in return. She would trust God for direction from now on. He bent and kissed her, this time allowing their lips to mesh softly. Mandy melted into his embrace, unfamiliar delights racing through her. Incredible joy filled her heart, threatening to overflow and spill out of her.

She recalled the passage from Song of Solomon that warned against awakening love before its time, and regret swelled within her for her time with Richard, warring for space with her newfound happiness.

But she pushed the disturbing thought away and thanked God for his mercy, which was new each morning. God had forgiven her for her past, and she was new in Jesus, free to start again with a good Christian man, one that the Lord had brought to her rather than the one she'd hunted down and captured on her own.

Carlos reentered the sitting room with a steaming cup in his hand. "So? You two have finally come together. I knew it was only a matter of time. When is the happy day to be, then?"

Mandy felt a sudden thrill shoot through her. She'd never had a wedding day. She pushed back from Brian and said, "Oh, yes, please let it be soon. Now that I know what my heart desires, I don't want to wait."

Renewed Redemption

Mr. Vallejo sat in his favorite chair, sipping his drink. "As long as there will be good food after the ceremony."

Brian took her hand in his own and looked tenderly into her eyes. "I don't want to wait, either. Let's make it soon. We can tell the boys today and ask them what they think is best."

Sam and Jack were informed of the wedding plans later that day. Both boys were excited and whooped their delight at the upcoming union.

"I've been thinking of you as my father for some time," Sam confided quietly, his eyes on Brian.

"I'm just glad we can stay here forever," Jack said.

With the boys' approval, Brian and Mandy began planning their wedding in two weeks' time.

CHAPTER 28

The next day, Brian hitched the horse to the dray after breakfast. "I need to make an official visit to the Wilson farm," he explained with a look of fear in his eyes. "It's the least I can do, under the circumstances."

Mandy watched him drive from the yard, a sense of trepidation assailing her as well. She never liked Miss Wilson but wished the girl no ill will. To have your hopes dashed by another person taking your boyfriend cannot be easy, Mandy reasoned as she returned to the kitchen.

For herself, however, she felt only excitement and joy.

A thousand times since yesterday, she'd pinched herself to see if it was real. She was in love with a man who loved her in return. Mandy couldn't easily believe it, and she dwelled on it all day, astonished at its truth.

Happy tears came to her unbidden now, and Mandy smiled. These tears were not for her woeful struggles but rather for her incredible blessings. She didn't deserve such happiness, yet God had shown her mercy and forgiveness. God was good.

The breakfast dishes were no difficulty today. Laundry seemed easy as she hung clothes on the line outside, humming to herself. Sweeping and mopping the floor was an enjoyable task that allowed her to ponder her new emotions and reflect happily on her unexpected situation.

Quail Valley was like a fairy tale. Mandy surveyed her surroundings with new realization and was filled with contentment.

Except, she thought suddenly, that she wished her parents could see her now.

Renewed Redemption

Mandy had done things right this time and wished to show her parents her growth and the changes Christ had performed in her. If only her father could meet Brian, she was sure they'd like each other tremendously. They had so much in common. The two men were both farmers, both Christian men, both kind and thoughtful.

More than anything, Mandy wished her parents could know her as the new creation in Christ she'd become. Sam and Jack were Christians too, and Mandy was certain her parents would love their two grandsons.

∞∞∞∞∞

That afternoon, Mandy watched while she swept the sitting room, the front door open to the warm, early summer day, as Brian returned. He pulled the reins and halted the wagon in front of the barn. Even from here, she could see the troubled look in his brown eyes.

Dismounting stiffly from the dray, he pivoted and strode slowly toward the house. With a limp, he crossed the yard and entered the house. Mandy watched him coming, observing the limp with apprehension.

"What happened to you?" she asked as she handed him a steaming cup of coffee.

Brian sighed heavily and blew on the hot mug. "Miss Wilson threw a skillet at me when I shared my joyful news. She didn't think my news as joyful as I did." He rubbed his leg and lowered himself onto the couch, stretching the leg before him. "Thanks for this." He held the mug aloft. "It's been a hard day."

Brian closed his eyes and leaned his head back.

Mandy reached for the broom once more and glanced at him, a sly smile on her face. She leaned the broom against the wall again and came to sit on the arm of the couch.

"Her sad news is my happy tidings."

Brian opened one eye and grinned as he slid an arm around Mandy's slender waist. His comforting touch made her pulse quicken, and she could feel herself blush. Quickly, she glanced over her shoulder to the hallway.

Brian winked at her. "I doubt if Ruby appreciates your happy tidings." Mandy said nothing to this, watching Brian take another sip of coffee. "But they are my happy tidings, too, dearest," he added as he handed her the empty mug. "I thought of you all the way to Ruby's farm and all the way home. You've made me so happy, Mandy."

"Well, you don't look so happy," she observed glumly, seeing the apprehension in his eyes. Brian nodded in agreement, and Mandy could tell he hesitated to say something more. She waited patiently, knowing he'd share when he was ready.

"I stopped in town and heard some worrisome news," Brian explained, shifting his sore leg. Mandy hurried around him to place a cushion under his foot. She moved to his side and seated herself near him, eyeing him expectantly.

Brian hesitated again, his gaze fixed on the dead ashes in the fireplace, and then turned to face her. "The Confederacy has fired on Fort Sumter. It's a small fort that guards Charleston Bay. The war has begun."

Mandy felt her blood run cold as a knot formed in her belly. Her excitement at Brian's nearness turned abruptly to fear and concern. The war would certainly engulf her parents' small family farm outside Richmond.

She reached a trembling hand for Brian. He took and clasped her hand tightly with his own, while he peered intently into her eyes.

Even in the midst of this disturbing information, Mandy felt safe and secure in Brian's presence. He was strong for her, and she marveled, drinking in the feeling, like a woman dying of thirst in the desert.

Mandy had been forced to stand on her own before she accepted God's forgiveness. Now the Lord had provided Brian to be her helper. Silently, she thanked God again for this kind farmer beside her. How had she ever managed before him?

Renewed Redemption

"This is what I was afraid of," Mandy whispered. "I'm worried how this will affect my folks in Virginia."

Brian squeezed her hand. "They'll be all right, Mandy."

She shook her head. "You don't know that."

∞∞∞∞∞

The anxiety Mandy felt at the news of the war was still with her when she ventured into town three days later.

Brian had sold another two wagonloads of hay, and the teamsters could only talk about the war. Mr. Vallejo had also reported some of the local men were considering moving back east to join the war, some for the south and some for the north.

"This will divide the nation," the old man warned and walked away, shaking his head.

Now, the honey he'd harvested from the bee boxes needed to be delivered to town, and, truth be told, Mandy hoped there would be some update about events back east. Possibly the long-sought-after letter from Virginia had arrived.

She trudged to town, mindless of the deep blue sky overhead and the sound of birds singing along the road. Mandy's thoughts were heavy, causing her to ignore the beautiful summer day around her.

Mrs. Bricker waved at her as Mandy entered town. Wagons rumbled through the dusty street, and Mandy waved in return, lifting her voice to be heard across the road.

"I need to get this honey to the market." Mandy hefted the heavy basket for the blacksmith's wife to see. "I'll stop on my way back." Mandy shouldered her way into the crowded shop. Men stood in groups, some whispering conspiratorially with each other, afraid to let other groups hear what they were saying. Other men discussed the best route in traveling east.

"Around the horn will take at least eight, maybe nine months," one bearded miner shouted.

"Over land is shorter but more difficult, at least six months," another man in a broadcloth suit called loudly.

"Well, if we don't get back there quickly, the Yankees will be beaten and there'll be no one for us to shoot." A man in suspenders with a beaver hat roared raucously, and cheers followed his boastful claim.

Evidently all the groups did not agree with this man's assertion as grumbling and muttering were overheard everywhere in the crowded room.

Mr. Ambrose climbed laboriously onto a counter and clapped his hands for attention. "Gents, everyone is entitled to his own opinions. But I must say that if you're not shopping, could you please move this outside. I have customers to wait on."

He continued to call to individual patrons and wave a hand toward the door, encouraging their departure. Slowly, the groups filtered out, and the crowd thinned so that Mandy could get near the counter. Mr. Ambrose himself attended to her.

The storekeeper mopped his red face with a handkerchief, looking as worried and anxious as Mandy felt.

"I didn't think they'd listen to me," the flustered shopkeeper admitted as he reached for Mandy's basket. "I don't want my store wrecked when those supporters go to fighting," he added as he lifted the golden jars from the basket. Mr. Ambrose tried to count the jars Mandy brought in but seemed terribly preoccupied with the men in his store and the talk of war. On his third attempt, he threw up his hands and motioned to a young clerk to take his place.

The clerk she recognized from before narrowed his eyes and studied her as he approached then paused to check the mailboxes along the back wall. He grinned as he finally strode to the counter where Mandy waited. She crossed her arms protectively across her chest and tapped her foot as he counted the jars.

"There's no mail for you, ma'am," he said, lifting each jar from the basket and arranging them along the counter.

Mandy frowned, impatient now to be on her way.

Renewed Redemption

"I was hoping to have a word with you, Mrs. Barrett."

Mandy steeled herself for what was coming, not liking the young clerk's mischievous smile. By now, the word would be out about her and Brian's engagement. Certainly, everyone in Yuba City would have an opinion on the matter.

"It's all over town about you and Mr. Dawson," he whispered with a bright gleam in his eyes. "My congratulations. But that's not what I wanted to say. No, not at all."

He paused and glanced over his shoulder as if he expected people to be listening in on this conversation. He leaned closer. Mandy felt herself lean forward as well.

"I saw Miss Wilson in here yesterday, and I asked if I could come calling this Sunday. She said she'd be pleased if I would." The young man stood straight again, pink coloring his cheeks. "There, I've said it. I wanted to thank you for fetching Mr. Dawson and leaving Miss Wilson for me. I've had my eye on her for a year," he confessed, a wide grin creasing his face.

"Glad I could help," Mandy mumbled. She snatched her empty basket before hurrying from the store.

She stopped at Mrs. Bricker's where the blacksmith's wife informed Mandy that news of her sudden engagement was indeed all over town, but folks were divided about the incident.

"Some people think you have the right since you lived and worked there and you're closer to his age. Others think Ruby had first chance because of longevity. She had her eye on Mr. Dawson long before you were even in the picture."

Mandy smiled with a confidence she did not quite feel. "Well, the deed is done," she announced merrily, suddenly happy to be able to announce her love of Brian openly to all who would hear. "Mr. Dawson has informed Miss Wilson of our engagement, and I will be Mrs. Dawson soon. My regrets to Miss Wilson, and I hope her every happiness in her next search for a husband."

With a wave, Mandy walked down the street and left Mrs. Bricker.

As Mandy worked her way around wagons and groups of bearded, noisy men, she slowed her gait. Few of the miners turned their attention to her now. They were too deeply engrossed in conversations and debates about the war in the east.

Her thoughts returned to the young brunette she'd bested, and Mandy felt a sudden remorse for the girl. Although thoroughly pleased she would marry Brian, she did feel sorrowful for the plotting Miss Wilson. Ruby had tried so hard to capture Brian.

The feeling quickly passed, and Mandy smiled as happiness swelled within her. She was overjoyed to marry Brian and wanted to shout. She did love him and thanked God again for bringing her to Quail Valley. Who would've guessed the turns life had in store for her when she first came to the little farm cottage?

∞∞∞∞∞

Later, after she'd returned to the cottage, Sam and Jack expressed their excitement about the upcoming marriage as well. Mandy watched Brian closely, an easy smile resting on his tanned face, as he listened to the boys.

"I've loved living here, Brian," Jack declared. "It'll be so wonderful that we're a real family."

"Maybe then I can have my own room," Sam said with a playful punch at Jack's shoulder.

Mandy understood the implication and glanced quickly at Brian, the color rising to her face. Did he understand what Sam meant? Another room would soon be available when Mandy moved into Brian's bedroom.

A tingle of excitement ran down her spine as Mandy thought of being close to this handsome man within the darkness of his private bed chamber. Immediately, she chastised herself for inappropriate thoughts.

Renewed Redemption

Covertly, Mandy peeked at Brian and blanched when she saw his smile widen as he glanced at her, a look of real anticipation in his eyes.

"Sam, I believe I can guarantee you'll have your own room."

He paused, and Mandy watched him from the corner of her eye. He grinned mischievously. "But then you'll have to move back in with Jack."

Mandy titled her head, wondering at his meaning.

"Why, Brian?" Sam also wanted to know.

Brian chuckled. "Well, when the babies start coming, we'll need room for them."

Mandy felt her eyes widen. Babies? She hadn't thought of that.

"Oh, it'll be nice to have a younger brother," Jack whooped.

Brian rose from the table, and Mandy leaped to her feet.

"Boys, if you don't mind doing the dishes, I'd like to sit on the porch with the prettiest girl I know," he said as he reached for Mandy's hand.

Brian led her outside to the bench where they sat and talked for hours about the future and children and what God might have in store for them.

Despite her worries about her parents back in Virginia, Mandy felt happy. And for the first time in a long time, she was content with the Lord. God had brought her to a point of brokenness and repentance. Only recently had she allowed herself to claim his forgiveness and grace. She was right with the Lord and was eager to be a part of the adventure in which God had called her.

∞∞∞∞∞

Finally, the big day arrived. A bright and clear sunrise topped the rim around Quail Valley and illuminated the entire basin. Excited and merry voices filled the little cottage as the quartet prepared for the special event to come.

Mandy left the breakfast table hastily to change once more into the blue dress, tossing the yellow one on the bed. The burgundy was too fancy, she felt. Besides, the blue was Brian's favorite.

"Come on, Mandy," Brian called from outside her closed door. "I liked the dress you had on."

"Hold your horses," Mandy called loudly. "It'll take only a minute."

She looked again into the mirror after donning the blue dress. Her long blonde hair was feathered, hanging down her back and secured with a matching ribbon. She wanted to look her best for Brian.

A blue and cloudless sky accompanied the little party as they rode in the dray to town.

The boys chattered unceasingly in the back while Mandy rode beside Brian on the high seat. Mandy smoothed the folds from her dress as they traveled. Brian told her this one was his favorite dress. She smiled. He said he liked how the gown highlighted the blue in her eyes.

Mandy's mind wandered to those early days long ago when she'd first come to Quail Valley. Sick, heartbroken, distanced from God—Mandy had been truly lost. Now, with Jesus again in her life, there was a sense of newness, an air of anticipation about the future. With God, all things were possible.

"Whoa." Brian startled her when he tugged on the reins, pulling the horse to a halt. With a twinkle in his warm eyes, Brian handed the reins to Mandy, ignoring her curious look.

He leaped to the ground and spoke over his shoulder as he moved to the edge of the trail. "I think some of these wildflowers will work as a bridal bouquet. They're so beautiful," he explained, hurriedly picking the different colored flowers.

Mandy smiled, touched by his thoughtfulness, as she watched Brian choose an armload of the pretty wildflowers. The boys called from the wagon, pointing to certain flowers they wanted Brian to select. Soon, he held an enormous bouquet.

Handing the multi-colored arrangement to Mandy, he clambered up the wheel of the wagon and took the reins from her.

She smiled at him, her heart full.

Yet a single note of sadness remained, a drop of heartache in this special day. Mandy wished her parents could be here.

Despite the festive mood, the hint of sorrow persisted. She knew she was doing the right thing marrying Brian—God had revealed this was a good thing. She loved Brian with all her heart, and she knew he loved her. But she could not help feeling a little remorse that her parents, once again, would not be sharing her wedding day.

She smiled bravely at Brian, trying to conceal her dismay. The pangs of regrets she felt for the past ten years haunted her now, and Mandy was afraid she'd be haunted again for not having her father give her away.

But this was Brian's happy day too. Mandy would hide her unease from this special man, wishing to give him the wonderful event he deserved.

Mr. Vallejo waved to them from the stoop of the general store as they passed. "I have a surprise for you," he called as they moved through the crowded streets of a Saturday in Yuba City.

"I wonder if he has the letter you've been waiting for," Brian pondered aloud as he searched for a place to park the dray. Mandy bit her lip and doubted if the long-awaited letter would actually arrive today. That would be too much to hope for.

The town was full of weekend shoppers, and there was nowhere to stop the wagon until they halted under the spreading branches of a big oak tree at the far end of town. The gentle roar of the Feather River drew Mandy's gaze, and she craned her neck, peering toward the bridge that spanned the river and led to the dilapidated shanty she'd lived in.

She cringed, remembering, and then joy overwhelmed her once more. She would never return to that horrible shack. Today, she was starting a new life with Brian Dawson at Quail Valley.

Brian leaped from the wagon and helped Mandy to the ground, his hands remaining on her waist as he looked into her eyes and then swiftly kissed her.

A sense of peace swept over her. Everything would be all right. God was with them. She was marrying the right man. Finally.

"I'll fetch the parson. I saw him near the café. I'll round up Carlos too. I wonder what his surprise is." Brian grinned as he turned toward town.

He walked back up the busy street while Mandy stretched her legs. Sam and Jack ran around the large tree, chasing each other and laughing.

Mandy held up her bright bouquet and inhaled deeply. Her wedding day had finally arrived. She was surprised at herself for doing this again after so adamantly refusing to consider love for so long. This was something she'd never expected but was fully aware of her immense joy at the prospect. Marriage to Brian Dawson filled her with great happiness and fulfillment. God had plans for them, and she was excited to be a part of the journey he had in store for the newlyweds.

Glancing up, Mandy peered again along the river, down where the trail to Sacramento passed the familiar shack. A smile tugged at her lips as she recalled when she and Brian had first met. Who could've guessed back then where she'd be now?

She glanced over her shoulder. Brian should be back by now. He'd been absent longer than it should've taken to secure the parson. Perhaps Brian couldn't find the minister.

Dread and anxiety crept into her mind and nagged at her. She glanced fearfully uptown. What was taking so long?

Was God testing her? After all she'd endured, was there still more for her to suffer?

Renewed Redemption

She finally caught sight of him walking through the crowded streets with Carlos Vallejo in tow. A sense of relief swept over Mandy, and she relaxed, her shoulders loosening the tension she hadn't been aware she felt.

She looked at the beautiful flower arrangement in her hand for the hundredth time, marveling that Brian had chosen each one specifically for her. Smelling them again, she turned from the fragrant flowers to search for the boys.

As Mandy looked for Sam and Jack playing under the massive oak tree, she caught movement from the corner of her eye, and she gasped. She squinted at the man beside Brian, recognizing the familiar walk. A walk she'd watched a thousand times, a walk she'd longed to see again. Her clouded mind fought to focus, and she blinked several times, trying to clear her dimming sight.

He was really here. Her father strolled beside Brian, chatting merrily, as if they were old friends.

Was her mind playing tricks on her? No. She would've known that walk anywhere.

Mandy panicked, her eyes widening. What could he be doing here? Her usual feelings of dread and self-reproach flooded momentarily over her, and then she brushed them aside with the truth.

She was loved by Jesus. She was forgiven. She had repented of her stubborn heart and was living for God. It was all right and good to see her father.

Suddenly, she also recognized her mother walking beside the men. Mandy felt her knees weaken.

"Dearest," Brian called cheerfully as he approached. "Look who Carlos met in the store this morning while checking on the mail. They're here in time for our wedding. Isn't that wonderful?"

Mandy stared at her parents as they neared. What would they say? Why were they here?

They halted before her, silent and expectant.

Tears welled in her mother's eyes. She was older, but kindness and love still shone in her bright eyes.

"Mandy, darling. It is you," her father whispered softly, reaching suddenly for her free hand. The older man gripped it tightly, staring intently into his daughter's eyes. She peered up into his weathered face, the lines deeper now than she remembered. His hair still lay thick but grayer, his eyes gleaming with happiness.

Suddenly, a desire filled her to hold him, to be held by him. With a sob, Mandy launched into his arms. Without a word, he clasped her tightly, squeezing her so hard she struggled to breathe. Mandy sensed his forgiveness.

"We've prayed for this day for years," she heard him say into her hair.

Mandy stepped back, wiping her eyes on her sleeve before embracing her mother. "I'm so happy. I can't believe you're here."

Mandy's mother smiled, unable to speak as the tears streamed unchecked down her rosy cheeks.

As Mandy's own tears flowed, she laughed and then turned to her father, questions bubbling to the surface as she tried to speak.

He nodded with understanding.

"When we received the letter from Mr. Dawson some months ago, I swiftly replied, and then we both realized we didn't want to lose you again. What with the political unrest back east and discovering your situation in California, it seemed a good time to move. I sold the farm, and we took passage on the next steamer to Panama," Mr. Mulligan explained.

"We'd lost you for ten years, and Mr. Dawson's letter was a Godsend. Coming to California to find you seemed the thing God wanted us to do," he added softly, his gaze turning to include his silent wife.

Mandy looked from her father back to her mother. "I can't believe you're standing in Yuba City. It's been so long. I'm happy you've come." She leaned into her mother and embraced her again.

Then she released the older woman and stepped back. Sniffling, she dried her eyes. "You've met Brian. It's true, we are to be married today. Let me introduce you to your grandsons."

The boys stood behind Mandy, eyes wide and attentive. She reached for Sam and pulled him forward, Jack followed hesitantly.

"This is Sam. You knew of him before I left Virginia. And this—" Mandy moved her hand from Sam's shoulder to Jack's. "—this is Jack. He is eight."

Her mother brought a hand to her mouth, and Mandy saw fresh tears spring to her eyes. Her father stepped forward and then stiffly knelt in front of the two apprehensive boys.

The older man looked at the two young boys, his eyes filling with gentleness and kindness. He stuck out his big gnarled hand and shook each of the boys' smaller hands.

"Hello, Sam. Hello, Jack. I'm Jack Mulligan, and I'm your grandfather. I'm very pleased to meet you."

"Sir?" Jack queried, his small head leaning to one side. "Am I named for you?"

The older man stood and chuckled. "I reckon so, Jack. It's a strong name, and I'm proud to share it with you. After this here wedding, I'd like to take you two boys over to the store and buy you some candy and a pocketknife, if you don't already have one."

Sam rubbed his hands. "Well, let's get this thing done with!"

And, so they did. The parson stepped forward, and in a few minutes, Brian and Mandy were married. Her father stood up for her and gave her away while her mother quietly wept tears of joy.

As Brian and Mandy kissed, the moment felt magical, a moment in time she would never forget.

Mandy was overwhelmed with complete happiness. Everything came to pass better than she could have ever dreamed. God had given her the desires of her heart, even the desires she didn't know she had. But God, who knew her better than Mandy knew herself and loved her so much that he gave his only Son for her, wished Mandy to have this joy.

Brian turned to Sam after the ceremony was concluded. "Well, Sam, I guess you will not be having your own room. It looks like we'll be having guests."

Sam didn't seem to mind, though, as a happy hour ensued in the general store. Candy and a new jack knife were soon procured for each grinning boy, and then the group moved to leave the small town.

Mandy's eyes shone with wetness as she and her mother climbed atop the dray. The men loaded the little wagon with the bags and trunks Mandy's parents had brought with them. They would be moving into her vacant room, and Mandy would have her entire family around her.

As the dray rolled slowly through the crowded streets toward the little cottage in Quail Valley, Mandy thought back on the months that had passed. She'd come to the small farmhouse a broken, lost, and sick woman and became a housekeeper for a Christian man. Now she was a daughter of the living God and the wife of a Christian farmer. Her two boys now had a father, a home, and her family was reunited.

Happiness welled within her as she wept tears of contentment. Joy surged, overwhelming her heart.

God was good, and for the first time in a long time, Mandy knew she was loved by many people.

Yes, God is good.

Andrew Roth

DISCUSSION QUESTIONS FOR
RENEWED REDEMPTION

1. In the beginning of the book, Mandy faces catastrophe as her health, her income, and her housing are taken from her. Do you remember a time in your life when you felt everything was going against you? How did you respond? Think of Bible characters who faced overwhelming challenges. How did they handle them?

2. Mandy has allowed bitterness and resentment to take root in her heart and finds coming back to a loving God difficult. What obstacles have you allowed to fester in your own walk with God that interfere with healthy spiritual growth? Is there an area of bitterness in your life God wants to heal?

3. Mandy believes that only through her hard work and efforts is her family provided for. Where in your life do you feel that success is based on your efforts alone? How can you release this to God's control?

4. Brian's solution to Mandy's problems is to trust Jesus, but Mandy wants her problems solved without the Lord. Have there been times in your life when you wanted a "quick fix" rather than waiting on God's help? Is there currently an issue in your life that God is trying to guide you through, but you want an easier path?

Renewed Redemption

5. Eventually, Mandy allows the redemptive work of Christ to work anew in her heart. She is reunited to the Savior who had never let her go. Has there been a time in your life when your stubborn heart led you astray? What emotions did you experience when your relationship with God was restored?

6. Brian is compelled as a Christian to share his faith with Mandy and her boys. Through his words and actions, he points them to Jesus. Who shared Christ with you? Think of someone in your life who needs to experience God's redemptive work. Is God calling you to share your faith with them?

7. Mr. Vallejo acts as a wise mentor to Mandy. Think about someone who is a respected spiritual guide in your life. How have they impacted your walk with the Lord? Are you being called to be a spiritual mentor to someone?

8. Mandy's redemption was renewed through sorrow and hardships. Her faith was shaped through trials. What trials have you experienced that refined your faith and drew you closer to the Redeemer? Are you facing a trial that you need to surrender to God?

9. What predominant lesson did you learn about God or yourself from this book?

10. At the end of the book, Mandy finds many blessings as she falls in love and her family is reunited. What blessings can you thank God for in your life?

ABOUT THE AUTHOR

ANDREW ROTH taught American History for twenty-two years at the middle school level before beginning his literary career. He lives in Bakersfield, California, with his wife and is a proud father and grandfather. A native of Kansas, Andrew was raised with a deep love and appreciation for history, particularly the Old West. A Christian for more than three decades, Andrew's hope is that his writing will encourage readers and rebuild lives. The passage he feels is his guiding verse is Jeremiah 31:4, "I will build you up again and you will be rebuilt." Andrew's website is: http://andrewrothbooks.com.

Made in the USA
Middletown, DE
14 April 2021